"You cannot close the game, mister," Lieutenant Gonzalez said.

"Watch me."

"Then you mus _____"

I smiled at him. _____. But if you aren't, I have _____ to you. Go to hell."

Gonzalez reached for his pistol. There were a couple of candles on the table and for some reason he took a swipe at them with the barrel of his gun. I assume he did it in an attempt to plunge our corner of the cantina into darkness, though why he needed more of an advantage than to have a half-dozen of his *compadres* backing him I could not say. But that was his mistake, because in a gunfight, one should use his hardware for one thing and one thing only—and knocking over candles wasn't it.

GUNMASTER

JASON MANNING

St. Martin's Paperbacks

GUNMASTER

Copyright © 2001 by Jason Manning.

All rights reserved. No part of this book may be used or reproduced in any manner whatsoever without written permission except in the case of brief quotations embodied in critical articles or reviews. For information address St. Martin's Press, 175 Fifth Avenue, New York, NY 10010.

ISBN: 0-312-97980-0

Printed in the United States of America

St. Martin's Paperbacks edition / September 2001

St. Martin's Paperbacks are published by St. Martin's Press, 175 Fifth Avenue, New York, NY 10010.

10 9 8 7 6 5 4 3 2 1

A MESSAGE TO THE READER

I, JOSEPH GLOVER, attorney, do hereby warrant that the following is an autobiographical account of the life of Ben Thompson, penned by the subject himself in the last year of his life. Considering all the sensational accounts of Ben Thompson's career that have been produced in recent years, I came to the conclusion, in concurrence with the wishes of his widow, that this work be published. As one who knew Thompson well, I can vouch for the accuracy of much that transpires within these pages. I cannot assure the reader, however, that Thompson ever wanted this material to be made public. This is a consideration that has caused much soul-searching on my part. However, as I am confident that my friend believed himself to be misunderstood and misrepresented by his peers, and since several writers have profited immensely from manufacturing lurid tales that I fear will only enhance the misperceptions currently held by so many about him, I have laid my reservations aside. It is my firm belief that all Ben Thompson ever wanted was to be accepted into society. He could not perceive any difference between himself and the average man on the street. Of course, there was a significant difference. I doubt any man was a more gifted master of the gun. I suppose that alone was sufficient to ensure that Thompson would never get his wish.

Joseph Glover
Austin, Texas
April 1, 1888

Chapter 1

I WAS SIXTEEN years old when they put me on trial for attempted murder.

It was early in December in the year 1858 when Judge A. W. Terrill presided over my trial. He wasn't the first judge to hear the case, though. Right after I shot Joe Smith, the Austin sheriff hauled me up before a justice of the peace named Calhoun, but since there had been no witnesses to contradict my statement that the deed had been done in self-defense, Calhoun let me go free. But about a week later the local badge-toter came for me again, and I was brought before Justice Graves. It seemed that some of the more enlightened members of the community had balked at the notion that a fellow could unload a single barrel full of buckshot into someone and not be called to account for doing so. It didn't help matters that the buckshot had lodged in Joe Smith's back. Some folks could not see any possible justification for back-shooting, I guess. Justice Graves listened to some of the evidence before deciding to pass the case on to the circuit judge—Terrill—who would be open for business in Austin in about a month or so. I awaited Judge Terrill's arrival in a jail cell, so it felt like he took a lot longer than a month to get here.

When my day in court finally arrived, they put me on the witness stand and made me swear to tell the truth, the whole truth, and nothing but the truth while resting my hand on a Bible. I had no problem swearing to that, as I genuinely felt that I had been within my rights to shoot Joe Smith.

The city's prosecuting attorney got first crack at me. His name was Stapleton. He was a young man, tall and reed-thin, with a handsome set of side whiskers covering his gaunt cheeks and a tic at the corner of his mouth that grew more pronounced when he became agitated. He didn't appear at all agitated to me, however. At least not in the beginning. In fact, he acted very confident, as though this was a mere formality in an inevitable process that would result in my spending a lot more time behind bars. In other words, he was a cocky bastard, so naturally I took an immediate dislike to him.

"State your name for the record, if you please," said Stapleton.

"Benjamin Thompson."

"Where were you born?"

"A town named Knottingley, on the River Aire in Yorkshire. That's in England."

"Yes, I know. And on what date were you born?"

"November eleventh, 1842."

"And when did you arrive in Texas?"

"Last year. My family came here to Austin. We have relatives nearby, my aunt and uncle, and the things they wrote in letters to us convinced my parents to give Texas a try."

"Your family—are they here today, in this courtroom?"

I avoided looking directly at my parents, who sat near the front of the crowd that had come to witness the proceedings. With them was my younger brother, Billy, and my sister, Ellen. I was ashamed of what I'd done only to the extent that my actions had caused them grief.

"Yes, they're here," I replied.

"Including your aunt and uncle?"

He already knew the answer to that, and I wanted to tell him that I realized what he was up to. But my lawyer, old John Glover, had told me that a smart mouth would not do much to endear me to either the judge or the jury, so I bit my tongue.

"No, they are not here," I said. "Because they're dead."

"How did they die?"

I glanced at John Glover, a big-bellied, white-bearded, ruddy-cheeked man in a seedy tweed jacket, a cold briar pipe clenched in his teeth. Leaning back in his chair, hands resting on his belly with chubby fingers laced together, he just looked at me and raised a single eyebrow in a what-are-you-waiting-for-answer-the-man expression.

"They were murdered in their sleep by a runaway slave," I said.

A murmur of compassion rippled through the on-lookers. There were a lot of people present, but very few of them were genuinely interested in the outcome of my case. In a frontier community like Austin, a trifle short on civilization's amenities, trials were just about the best form of entertainment available, a substitute for theater.

"Oh, yes," murmured Stapleton. "I remember now. The runaway was captured and lynched, as I recall."

Since that wasn't a question, I didn't say anything. Glover had warned me only to respond to direct questions and keep all comments to myself. Being a friend of my family, he knew me well—knew that I had a tendency to talk too much, and that I had a sharp tongue that more often than not just got me into hot water.

"This young man that you shot," said Stapleton. "He was a Negro, too, wasn't he?"

"Yes, Joe Smith was a Negro. But he was a freeman, not a slave."

"I would think, after what happened to your aunt and uncle, you wouldn't care much for Negroes. Is that true?"

"I didn't shoot Joe Smith because he was a Negro."

"No?" Stapleton laced that single word with plenty of skepticism. "Then why did you shoot him?"

"Because he said he was going to kill me."

"But he was unarmed, and you shot him in the back. He claims he was running away."

"When I went home and got the shotgun and went back—that's when he tried to run away."

"And yet you shot him anyway."

I nodded.

"You were trying to kill him, were you not?" asked Stapleton.

"You bet. I wanted to kill him before he killed me."

Smirking, Stapleton turned his attention to the jury. I glanced at those twelve good men and tried to read my fate in their expressions, without much success.

"Personally," said Austin's prosecutor, "I don't find your story credible, young Mr. Thompson. And I doubt that the gentlemen of the jury do, either. I will tell you what I believe to be true. I believe you harbor a murderous rage toward those of the Negro race because of what happened to your relatives nearly one year ago. That rage festered in your heart until the day you spotted Joe Smith, and you fetched that shotgun and sought him out and attempted to murder him in cold blood. We are fortunate that he survived a load of buckshot in the back, or today you would be facing a hangman's noose." He glanced at the gray eminence of Judge Terrill. "I have no further questions for this witness, Your Honor."

Terrill nodded curtly and glanced at Glover. My attorney didn't bother trying to elevate his bulk out of the chair.

"Ben," he said, his voice a benevolent rumble, "why don't you tell everybody here what happened between you and Joe Smith, before you went home to get that shotgun?"

"We met on the street. I just turned a corner and there he was. He asked me if I had any money and I said I did not. He called me a liar and when I tried to walk past him, he grabbed my shirt and told me I had better give him some money. I told him he could go to hell. Right then a couple of men came out of a store nearby and Joe Smith let go of me. But then he leaned in close and said that one night soon he would come to my home and geld me and my little brother—before he slit our throats. Then he laughed."

"And what did you do?"

"I walked away. At the end of the street I looked back to see him still standing at that corner, leaning up against a wall, watching me and grinning. So I went home, got the shotgun, and came back."

"So you took his threat seriously."

"Sure I did. Wouldn't you, sir? I knew all about Joe Smith. He's a bully. He almost killed a kid some months ago. And he is twice as big as I am. So I did take him seriously. And I was trying to kill him because I figured if I didn't, he would come looking for me and my brother, maybe that very night."

"Then the way you see it, you acted in self-defense."

"Yes, sir."

"I would think," murmured Glover, "that reasonable men would be inclined to agree with that."

Stapleton scoffed. "Shooting someone who is running away from you will give an entirely new meaning to the term self-defense," he opined.

"A few months ago Captain McNally of the Texas Rangers led an assault on a Comanche village," said Glover. "We all hailed him and his brave boys as heroes for defending our frontier. We did not ask that he wait until the Comanches were conducting a raid against our farms and villages before taking action against them."

"I don't see what that has to do with this," protested Stapleton.

"I do," said Judge Terrill, "so be quiet."

Stapleton did as he was told. That's when I saw the tic for the first time. He didn't look nearly as cocky as he had earlier.

"Anything else?" Terrill asked Glover. His expression made it clear that his preference was that there would not be. Glover astutely said that he was finished.

As I left the witness chair, Stapleton summoned a local sawbones to testify as to the wounds inflicted upon Joe Smith, followed by a fellow named Klinghoffer, a German immigrant who was a leading Unionist in the area as well as an ardent abolitionist—neither of which would make him a very popular hombre in Texas in 1858. But he knew Joe Smith, and testified that the rumors of Smith's villainy were wholly unsubstantiated, were in fact fabrications by proponents of the institution of slavery to assassinate the character of their worst nightmare, a free black man. Klinghoffer finished by claiming that he had for some time been fearful that Joe Smith would meet a violent end at the hand of some secessionist or Negro-hater. As he said this, he glowered at me.

This time John Glover got to his feet, and Klinghoffer watched the rotund lawyer's advance with some trepidation because Glover radiated the degree of righteous indignation one supposes must have possessed Moses when he came down from the mountain to find the Israelites engaged in an orgy of pagan worship.

"Mr. Klinghoffer," said Glover icily, "you are implying that my client shot Joe Smith because Smith was a freeman. You have any evidence to substantiate that accusation?"

"Well, no, I do not."

"Then it's mighty slender, don't you think? Of the same order as if someone were to suggest that you were a member of the Order of the Golden Cross because you are of German extraction. Surely you've heard of the Order. They say the founders and most, if not all, of its members are German immigrants. Like yourself."

"Yes, I have heard of it, but—"

"And the Order, I am told, has been promoting a slave insurrection right here in Texas," said Glover.

A large part of the crowd booed and hissed.

Klinghoffer lost all color in his face. "I am not—"

"You would agree, I'm sure," said Glover serenely, "that to even imply that you were affiliated in any way with the Order, or shared the views of its members, would be slanderous."

Completely stumped, Klinghoffer could only stare at Glover, who smiled benevolently at the witness before informing a stone-faced Judge Terrill that he had no further questions.

Stapleton then rose to announce that Joe Smith, though sufficiently recovered from his wounds to do so, had declined to appear in court. Terrill turned the case over to the jury. I avoided looking at the twelve men who held my future in their hands as they huddled to discuss the evidence and reach a verdict, their words masked by a hubbub from the excited onlookers who had packed the courthouse.

Fortunately, the jury didn't take long to reach a decision. Ten minutes later the foreman stood up, and when he did that, Judge Terrill gaveled the crowd into silence.

"So what say you?" asked Terrill.

"We find the defendant, Benjamin Thompson, not guilty, Your Honor."

I wanted to jump for joy, but somehow maintained my composure. Glover put a beefy hand on my shoulder. Behind me, my mother stifled a sob. She was like that, a very emotional woman, and I had already concluded that she would weep regardless of the jury's verdict.

Judge Terrill fastened his stern gaze upon me. "You are free to go, young man. I hope I do not see you in this court again. But somehow I think I will." He slammed the gavel down. "Let's move this show along. Next case."

My family and John Glover gathered around me outside the courthouse. It was a sunny day, but cold. I didn't care about the cold, though. I just marveled at the sensations of being free, of having escaped no telling how many years in a jail cell, and my senses seemed peculiarly attuned to every sight, smell, and sound in the wide and dusty Austin street.

My father, William Thompson, had been an officer in Her Majesty's navy, and no matter what the circumstances, there was always a stiff formality about him. It was evident now as he gravely commended Old John for a job well done, and he even extended a hand, which was about as much of an open show of affection as I'd ever seen from him. Glover, who understood my father better than most in Austin—they thought he was a rather stuck-up gent who put on entirely too many airs for a man who barely made a living by selling fresh fish caught in the Colorado River—and the lawyer gratefully accepted the proffered hand, shook it once, and let that be that.

"We were lucky," he said, "that Joe Smith was the injured party in this case. He had two things going against him. Everybody knows he's a troublemaker. And, of course, he's a Negro."

My mother was a handsome Scotch-Irish woman. Her warmth and compassion stood in stark contrast to the rigid impassivity of my father. She was in the process of smothering me with hugs and kisses, when something Glover said drew her attention—thankfully— away from me.

"But Ben was only defending himself and protecting his brother, Mr. Glover," she said.

Glover nodded. He knew my mother, too—well enough to have expected this spirited defense of her eldest son. As far as she was concerned, her children could do no wrong.

"You're a good and decent woman, Mary," said Glover, "and loyal to your boy, as you should be. I value our friendship, so I hope you will not take offense when I say that Ben, though he is a bright boy and I like him, has always had a violent nature. Long before this unhappy event, I feared that something like it would occur." Glover again rested a hand on my shoulder. "I hope you understand, Ben, that I say this only out of concern for your welfare."

"All I know is I took Joe Smith at his word," I said

grimly. "So I decided I had to kill him before he killed me and my little brother."

"I have always tried to teach my sons to stand up for themselves," said my father. "They are British and well-educated, and that sets them apart from the local youth. Tends to make them the brunt of ridicule, occasionally even contempt."

Glover nodded. "Yes, I am well aware of that." He was also, I sensed, well aware that my father's experiences in the service of the Royal Navy had made of him a man who saw nothing amiss in the resort to violence. Life on the high seas, even for an officer, was no tea party. I believe in some respects that Glover, while fond of us boys and my sister and my mother, was more than a little critical of my father. Old John could quaff a shot or three of rotgut whiskey with the best of them. Even so, he was not nearly the drinker that my father was, and he did not approve of the fact that William Thompson spent entirely too much of his profits from the sale of the fresh fish on bottles of liquid brave-maker, leaving barely enough to feed and clothe and house his family. Everyone knew this, but no one—least of all my mother—ever called him on it. In fact, she always made excuses for him, pointing out that as a boy even younger than I, her husband had first gone to sea and spent a quarter of a century there, and like all other Royal Navy sailors had come to rely on a daily ration of grog to ease pains both physical and emotional. My father these days was an unhappy man. He had left the navy under a cloud, though I was ignorant of the specifics. Still, the sea was in his blood and he longed to feel the pitching deck beneath his feet and to hear the whip and snap of canvas sails as they captured the trade winds. There was in my father's soul a tortured and constant discontent and quite naturally, considering his background, he sought solace in strong spirits.

Glover knew all this. Knew, as well, that my father was too consumed by his own misery to concern himself overly much with the upbringing of his children, and with my mother being as she was, that left us without what Old John considered sufficient discipline in our lives. Spare the rod and spoil the child—and I suppose he was right about me. I was too proud, and therefore entirely too quick to take offense. I was too brave, and therefore prone to rash acts, for it never occurred to me that I would not prevail in a scrape. And I was too violent, and therefore likely to find myself, one day, in serious trouble with the law again.

But as my father liked to say, there was nothing to be gained by going against your nature. I had been born with a mean streak, as Joe Smith had been—which was why I had understood the need to take his threats seriously. And, again like Joe Smith, I would probably meet a bad end. Perhaps, like him, I would be gunned down from behind, by someone who had decided I was too dangerous to let live.

Chapter 2

BECAUSE MY MOTHER had paid particular attention to the matter, I was well-educated—very much so by the standards of the Texas frontier. For that reason I got a job at the *Southern Intelligencer,* Austin's daily newspaper, setting type. That required someone with more than just a passing interest in the King's English, and since I happened to be one of the few in the area who could actually spell the word "journalism," the editor of the newspaper paid me a very fair wage, all of which I dutifully turned over to my mother. It almost made up for the money my father squandered on liquor as he spent his nights regaling other saloon patrons with tall tales of adventure on the high seas, and so our lot was somewhat improved.

I never saw Joe Smith again. He left Austin, and about a year later I heard that he had been gunned down in Waco while attempting to rob a general store. That, however, did nothing to vindicate me in the eyes of a sizable portion of Austin's population, the ones who had decided I was just plain old trouble. Half of Austin didn't care that I had shot Joe Smith in the back—after all, he was a no-account and a Negro besides, and somebody had been bound to do it eventually. But there was a code of conduct even out here on the verge of civilization, and part of that code spoke to the subject of back-shooting. In short, that was just not acceptable to a lot of folks, regardless of the circumstances, and any man who stooped to it became a social pariah. I learned a valuable lesson. It mattered less that you shot a man than it did the manner in which you performed the deed.

In 1859 I had what I thought was a chance to redeem myself. For years the Comanches had been carrying out bloody raids up and down the frontier. They were fierce warriors and superb horsemen—in my opinion the best cavalry the world had ever known—and they were truly audacious and implacable in their resolve to halt the encroachment of white people westward into their lands. In spite of the best efforts of the Texas Rangers to stop them, the Comanche raiders seemed close to achieving their goal. Farms and even whole villages were being abandoned. Many pioneers were burying their dead loved ones, loading up their wagons with belongings—assuming they had anything left to their name after an Indian raid—and were heading east for safer environs.

Met with this success, the Comanches became bolder than ever, and one day in the early summer of 1859 a band of them rode into the outskirts of Austin, killed a couple of men and one woman, and made off with five white children. That stirred up a real hornet's nest. Seemed like every able-bodied man in Austin was grabbing his guns and his horse and charging off into the hills. The pursuit was by no means organized— there was no posse, just several bunches of mad-as-hell Texans racing hither and yon looking for Indians to kill. I wasn't about to sit on my hands, either. I went home, got my shotgun and a pistol, told my worried mother not to be concerned, and my little brother, Billy, that he could not come with me. My father was in San Antonio at the time, which was just as well. Even sober he was a poor horseman, but might have felt obliged to come along, and then I would have had to look out for him, because he couldn't shoot worth a damn, either.

As I was leaving town, a group of riders, about a dozen, led by an elderly but tough-as-nails gent named Major Seth Walton came along.

"Thompson," called Walton, his voice stentorian. "We are going in pursuit of the those redskins and you are welcome to ride with us."

I nodded. Walton had fought in the Mexican War and was highly respected as a military man by the local folk. He had not attended the military academy at West Point, but he was well-read on the subject of war, and he knew me, as I had on occasion borrowed a book or two from him. So I agreed to ride along for a while. I wasn't interested in galloping around the countryside eating dust all afternoon, but I noticed Toby Willis was with Major Walton, and Toby was a tracker of great repute, so it was possible that this group might have a fairly decent chance of catching up with the Comanches, and if so, I wanted to be with them when they did.

Sure enough, Toby found the trail of the raiders and after we had followed it for a while, we all agreed that the war party seemed to be heading for a crossing of the Colorado River called the White Wolf. They were about an hour ahead of us, so we decided that our best chance of catching up with them before darkness fell would be to cut across some rough country. This turned out to be a ride demanding a lot from men and horses alike, so that by the end of it there were only seven of us left. The others had fallen behind. As we reached high ground above the crossing, the Comanches came into view—about thirty warriors in all, and I could tell that the odds gave the men I rode with pause.

"If they get across the river into open country, there'll be no catching them," I pointed out. "Our horses are about done for, so we need to stop them here."

Walton was no coward, but he felt a responsibility for the lives of the men who followed him, so he hesitated. "I am afraid there aren't enough of us to get the job done, Ben," he said regretfully.

"Well," I replied tersely, "one of those little ones could have been my brother or sister, and I can't just stand by and watch them be taken off like this."

With that I kicked my horse down the hill in the direction of the crossing. The terrain was such that the Comanches could not see me, so I figured I could beat them there and, I hoped, find a good place to make a stand before they arrived. Looking back, I saw Walton and the others following me. Though they thought what I was doing amounted to suicide, they weren't about to let me do it alone, for that would have brought everlasting shame down upon them.

I reached the crossing just minutes before the Comanches arrived, and Walton and the others were right behind me. We left our horses in Toby's keeping and then fanned out in the brush on either side of the trail. We agreed we had to let the Indians get close before opening up on them—there were five white children among them, and no one wanted to shoot a child by accident.

Then the Comanches came into view, moving down the trail on their painted ponies, and they didn't appear to be in too big of a hurry. I wondered where all the other men from Austin were, and if any might be close enough to hear the gunplay about to ensue, and decided I better not count on that happening. The Comanches certainly weren't acting as though anyone was in hot pursuit.

I figured for sure that one of my companions would lose his nerve and shoot long before the Indians got close, but no one did. When the buck in the lead was about twenty feet away, I stepped out of the brush, leveled my shotgun, and blew him right off his pony. All hell broke loose then, pistols and rifles going off left and right, men shouting, horses bucking and snorting, but I stayed focused on the task at hand, which was killing Comanches. I tossed away the empty shotgun, drew the pistol from my belt, and walked up the trail, picking a target and firing, and each time I fired, a raider went down. When the pistol was empty, I grabbed up a rifle that had belonged to a dead Comanche and dropped a couple more. I was drawing a bead on yet another when I saw him reach back and drag a white girl, about age five, in front of him, using her as a human shield, so I lowered my sights and killed his pony instead. Rushing in, I clubbed the warrior so hard that the rifle's stock shattered, snatched up the stunned little girl, and plunged into the nearest cover. The ground abruptly dropped out from under us and we toppled into a brush-choked ravine and she cried out, but it was more in fear than pain, as she appeared to be uninjured. I told her to stay put when we reached the bottom, and told her again, and yet again a third time, until she nodded that she understood. Scrambling up the steep bank of the ravine, I got to the trail in time to see about half of the Comanches beating a hasty retreat. The rest lay dead or dying.

One of my companions had been killed outright, and another one was slightly wounded. We retrieved a second child, this one also a girl, no more than three years old, who stood weeping amidst the carnage. To our chagrin, we found a third child crushed beneath a dead horse. The wounded Comanches were quickly dispatched upon Major Walton's orders. It was just as well. Had we taken them back to Austin, they would have met the same fate. In this way they died as warriors should die—on the field of battle.

It was nearly dark, so we moved down the river a ways before making a cold camp, bringing the dead man and child as well as the two little girls we had rescued with us. That night Walton came up to where I was sitting on the bank of the river and complimented me on my shooting. "You brought down a Comanch' every time you pulled the trigger, Thompson. Where did you learn to shoot like that?"

"I didn't learn it. I've just always been able to hit what I aim at."

"At long range, too?"

"No, sir. I'm no sharpshooter. It's strictly close quarters for me."

He nodded. "A pistoleer. A few are born to it. Some of it has to do with nerve. And you've got plenty of backbone, I'll give you that. You didn't appear to be at all scared of dying today."

"I wasn't," I replied, without bravado. It was merely a statement of fact. "Because I'm pretty sure I can kill a man before he can kill me. If I can get close enough, that is."

Walton pondered my words in silence for a moment. Then he said, "You should consider a military career. It's the only profession where a born killer can earn praise rather than condemnation for what he does best."

The term "born killer" threw me off a bit. I had never looked at myself in that light, but after what had happened at the crossing, and that business with Joe Smith the previous year, I could see how Walton might reach such a conclusion, and I didn't take offense, because I wasn't sure but that he might be on to something.

"Well," I replied at length, "looks like the war might be coming soon enough, and I'll get my chance."

"True words," allowed Walton. "Slavery and states' rights are tearing this country apart. But war is a grim business, son. There's not much glory in it."

"I'm not looking for glory, sir. But I don't want to be a typesetter all my life, either."

"Thompson, if I can ever be of help to you in any way, you just let me know."

We returned to Austin the following day, and were greeted by an enthusiastic crowd, as well as some good news—another group of Austinites had met up with the Comanches not long after our scrape with them at the river crossing. More warriors had been "converted," and the two remaining children were rescued.

You might have thought that once Major Walton told what had happened at White Wolf Crossing that I would have become the toast of the town, and indeed some folks proceeded to speak of me as a hero. But others were of quite a different view. The story started to go around that because of the way I had acted so recklessly, I was somehow responsible for the loss of the child who had been crushed by the dying horse. Major Walton wrote a letter for publication in the *Southern Intelligencer*—I set the type for it myself— in which he came to my defense, claiming that had I not acted, and by so doing prompted the others who rode with me to act, that the Comanches would in all likelihood have gotten away, and none of the five kidnapped children would have been recovered. But it did little good. The story persisted. Apparently there were some in Austin who were just dead set against me, and nothing I did, no matter how courageous or honorable, would change their minds where I was concerned.

It soon got to the point where I felt the need to leave Austin. My mother, though she hated to see me go, felt it was for the best, too. It was she who wrote a family friend named Samuel Slater, who had once owned a bookbindery in Austin, but who had recently relocated that enterprise to New Orleans. Slater wrote back that he would be more than happy to take me on as an apprentice. I suppose my mother consoled herself with the belief that in such a civilized place as New Orleans I would have a much easier time of staying out of trouble. At least there would be no Comanche war parties to go chasing after.

So it was that in the spring of 1860 I left the Texas frontier for the city of New Orleans. I was not yet eighteen years of age. I had no expectations with regards to how long I would stay in the city, or if I would ever return to Austin. Life is a mystery that unfolds one day at a time, and I had learned to live for today, without concern for yesterday or speculation on what tomorrow might have in store for me.

Chapter 3

TO MY MOTHER'S way of thinking, since New Orleans was a very large and cosmopolitan city, it would be less likely that I would come into harm's way during my stay there. But the Crescent City wasn't all that civilized, as I soon discovered. A thriving seaport and a melting pot of different races, cultures, and religions was by no means as staid as the only other metropolis with which I was familiar, London. In fact, I was astonished to hear of all the shootings, knifings, lynchings, and intentional drownings that occurred every week in New Orleans. It turned out that the city was no safer than the Texas frontier, and so I made a habit of carrying a pocket pistol and a dirk with me everywhere I went. Just a matter of time, I thought, before something happened. And, of course, I was right.

I had been in New Orleans less than two months when one day, riding in a mule-drawn omnibus, I intervened when a fellow, who was obviously drunk, insisted that a pretty girl traveling alone give him a kiss. When the girl refused, the man decided to take what he wanted. But before he could lay a hand on her, I stepped between them. When I suggested that he mind his manners, he struck me. I drove the blade of my knife into his shoulder, which abruptly ended the altercation. The man's friends hustled him off the omnibus and, I presumed, to the nearest physician.

"Don't concern yourself," I told the shocked girl. "It

looked much worse than it really is. He will survive."
Touching the brim of my hat, I also disembarked, and
made my way through the cobbled streets of the Vieux
Carre to Sam Slater's bindery, assuming that the matter
had been concluded and that nothing more would ever
come of it. When I told Mr. Slater what had happened,
he became very concerned.

"By your description of this fellow's accent and his
attire," said the bookbinder, "he sounds to me like a
Creole, probably from a local family of old money. The
New Orleans aristocracy, if you will."

"I would have thought an aristocrat would have better manners."

"Manners are not congenital," said Slater, with a
worried smile. "They have to be learned. And learning
depends on the individual, not his station in life."

"Then you think he will involve the authorities?"

"Certainly not," replied Slater. "That would not be
the course of action a 'gentleman' would resort to. No,
he is much more likely to challenge you to a duel."

"He will have a hard time finding me. This is a big
city and I am new here. No one knows who I am."

"Don't count on that, Ben."

A week later Slater presented me with a copy of the
newspaper, the *Picayune*. Amongst the advertisements
for slaves and tonics was this announcement:

A friend of Emil Latour wishes to call upon the
gentleman who on Monday last wounded M. Latour with a dagger on the Charles Street omnibus.
Unless he is a craven coward, said gentleman will
notify me of his identity and present address in
writing or in person. Louis Delacorte.

There followed an address on Canal Street.
My first inclination was to pay a call on Mr. Dela-

corte, but Sam Slater talked me out of it.

"You're hot under the collar, Ben, and if you charge over there now, there's bound to be trouble."

"Trouble? Isn't that what he wants?"

"Let me go find out what it is that he wants."

"I don't need anyone to fight my battles for me."

Slater shook his head. "I'm no fighter, believe me. Use your head, Ben. Mr. Delacorte is representing this fellow Latour, if I'm reading this right."

"You mean they want a duel."

"That would be my guess. Now, while it is true that dueling is against the law in the state of Louisiana, the fact is that the authorities will look the other way as long as things don't get out of hand. But if you go charging over to Canal Street, that is exactly what will happen, and you will wind up in jail—or worse."

The thought of jail cooled me down a lot. I had spent enough time in an Austin jail cell a while back to know that more time behind bars was the last thing I wanted to endure. So I agreed to let Mr. Slater pay a visit to Louis Delacorte.

As it turned out, Slater was right. Delacorte was acting for Latour, who wanted to settle the matter that existed between us as gentlemen settle such things. This called for a meeting on neutral ground, and on the following day I met Latour and his second in a Bourbon Street saloon. It was a far cry from the watering holes one could expect to find on the frontier—the place looked as opulent as a ballroom in a French château.

Latour's left arm was in a sling, and his face was taut with anger. I could see that it was taking all he had to maintain control, and it occurred to me how easy it would be to provoke a fight right here and now and be done with it. But I decided to play by their rules, if it meant staying out of jail.

Delacorte stepped forward to speak for Latour. He was a tall, slender, pale, and almost ungainly fellow dressed to the nines in a plum-colored frock coat, yellow doeskin trousers, and a yellow cravat. He didn't look very dangerous, but then, he wasn't the one I had to worry about.

Sam Slater had accompanied me, albeit with some reluctance. But as I knew no one else in New Orleans well enough to represent me in an affair of honor, he had agreed to do so. I'd told him that I was perfectly willing to come to this meeting alone, but he informed me that the principals—Latour and myself—were not permitted to address one another directly. Such was the protocol of this bizarre and deadly ritual.

"Before we can proceed," said Delacorte, "we must have some indication that Mr. Thompson is a gentleman." He sounded very skeptical, and his glance in my direction was faintly contemptuous. "It would be a stain on my friend's honor to engage in a duel with a man who was not of proper breeding."

"Mr. Thompson's father was an officer in the Royal Navy," said Slater. "Will that be sufficient?"

Delacorte turned to discuss the matter, sotto voce, with Latour. They glanced at me a time or two—or rather, at my attire. I had spent most of what Mr. Slater had paid me on a wardrobe, so I at least dressed like a gentleman. I figured this business about my pedigree was merely designed to insult me—I mean, there could be no question that Latour would fight me; anyone who could read his expression would understand that this was a foregone conclusion. But I didn't rise to the bait. I knew I was no gentleman, and had no pretensions in that regard. And, sure enough, they accepted my bonafides, such as they were, so that we could get down to the real business at hand.

Since Latour was issuing the challenge, I had the right to name the weapons, so I opted for pistols at ten paces. I figured the Creole would gladly accept—Sam Slater had told me that he was a marksman of some repute. To my surprise, however, Latour rejected pistols, as was his right, and suggested swords.

"I don't know this to be true," Slater told me, as we consulted, "but my guess is that, considering his upbringing, Latour has been tutored by a swordmaster. He would be, I suspect, as adept with sword as with pistol."

I nodded. "Well, the Mexicans have an interesting way of solving quarrels like this. They give each man a dagger and lock them up in a dark room—and the men fight until only one is left standing."

When Slater proffered this alternative, Delacorte was taken aback. "That's just barbaric!" he exclaimed.

"Well, it does take a particular kind of courage," I drawled.

Latour took that as I had meant him to take it—as a challenge within a challenge. He pulled his second aside. They discussed the matter for a moment, and I got the impression that Delacorte was trying to talk him out of agreeing. But in the end it was Latour's decision to make, and finally it was agreed that we would meet a week later—time enough for Latour's arm to heal fully—at a place as yet to be determined. I didn't know New Orleans all that well, so I left it to my adversary to find an appropriate site for the duel.

A few days later Delacorte arrived at the bookbindery to inform me that a suitable location had been found, near the old slave cemetery along the eastern edge of the Vieux Carre. I agreed to be there in four days, at six o'clock in the morning.

Accompanied by Slater, I arrived at the appointed place at the appointed time. Latour and Delacorte stood before the green timber doors of a carriage house across a cobbled street from the crumbling wall of the cemetery, where the last shreds of night lingered beneath massive oaks draped with Spanish moss. We were well away from the main thoroughfares. I discovered that we were awaiting the arrival of a doctor, a man known for his discretion in such matters, if not for his punctuality. As we waited, Delacorte checked my weapon, the dirk with which Latour was already entirely too familiar. Meanwhile Slater inspected Latour's blade. This was a mere formality. Delacorte swung the doors open and I saw an empty chamber, about twenty feet square, dirt-floored, with brick walls on three sides and wood on the other and a single shuttered window in back. The physician arrived a moment later. He was a portly man huffing hurriedly around a corner, lugging his black leather bag.

"If you gentlemen are ready," said Delacorte, "we can now proceed."

As usual, Latour was dressed to the nines. No longer did he wear the sling on his arm. He shed his frock coat and unraveled his cravat. Placing these in his second's care, he rolled up the sleeves of his snowy-white linen shirt. I shed my coat—and my shirt as well. By his expression, Delacorte evidently disapproved of a gentleman fighting bare-chested. I noticed the physician checking his timepiece. The sun had not yet risen above the rooftops of the French Quarter, and I suppose the man was contemplating his breakfast and whether he would be late getting to it.

"Don't worry," I told him. "We won't be keeping you long."

Latour gave me a cold look and gestured at the carriage house. I walked in and he followed.

"When I close the doors," said Delacorte, "they will remain closed until one of you bids me open them, or until some time has passed since we have heard any sound from within."

"Close the doors and let's be done with this," growled Latour.

I turned my back and shut my eyes, walking deeper into the carriage house. The doors creaked on their rusted hinges. Only after I heard them come together did I open my eyes. It was very nearly pitch-dark, with only a ribbon of weak morning light slipping in beneath the doors. Moving silently, I put my back up against one of the walls, opened my eyes wider, and breathed tidally, straining to see the telltale glint of Latour's blade, or the whisper of his shirt's fabric.

A moment passed, and then I heard something, just the hint of a sound so faint that I could not distinguish it, and the blackness in front of me seemed to shift. I dropped into a crouch just as Latour struck, a broad lateral sweep of his knife, so close, I could feel the wind of its passage. His blade grazed the brick wall, making sparks, and I lunged, thrusting with my own dagger. But Latour was agile and quick, and though my blade caught and ripped the fabric of his shirt, he escaped unscathed.

I moved immediately, hurling myself to the right and then throwing myself to the ground, because I could hear him coming after me, or after the sound of me—and he tripped over my prone body and sprawled. We were both on our feet in an instant, and I stood there, very still, straining to hear something, anything, that might provide a clue to his location. I heard the barest whisper of fabric—Latour's shirt, I thought—to my left, and then behind me. He wasn't circling, I realized, but moving slowly past me, assuming perhaps that I had retreated to put my back against a wall yet again. I swiveled and took several steps, thinking this had to bring me close behind him. Switching the dagger to my left hand, I kicked at the dirt with the toe of a boot. When he felt the dirt strike the back of his trouser leg, Latour whirled and lashed out with the knife. I had already made note of the fact that he was right-handed, and so expected him to lead with the right shoulder as he turned. Raising my right arm to deflect the knife stroke, I stepped in and plunged the blade of my dagger to the hilt into his body.

Latour made an incoherent sound, a mixture of pain and fear and rage, and fell back, but I pressed forward and thrust the blade into him again, and this time he uttered a wheezing gasp—before I heard the heavy *thump!* of his body hitting the ground.

I waited a moment, not moving, scarcely breathing—but he made no further sound. Stepping forward cautiously, I felt my boot brush against something—Latour's leg. I kicked it—and got no response. Turning, I groped my way to the carriage house doors and struck at the timbers with the pommel of my knife, calling out for Delacorte to throw open the doors. This he did in haste. Sparing me a shocked glance, he looked past me and then rushed to Latour's fallen form, the physician in his wake. I looked at Slater. He was gazing at the knife in my hand. It was covered with blood. Taking my shirt from him, I wrapped the weapon in the shirt and handed it to him before shrugging on my coat. No words passed between us. There was no need for words. The physician emerged from the carriage

house to inform us that Emil Latour was dead. My
blade had pierced his heart, killing him instantly.

"Then I think this matter is settled," I said coldly,
and turned away, my nerves settling down, but feeling
queasy from the adrenaline still coursing through my
body.

News of Emil Latour's death became the talk of the
town, and once my name became associated with it, I
found I could scarcely walk the streets without being
confronted by someone, either a hostile friend of the
dead man's seeking to provoke a quarrel with me, or
a member of the press. I was not, however, bothered
by the constabulary. Still, it became apparent that my
notoriety caused disreputable sorts to gravitate to me
while the good folks made every effort to give me a
wide berth. I began to discuss with Sam Slater the possibility of my leaving New Orleans. I had a notion to
pay a visit to California. There were two possible
routes—one was overland while the other would take
me first by ship to a Central American port, where I
would disembark, make an overland journey to the Pa-
cific coast, and take a ship there for California. The
Gold Rush was long over, but California still had an
exotic aura, and the possibilities for an enterprising sort
were endless there.

Then, as usual, something happened to change all
my plans. Abraham Lincoln was elected President of
the United States, and secessionist fever swept the
South. One Southern state after another announced
plans to hold a convention for the purpose of considering ordinances of secession from the Union. Sam Slater pulled me aside one day to tell me that I would
have to give some thought to the role I wanted to play
in the war that was coming—and, just as importantly,

where I wanted to be when I played that role.

"Don't listen to those hotspurs who claim a single victory will secure the South's independence," Slater warned me. "This will be a long and bloody struggle. I expect that every able-bodied man will be drafted into the armies. If you remain here, you'll wind up in a Louisiana regiment, Ben. Is that what you want?"

"No," I replied. "If I have to fight, it should be under the banner of Texas."

Slater nodded. "I thought as much. I will be sorry to see you go, Ben. You've been like a son to me. But if you're going to go, you had better make it soon. There is no time to waste. Events will come at break-neck speed from here on in."

I, too, hated to part company with Sam Slater. He had been more of a father to me during my sojourn in New Orleans than my father had managed to be for my entire life. But I knew he was right. I dared not linger. So I returned to Texas, and not a moment too soon, for in January a convention was assembled in Austin, and on March 18 an ordinance of secession was passed. Along with the ordinance was authorization for the re-cruitment of a regiment of mounted men to protect the Texas frontier during the conflict all knew was coming. I enlisted that June as a private in the Second Regiment, Texas Mounted Rifles.

Chapter 4

THE ISSUES FOR which so many men were to fight and die in the bloody Civil War that came in the wake of Abe Lincoln's election as President did not, I must confess, hold much interest for me. I was ambivalent about slavery; I had not ever owned a slave nor did I aspire ever to do so, and as for those who came from Africa and their descendants, I had no particular animosity. I had known some decent ones, and some bad ones— like Joe Smith. Many of the men who, like me, joined the Confederate cause believed that Negroes were inferior beings. Of that I was not convinced. The black man who labored from dawn to dusk was probably not going to be as educated as the Southern landowner who had the leisure to acquaint himself with the knowledge contained in books, but that field hand was likely a lot smarter than the cavalier when it came to survival. I suppose my own book-learning had a lot to do with why my point of view in this respect was so different from that of most of the men with whom I served. It's worth bearing in mind that there were very few among them who were, as they say, to the manor born. The majority were poor, unlettered, frontier folk who would never be in a position to own a slave even had they wanted to. But they thought blacks were inferior, and my mother was of the opinion that this was because everyone needs to have someone they can look down on. I suspect there might be some truth to that.

Of course, many claimed that they supported the Confederacy because to do so was to defend the basic principles upon which the nation had been founded. The federal government had no right under the Constitution to encroach on state sovereignty, they argued, and those Yankee shopkeepers were simply trying to ruin the economy of the South for their own profit, and using slavery as a stalking horse to get the job done. I never could find a soul who was able to satisfactorily explain to me how the Yankees would profit by destroying the Southern economy, but by 1861 it was probably a fool's errand to seek anyone who still had his wits about him anyway. My guess was that the majority of Northerners were bound and determined to keep the Union together because they feared the whole grand experiment in democracy that was the United States would collapse if the willful and wayward Southern states were allowed to leave the federation at their whim.

So what *were* my reasons for joining the Second Regiment, Texas Mounted Rifles? One was that there were no Yankees to fight on the frontier of Texas; the regiment's duties revolved around making the state safe from the depredations of Comanche raiders and Mexican bandits. Some men grumbled because they had not been called to the battlefields of the east, where the fate of the Confederacy would be determined. But I was not among them. On the contrary, I was content to be far removed from those cataclysmic clashes in which tens of thousands fell in a single day of fighting. Sam Slater wrote me on three occasions during the course of the war, and each time he would meticulously note the extremely heavy losses suffered by regiments that had been recruited in and around New Orleans— this to remind me that my decision to return to Austin before war broke out had been an eminently wise one.

It wasn't that I wanted to avoid action, mind you. Not only did I long for it, I knew the Second Texas would do plenty of fighting. The Comanche tribes were aware of the strife among their enemies, the white men, and wasted no time in taking full advantage of the situation, stepping up their raids all along the frontier. However, the more immediate problem was a Mexican by the name of Cortinas.

Juan Cortinas had been born at a rancho north of the Rio Grande, not far from the town of Brownsville. Unhappy with the influx of Anglos into the area during the 1840s, he took offense at the way the white interlopers treated his people. One day in 1859, when he witnessed a Brownsville deputy sheriff assault an old Mexican who'd had a little too much to drink and as a result failed to respond as quickly as the badge-toter thought he should have, Cortinas snapped. Flying into a rage, he shot and seriously wounded the lawman, thus beginning a chain of events that would come to be known as The Cortinas War.

Cortinas escaped the wrath of the Brownsville whites, but other Mexicans who lived in the vicinity weren't so lucky. The mistreatment they suffered prompted Cortinas to return. He brought a small army of *pistoleros* with him. They seized the town and Cortinas would have hunted down and killed some of the leading citizens of the community, whom he held responsible for the pain and suffering inflicted upon his people, had not some of his friends from the village of Matamoros, located right across the river from Brownsville, intervened. Cortinas settled for ransacking the town, freeing all the prisoners from the jail, and burning down some buildings. Then he retired to his family's rancho, which he turned into a heavily armed and fortified camp.

Eventually, Texas Rangers and U.S. Army troops managed to dislodge Cortinas from his fortress, but the wily renegade managed to escape again, this time into the mountains of Mexico, where he continually eluded Mexican troops. Then, in May of 1861, he was back in Texas, conducting raids up and down the Rio Grande.

Colonel John "Rip" Ford was the commanding officer of the Second Texas, and his orders were to proceed immediately to the border country, confiscate all federal property there (including guns and ammunition, of course), and put an end to the Cortinas problem once and for all. Colonel Ford was a respected Indian fighter, and confidence was high that he could get the job done. He wasted no time, marching for the Rio Grande as soon as one battalion had been formed. I was one of the new recruits he intended to whip into shape while on the trail.

Like the others, I was responsible for providing my own horse and weapons and a good deal of the rest of the things a soldier needs. About all the state could afford to provide us were provisions and ammunition— if and when either came available. It quickly came to my attention that army life was ninety percent boredom and privation and only ten percent action and excitement, with a slim chance of glory thrown in for good measure. There was a far greater chance of being maimed for life.

I do not recall a single time when we ever had enough of either beans or bullets. To make matters worse, my company's quartermaster was a sergeant by the name of Vance, and Vance was as crooked as a dog's hind leg. If he liked you, you would get your share of the provisions, and if he didn't, you would always get short-changed. The way to make Vance like you was to do something for him. If you were a private, that might mean giving him half of your hard twist of tobacco, or some of your winnings if you happened to get lucky in a game of poker or three-card monte. If you were an officer, you automatically got special dispensation from the sergeant, because an officer had the authority to give him light duty. I thought the whole business was despicable, and refused to kowtow to a rancid man like Vance. As a consequence I often got fewer of the provisions than many of my companions, and that rankled something fierce.

It was a long and grueling march across the arid southern plains of Texas in the heat of summer. Some of the horses and even a few of the men didn't make it. I left Austin the epitome of the dashing cavalryman, with a new butternut-gray tunic sewn by my mother, and fat and sassy after several months of being lazy, eating regularly, and also regularly winning at the gaming tables available in every saloon in town. But by the time I got to the Rio Grande, I was lean, hungry, bearded, dirty, bone-tired, and feeling meaner than the devil.

We met with some luck in dealing with Cortinas, catching him red-handed as he led his men in an ambush of a sternwheeler riverboat carrying gold from the mines located in the mountains out west, and headed downriver for Brownsville. Showing up unexpectedly on the north bank of the river, we bled the bandits pretty good in a short but fierce fight. What I remember most about that day was seeing Cortinas himself, astride a big white horse and as fine a target as you could hope for as he rode across a mud flat trying in vain to rally his retreating men, and yet seemingly im-

pervious to our bullets. And believe me, just about
every man in the battalion took at least one shot at him.
I know I did. I think it was the first time I had ever
missed what I was aiming at.

Cortinas wasn't able to rally his troops and eventually gave up, firing what I imagine was a disdainful
look in our direction before riding away. We learned
later that most of his men deserted him shortly
thereafter, and Cortinas went into hiding in the mountains. Some years later, following the ouster of Emperor Maximilian, Cortinas became governor of one of
Mexico's northern provinces. His animosity towards
Anglos never faded; as governor he reportedly fi-
nanced—and may have, on occasion, even led—raids
across the border to steal Texas horses and cattle. Viva,
Cortinas. I was always glad I had missed that shot.

With the Cortinas problem resolved, Colonel Ford
proceeded to occupy various forts abandoned by federal forces. That meant one company garrisoned Fort
Bliss out El Paso way, another set up shop within the
walls of Fort Davis, while I went with Company H to
Fort Clark in Kinney County. That's where I finally
had my reckoning with Sergeant Vance.

About a week after our arrival at Fort Clark, a supply train arrived, and the following evening I went to
the quartermaster's tent to request my ration of bacon
and candles. Vance curtly informed me that there was
very little left, and that if I had wanted a full ration, I
should have come begging sooner. With that he provided me less than half of what I deserved. I made no
protest—but on the way out of the tent I took some
bacon that was lying on top of a crate.

A moment later Sergeant Vance discovered that the
bacon was missing and bolted out of the tent, pistol in
hand.

"Some damn thief stole bacon!" he roared, loud enough to draw the attention of the entire company, most of which was gathered around evening cook fires. "Where is that son of a bitch Thompson?"

I turned and retraced my steps, stopping about twenty paces from Vance.

"I took the bacon," I said. "But I didn't steal it. You owed it to me."

"That bacon was set aside as a ration for the laundress. Surrender it right now or I'll take it from you."

I smiled tautly. "The laundress. I should have known." In fact, I knew what everyone else in the company knew about the special favors the laundry woman, a plump and profane camp follower named Anne Brown, showed the sergeant.

"Give me back that bacon, you bastard," growled Vance, advancing on me.

"Stop right there," I warned him. "If you don't, you'll regret it."

Vance did not heed my warning, instead made the mistake of raising his pistol. We fired simultaneously. His bullet missed me and struck a soldier standing near a fire a few feet behind me. My bullet hit Vance in the chest and knocked him off his feet.

But it wasn't over. Someone shouted a warning and I whirled to see a lieutenant by the name of Hagler coming at me with saber raised. I didn't hesitate, and dropped him with a bullet in the leg.

"Thompson!"

I turned to see Captain Hamner, the company's commanding officer, standing near Vance's fallen form. He had neither pistol nor sword in hand, which I took to be a good sign.

"Drop that pistol, Private," said Hamner.

I did as he told me. "I'll surrender to you, Captain.

I would have to them, had they not been trying to kill me."

Hamner made no comment, other than to order a couple of men to escort me to the guardhouse before turning his attention to the wounded. There I was put in irons. The shackles on my ankles were bolted to the floor, so I had no freedom of movement. I could lie down, sit, or stand still, but could not move around. The guardhouse was built of stone, without windows, save a slot on the door through which the guard on duty outside could peer in to check on me. I was given a bucket half filled with water and a plate of mush each day to sustain me. All in all, these were the worst accommodations I ever had to endure.

A few days after the incident, Captain Hamner came to see me.

"It appears that both Lieutenant Hagler and Sergeant Vance will recover from their wounds," he said. "Had either man died, you would have faced a firing squad."

I shrugged. "There were both trying to kill me. I only did what I had to do."

Hamner nodded. "Most of the men who witnessed the shooting say you were just defending yourself. However, both of the men you shot were officers. I've sent a dispatch to Colonel Ford, explaining the situation. Until I hear from him, I'm going to have to keep you confined. I have not much knowledge of military justice, but the colonel does. He will know what's to be done with you."

I didn't say anything. Just made up my mind then and there that I was going to have to desert.

About a week passed before an opportunity presented itself. The captain visited me again, this time to say that a friend of mine, a private named Dick Richards, had come down with the pox. He had been placed

in a tent about a mile from the fort. No one wanted to
tend to him—indeed, most assumed that he was as
good as dead. Hamner offered me the option of remaining in shackles or going out to that tent to nurse
Richards back to health, if possible, risking exposure
to a highly contagious disease. I made up my mind
immediately. I would go.

Hamner nodded. "Suit yourself. I advise you not to
try to run away, Thompson. There's a hundred miles
of desert between us and the nearest civilization. Not
much out there except Comanches and scorpions and
diamondbacks. I doubt you would get very far."

I spent more than a week out near that tent with
Richards. Every day they would bring supplies—food,
coffee, candles—leaving these stores on a rock a few
hundred yards away. To my amazement, Richards
slowly recovered. Even more amazing was that I did
not contract the pox. When his fever broke and he
could talk coherently rather than babble deliriously,
Dick and I discussed desertion. I told him what my
intentions were and he wanted to throw in with me.

"Those cold-blooded bastards would have left me
out here to die," he muttered resentfully. "If it wasn't
for you, Ben, I would not still be above snakes. So to
hell with them, I say. If you're going, I'm going. But
where are we going—and how are we going to get
there?"

"I don't care where we go," I replied. "But I do
know how."

Each day the company's horses were brought out of
the fort and herded along a nearby creek where they
were allowed to graze on the sparse grass located there.
Two men were assigned to watch over the herd. After
a few hours they would grow tired and careless, as
sentries tend to do, and it would be a fairly easy matter

for me to make off with a couple of horses at the edge of the herd.

And so it was that by sundown Richards and I were thirty miles away from Fort Clark. I didn't know how long it would take them to discover that we and the horses were missing, and whether Captain Hamner would even try to catch us. But we saw no signs of pursuit in the days to come. We bought some clothes and provisions at a trading post—regretfully I disposed of the gray tunic my mother had made—and a week later arrived in San Antonio. We were deserters, but not a soul in that town knew it.

Chapter 5

DICK RICHARDS AND I SPENT some time in San Antonio together before he decided it was time to head south across the border. Part of it was his concern that he would be caught and hanged for a deserter. The army was in such disarray that there was little chance of that, though, and I tried to convince him that we were about as safe as one could hope to be in a big town like San Antonio, but I did not succeed. Then, too, Dick wasn't nearly as lucky as I was at the gaming tables. Well, it wasn't entirely luck—I had become a damned fine poker player if I do say so myself, and wasn't bad at bucking the tiger at the faro wheel, either. So I won consistently, while Dick lost just as consistently, and he soon soured on San Antonio in general.

"I am just going to go on down there and find me a pretty, brown-eyed señorita to keep me company," he told me. "There are worse ways to wait out this damned war."

"Well, I won't stand in your way," I said, "but I'm sorry to see you go."

Dick clasped my hand in his. "You've been a good friend to me, Ben. We'll meet up again."

"Of course we will," I said, and laughed. "In hell. And who knows, maybe even sooner."

I gave him a grubstake out of my winnings and saw him off with a big fandango at a cantina on the south side of town, and I think it is safe to say that those were festivities Dick Richards did not soon forget.

I was perfectly content to ply the trade of gambler. If anyone asked why I wasn't fighting for The Cause, I replied that I had done so, had been at Bull Run with Beauregard, and had suffered a grievous wound that had gelded me. This outrageous lie earned me a good deal of sympathy and any number of free drinks—and no one ever thought to call me on it. Of course, it also meant I had to forego the pleasures provided by the town's soiled doves, for fear the truth would out. But there is always a price to pay.

I might have spent the rest of the war in the saloons and gambling dens of San Antonio if the Yankees hadn't seized the island of Galveston.

Early on in the conflict, President Lincoln had called for a blockade of the Confederacy, and by the middle of 1862, a federal fleet had effectively done the job of closing all the Texas ports, chief among them being Galveston. By October, the small garrison of Confederate soldiers holding Galveston Island had been bombarded by Union warships long enough. When word reached them that an invasion was imminent they abandoned the island altogether. In December several companies of the 42nd Massachusetts occupied and fortified Galveston, supported by a fleet consisting of the frigate USS *Harriet Lane* and several schooners.

About that time a southern gentleman named J. Bankhead Magruder, a major general who had served with Robert E. Lee in the campaigns to defend the Confederate capitol of Richmond, Virginia, was assigned to the command of a district that consisted of Texas, New Mexico, and Arizona. Magruder, being the die-hard Confederate and dashing cavalier that he was, simply could not abide the thought that Yankee soldiers were occupying—and therefore defiling—Southern soil, and resolved to drive the federals from Galveston Island. His decision was well-received in Texas, as we weren't too thrilled about the Yankee presence, either. You might say it was an affront to our dignity. The fact that the blockade rendered Galveston practically useless from a strategic sense made absolutely no difference whatsoever. To make such an argument would have been to miss the point entirely.

Magruder knew that wresting Galveston from the unclean clutches of the federals would require an assault by both land and sea. One problem with that was the unhappy fact that there was no Confederate navy to speak of. So Magruder proceeded to transform a couple of river steamers, the *Bayou City* and the *Neptune*, into gunboats. We called them "cotton clads" because bales of cotton were used in lieu of nonexistent iron plating to protect the vehicles and the men who would be on them. Magruder even found several twenty-four-pounder cannon with which to arm his "fleet." Even so, one had to wonder how the "cotton clads" would fare against a powerful warship like the *Harriet Lane*.

Meanwhile, Magruder reorganized the Second Texas, brought some other units in from New Mexico, and called for five thousand more volunteers. The whole idea of this crusade to rescue Galveston from the Yankees was too much for me to resist. So I made some discreet inquiries and learned that Sergeant Vance had himself deserted, taking off with some stores and the laundress Annie Brown and God knows what else. Lieutenant Hagler had decided not to reenlist after his twelve months were up—due, it was said, to the lameness of his leg. And Captain Hamner had died of a fever. As far as anyone could tell, there was no record of my contretemps with Vance and Hagler, or of my desertion. Paperwork was never the Confederate army's strong suit. With the reorganization, most of the men I knew in Company H were scattered among other units. Learning all this, I wasted no time in enlisting, once again, in the Second Texas. When I gave my name to the recruiting sergeant, he didn't even lift an eyebrow. This time the reenlistment period was for three years, or the war's duration. I wasn't worried about that. There was, after all, always the option of desertion if I got bored and decided not to stay the full term.

Having reorganized, the Second Texas Cavalry marched for Houston to join General Magruder. As was so often the case in the army—any army—it was a lot of hurry up and wait. We were under the mistaken impression that all Magruder was waiting for before launching an attack on the federals on Galveston Island was our arrival. We soon learned differently. Magruder had no intentions of attacking until he had his five thousand volunteers. I wasn't the only one who came to the conclusion that the general was full of bold talk but entirely too cautious when time came to turn words into action.

My regiment made camp among the swamps and bayous, and it was a generally unpleasant experience all around. Though it was November, the days were still warm and humid there on the coastal plain, while the nights were cold and damp. Before long it seemed like at least a third of the regiment was listed on the sick rolls. The only thing we did was drill, and then drill some more. I began to regret the decision to reenlist, and, as were all my companions, I was immensely bored. That's my only excuse for becoming involved in a scheme to smuggle whiskey into the camp.

There were several towns in the vicinity of our encampment, and a good many trading posts, as well. The traders had plenty of rotgut to peddle, and they were eager to have every enlisted man for a customer. While we had no objections, our officers did, and after a trader was caught trying to haul whiskey into the camp, they were all issued strict orders to steer clear. In addition, the officers posted heavy guards to make sure none of us slipped away for a visit to the trading posts. That didn't stop some soldiers from trying. Whiskey was an awfully strong temptation. But no one succeeded in getting through. Eventually the other men in my company turned to me to get the job done. Some of them knew me from the months I had spent in San Antonio, between my periods of service, and I had a reputation for being a real clever fellow.

I managed to succeed where those before me had failed because I braved a cypress swamp south of the camp, the haunt of alligators, cottonmouths, and any number of cutthroats, or so the locals claimed. The officers didn't think anyone would be foolhardy enough to attempt crossing the swamp, but I not only attempted, I got through. The men in my company were so desperate for liquid bravemaker that they had offered me a reward if I brought them what they had a hankering for, and I fully intended to profit from this enterprise.

Before daybreak I was back in camp with six jugs of strong spirits. It was a far cry from bonded liquor, but my fellow soldiers weren't inclined to quibble. I got my reward, the boys got drunk, and the officers posted extra guards. They had no idea who the responsible party was, but they were bound and determined to prevent him from succeeding a second time. I had not intended to press my luck and make another nocturnal excursion through the swamp for a second load of whiskey, but that's exactly what I ended up doing. Somehow the boys pitched in to make up an even bigger pot than before, and then they made me an offer I could not refuse. So about ten days after my debut as a whiskey smuggler, I was riding back through the black, noxious bog on a rainy night, with nothing to guide me but my infallible sense of direction.

Reaching the trading post at which I had acquired the first load of snakehead whiskey, I woke up the proprietor and told him what I needed. He struck me as a little on the nervous side, but then some people are just like that when they get awakened in the middle of the night. I paid for the six jugs of good cheer, tied them to my saddle, three on either side, joined by a length of hard twist passed through the thumb hole. Since it was the middle of the night, the trader came out with a lantern, which he held aloft to provide illumination for my endeavors. Or I assumed that this was what he was doing. When I told him to put the light out, he did so, then went back inside the trading post muttering a hasty "So long."

At that moment mounted men came out of the nearby woods and one of them shouted at me to throw down my guns. I suspected then that the lantern had been a signal, and that I had walked right into a trap.

In the darkness I couldn't tell who they were or how many of them were closing in on me, but I decided there were two possibilities. Either they were army or robbers in cahoots with the trader. As though I would be foolish enough to carry a lot of money, assuming I had a lot, with me on an excursion like this. Still, I wasn't planning to stick around and find out who they were. I swung aboard my horse and kicked it into a gallop and headed down the road from whence I had come.

They chased after me but they didn't do any shooting, and I briefly entertained hopes of getting away—until my horse fell. It had rained that afternoon, a heavy shower, and the road was muddy, and as it rounded a bend in the road my mount slipped and fell sideways. I had no time to jump clear, and the animal landed on my left leg, breaking it. The chase was over.

The men turned out to be soldiers. Second Texas, under a lieutenant's command. I did not find out until later that someone in my company, in trouble for an infraction of his own, had bought leniency by telling of my plan to smuggle in more whiskey. No one knew exactly which trader I was dealing with, so they had posted details at each of several likely trading posts.

You might expect that I was relieved to discover that my pursuers were soldiers and not robbers, but I wasn't. I faced another long stint in jail and that didn't appeal to me one bit. Getting my throat cut seemed to be preferable to that fate.

I wasn't put in a cell this time, as had happened at Fort Clark, and Austin before that. My prison was a tent from which I was forbidden to stray, and a pair of guards were always present to make sure that I stayed put. Luckily, I didn't have to endure this arrangement for very long. On the third day of my incarceration, a stout bearded man in a shabby longcoat paid me a visit.

"My name is Drumm," he said. "Aloysius Drumm. And you would be Ben Thompson."

I nodded. "Pardon me for not getting up."

I was laid out on a narrow wood and canvas cot, my leg bound in a splint.

Drumm looked about in vain for something to sit on. There wasn't anything else in the tent besides the cot.

"The accommodations leave a lot to be desired," I said dryly.

"I see that. Well, no matter. The doctor seems to think your leg will heal up nicely. It was a clean break, fortunately. We can only hope that infection can be kept at bay."

"Well," I said, "it's not like I need to go anywhere any time soon."

"That will be entirely up to you, Thompson."

"How do you figure?"

"You have a choice. You can work for me, or you can spend the rest of the war in a prison camp."

"Work for you. And just who are you and what do you do, anyway?"

Drumm smiled faintly under his dense salt-and-pepper beard. "I am a native of the Commonwealth of Virginia. I was educated at Dartmouth College. I traveled extensively in Europe as a young man. I have been a smuggler, like yourself. In addition, I have dabbled in blackmail, theft, and kidnapping. I am wanted for crimes committed in several countries. And at present I am a spy who holds the rank of major in the army of the Confederacy."

"That's very impressive. But what do you want with me?"

"You're a clever man, Thompson. Devious when you have to be, bold when boldness is called for. I need just such a man to undertake a mission of the utmost importance to the success of our endeavors against the federals. A mission, I might add, that promises to be extremely dangerous. But if you can pull it off, I'll see to it that all charges against you are dropped. I have already discussed the matter with General Magruder, and he has agreed to that stipulation."

"No offense, Major, but I would like to have that in writing."

Drumm chuckled. "I would be disappointed in you, sir, if you did not."

"And exactly what is this mission?"

"I have an associate in Galveston who is in possession of detailed information regarding the federal forces occupying the island. We desperately need that information. In fact, the general insists upon having it before he will move against the enemy. The agent cannot bring this information out to us. So someone has to go in and get it. I think you are the man for the job, Thompson."

"I have a broken leg, Major, remember?"

"In a couple of weeks you will be on your feet, albeit with help from a walking stick, I'll warrant. That will give me time to make preparations to get you onto the island. Once there, however, you will be on your own."

I didn't have to think it over. "You've got yourself a deal."

"Make no mistake. The risks will be exceedingly high. The chances of success are probably slim. And if the federals catch you, well, you will most certainly be executed for a spy."

"Then I'll just have to make sure I don't get caught," I said.

Chapter 6

As I LAY there waiting for my leg to heal sufficiently so that I could embark on a suicide mission for Major Aloysius Drumm—or should I say for the honor and glory of the Confederate States of America?—I learned more about his network of spies on Galveston Island.

Apparently, in the weeks prior to the federal invasion and subsequent occupation of the island, Drumm had visited the city of Galveston and recruited several women to gather intelligence for him in the event that what happened did actually come to pass. These valiant Southern belles, as Drumm liked to call them, were to learn all that they could about the enemy's disposition on the island. Who better for that task than women? They could walk the streets and observe the bluecoats without arousing the level of suspicion that would naturally attend a man who conducted himself in a like manner.

My job, on its face, was simple enough. Once I arrived on the island, I was to make my way to the residence of a Mrs. Lorelei James, who was responsible for gathering all the reports produced by Drumm's bevy of petticoat-and-parasol secret agents and putting them in writing. Mrs. James would give me her report once I handed her a coded missive from Drumm, which would serve as proof that I was the genuine article. Then I would smuggle her report out of Galveston. Drumm provided me with a map of the island, which

I spent long hours perusing, as well as one of the city itself, which I studied until I had every street memorized. The difficulty, then, would not rest in finding the residence of Lorelei James, but in getting there—and getting out again.

At least Drumm had made suitable arrangements to transport me to the island. A small boat manned by two reliable men would deliver me to within one hundred yards of a sandy point at the far western end of the island. That part of the island was largely uninhabited, and all I would have to do, once I swam ashore, was to elude an occasional patrol on the long trek to the city. Shallows at the western end prevented the federal warships from cruising those waters, so Drumm reasoned that under the cover of night the rowboat could come and go unobserved. I hoped he was right. Getting from that western point to Lorelei James's house would be entirely up to me. When I had her report in my possession, I would make my way back to the point on the following night, swim out into the sea one hundred yards due north, in the direction of the mainland, and there find the same rowboat manned by the same two reliable associates awaiting my arrival. Fortunately for all concerned, I was a fairly good swimmer, having learned in waters off the English coast as a boy, and later honed that skill in the Colorado River, which made its serpentine way through the arid hills surrounding Austin.

After a couple of weeks of calculating the odds of my surviving this endeavor, I concluded that they were, at best, five to one against. Galveston was swarming with enemy troops, and getting to and from the home of Mrs. Lorelei James without being apprehended was highly unlikely. But it was worth the chance to avoid spending no telling how long in a stinking prison camp.

The survival rate in those places was not good at all. And once Drumm had shown me the letter signed by General Magruder absolving me of all my sins against the Confederacy, I never had a second thought about going through with his risky scheme.

In a fortnight I was up and around, and at my request Drumm arranged for me to be able to take long walks—accompanied, of course, by a guard. I used a crutch at first. By the end of another week I was getting around pretty well, and using just a cane. During that time I grew a beard.

"It will make me look older," I explained to Drumm, "and if a Billy Yank stops me, I may get away with being there by saying that I'm a veteran of the Indian wars, and because of a bad leg wound I had to sit this war out."

"What Indian war?" asked Drumm.

"Take your pick."

He laughed. "It won't matter what story you tell if they find my coded letter to Mrs. James, or her report, in your possession."

"Maybe they won't find either," I said, and showed him the cane. By pushing down a copper ring, I could lift the curved handle off, exposing a hollowed-out space I had spent all week carving.

"That will hold my letter," said Drumm, nodding approval at my ingenuity, "but I doubt it will the report."

"If I can get in, I'll get out the same way. Just make sure the boat is waiting where it's suppose to be."

"If for any reason it isn't, just swim for it. It's but a mile to the mainland at that point."

"I've heard that sharks frequent those waters."

Drumm smiled. "Swim fast, then."

Late one afternoon he came for me. "You must go

tonight," he said. "The sky is overcast, but there won't
be much wind, so the sea should not be too choppy.
Are you ready?"

Having spent the past three weeks wondering
whether I would live to see another Christmas, I was
certainly ready.

Drumm personally escorted me to the coast, with a
pair of armed guards. He didn't trust me not to make
a break for the tall timber at the last minute, and I
couldn't blame him for that. In his line of work, Aloysius Drumm had not prospered by trusting anyone. And
who's to say that I wouldn't have tried something, absent the guards? I wasn't so committed to the Confederate cause that I was eager to get killed just to prove
my devotion to God and country.

It was around midnight when we reached the rendezvous point with the boat, and only then did Drumm
give me the coded letter I was to present to Lorelei
James as my bonafides. I placed this, rolled up tightly,
into the secret compartment of my cane, bid Drumm
farewell, and climbed into the boat. The two oarsmen
pushed off, clambered in, and put their backs to it, and
we were off.

It was a dark night indeed, and I could see nothing
of the island that was my destination save for a few
pinpricks of dim light to the southeast. These, I suspected, marked the spot where a ferry had once con-
nected Galveston to the mainland. When the boatsmen
stopped rowing and informed me that we were a hundred yards from the western point, I still had to strain
to see land—low dunes with an occasional wind-
twisted palm tree.

I had rolled a long black cloak tightly around the
cane and a five-shot Adams pistol that Drumm had
given me right before my leaving the mainland, tying

both ends of the bundle with a single length of rope. This I then slung over my shoulder, and went over the side without a word to the oarsmen, who did not strike me as men much given to polite discourse anyway.

The water was shockingly cold, so I wasted no time in striking out for shore, trying very hard not to think about sharks, and failing miserably—which motivated me to swim all the more quickly. Before long I was standing on the shoreline. I untied the bundle, shivering uncontrollably all the while. Putting on the cloak, I shoved the pistol in a pocket and, wielding the walking stick, moved deeper into the dunes before striking off for the east. The town of Galveston lay several miles away.

It was rough going through the sand dunes with a stiff, barely-healed leg, but I pushed on, wanting to reach the town before daybreak. I spotted only one Yankee patrol. They were easy to spot, too—camped out on the northern beach a mile west of town, all but one asleep in their blankets, and that one dozing off as he sat by the dwindling fire. Needless to say, I passed them by without any difficulty.

As I drew near the eastern end of the island, I cut across the dunes to the southern beach. I figured I had less than an hour's worth of night remaining, and so that left me with precious little time to waste. Getting into the town was not a problem, but eluding the Yankee patrols that roamed the streets was a different matter entirely. I had several close calls before arriving at the residence of Mrs. Lorelei James.

Persistent tapping on the back door finally roused the sleeping house. An old black man opened the door, but I spared him only a glance, because my attention was immediately drawn to the woman who stood behind him. She was very attractive. The light from the lamp the old man carried shone in her auburn hair and on her alabaster white skin. She wore a silk wrapper and held a pistol quite steady, aimed at my heart. I thought how ironic it would be, having eluded a Yankee army to get here, if I were shot to death by the woman I had come to see.

"Drumm sent me," I said, "and I hope you will give me time to prove that before you shoot."

"Who is Drumm?" she asked coolly.

"If you will allow me." I removed the handle of the cane from its shaft and extracted the coded message. The black man took it from my hand and gave it to her. She looked it over, apparently decoding on the spot. Then she lowered the pistol and bade me enter. The old black shut and bolted the door, then hurried to precede us into a sitting room, where he set about lighting other lamps.

"Would you care for a drink?" asked Lorelei James. "You look to me as though you could use one."

"At least one." I glanced longingly at a chair and sofa, but they were of top quality, and I was covered with dirt and sand.

"Please, sit down before you fall down," she said.

I sank into a chair with a grateful sigh. She arranged herself on the sofa facing me. The old black brought us our drinks—cognac. As soon as I'd had some of it, I began to feel a lot better about things.

"Feel safe?" she asked, with a faint smile. "You shouldn't, you know. Not entirely, anyway."

"Why not?"

"Drumm sent you just in the nick of time. The Yankees have begun to suspect something."

"Are they watching this house?"

"No, I don't believe they are."

In spite of that I had to wonder if I had walked into a trap rather than a sanctuary.

"So they think you're a spy?" I asked her.

"One of the ladies with whom I work caught the eye of a young officer. By the time we learned that he was watching her, he had come to believe that we were up to something. I don't know if he shared his suspicions with anyone before he died."

Something in the way she said that prompted me to say, "You killed him."

"Oh, no. Not I, personally. But I did pay the fee requested by the two men who did."

I stared at her for a moment. Lorelei James was the epitome of the Southern belle, and she was also a strikingly handsome young woman into the bargain. It was difficult to picture her as an accomplice to cold-blooded murder. Then I reminded myself that this was war, so maybe it didn't qualify as murder, after all.

"He was just a Yankee," she said, with a trace of venom in her voice. "He wore the same uniform as the man who killed my husband at Shiloh."

"I'm sorry for your loss. Now, if you'll give me the report I came for, I'll be on my way."

"It's nearly dawn. You're leaving the island in broad daylight?"

"No. I rendezvous with a boat at midnight, on the other end of the island."

"Then you must stay here until night comes."

"I'm thinking it might be safer if I find some other place to hole up."

"No," she said firmly. "The safest place for you is here. If the Yankees were to come, I would hide you where you could not be found, no matter how diligently they searched." The faint smile touched her lips again. "You will simply have to trust me."

"It would be ungentlemanly of me not to," I said.

She laughed. "Otis will show you to your room. Sleep as long as you like."

I finished the cognac, rose, thanked her for her hospitality, and followed the old black out of the room. He escorted me upstairs to a bedroom. There I stripped down, slid the Adams pistol under a pillow, and climbed into the four-poster, my body sinking into the feather mattress. I closed my eyes and instantly was asleep.

It was early afternoon when I awoke, to find my clothes cleaned and neatly folded at the foot of the bed. A meal awaited me downstairs—bread and stew. Lorelei James apologized for the plainness of the fare. "The Yankee officers are the only ones who eat well in Galveston these days," she said bitterly.

"This is far better than anything I've had in the last six months, so don't apologize."

Until I had a taste of the stew, I didn't realize how hungry I was. She watched me, amused, as I wolfed it down.

"Now I am the one who should apologize," I said with a self-conscious laugh. "I do have better table manners than this."

"I hear the faintest of accents. Where are you from?"

"England. My father served in the Royal Navy. We came to Texas about eight years ago."

"You have the vocabulary and diction of a gentleman. You have been well-schooled."

"My mother insisted on it. I just realized, I have you at an advantage. I know your name, but you don't know mine."

She shook her head. "Just a first name will do."

"It's Ben."

"Very well then, Ben. And you must call me Lorelei."

"This house," I said. "It's very quiet. You have no children?"

"No," she replied wistfully. "My husband and I were married less than a year before he died. Of course we both wanted children. Lots of them. We had a wonderful .future planned. We were madly in love, you see."

"Of course. Perhaps I shouldn't have . . ."

"Nonsense. I live here alone. Well, Otis is here, and his daughter, Beulah." She glanced pensively about the well-appointed dining room. "You're right, Ben. It is quiet. Very."

The mask slipped for a moment and I caught a glimpse of her loneliness and grief. Oddly, I felt a measure of resentment toward Aloysius Drumm. Knowing him as I did, I assumed he had known all about the fate met by this woman's husband, and no doubt he had used her hatred for the Yankees to his advantage in persuading her to engage in the dangerous work he'd had in mind for her. Now, if Lorelei was correct, and the federals had their suspicions, she was in very grave peril. A spy would be hanged or placed before a firing squad, regardless of gender.

"I think you should come with me tonight, Lorelei," I said.

She smiled warmly at me. "I appreciate your concern for my welfare, Ben. Really, I do. But I couldn't possibly."

"They're bound to come for you sooner or later. I have a feeling you know that."

"Yes. But until they do, I will stay here and fight for the cause the only way I am able. Besides, Drumm sent you to get our report because General Magruder is planning to liberate us. Is that not true?"

I admitted that it was. "But with Magruder I'm afraid there's not much telling when the liberation will take place. He might wait until all the Billy Yanks on this island die of old age."

She gazed solemnly at me. "You do not believe in our cause, do you?"

"Not the way you do, I'm ashamed to say." And I actually was ashamed to say it.

"Well, my husband believed, and so do I. And if I die, I know I shall finally be reunited with him. Have you ever been in love, Ben? Truly in love?"

"No, not like that."

"I hope one day you shall be."

There was nothing more to say. Lorelei James was quite willing to die because without her husband beside her, life held no allure. Though I could not really comprehend such depth of feeling, such grief, there could be no doubt that she was sincere. And it struck me as such a tragic waste.

Lorelei James had made arrangements to get me out of the city that night. About eight o'clock that evening a "dead wagon" came to the back of the house. Two men carried a pine coffin inside, into which I, along with the report I had come for, were placed. The lid of the coffin was nailed shut. She paid the men, who loaded me into the wagon and took me to a cemetery beyond the town limits. A federal patrol stopped the wagon once, but apparently the dead wagon was a common enough sight, and we were swiftly passed through. At the cemetery I was released from the coffin and sent on my way. I reached the western end of the island and at midnight caught the briefest glimpse of a lantern's light out on the water. I swam for the spot, and a short while later was being pulled aboard the rowboat.

Aloysius Drumm was waiting for me on the mainland. I gave him the report, in exchange for General Magruder's letter clearing me of all charges. As he turned away, I grabbed his arm.

"We need to take that island very soon," I told him. "Lorelei James doesn't have a lot of time."

I could not read the expression on his face in the darkness, but his voice was cold. "She is a very brave lady, and she knew the risks involved."

My exertions during the mission to the island caused considerable swelling in my still unhealed leg, so I was not involved in the battle to retake Galveston Island. Magruder launched his attack on the night of December 31, sending his troops, including the Second Texas, across the bay from Virginia Point in a flotilla of small boats. They made a landing against surprisingly light resistance and marched on Galveston. That's where the federals stiffened. The attack on Union positions the following day was a bloody one. Magruder's men were met with heavy fire from the federals behind their barricades, who were supported by the guns of their ships in the harbor. The outcome was in doubt—until the two "cotton clads" appeared on the scene. They had been delayed by the low tide. The *Neptune* was sunk, but the *Bayou City* rammed the USS *Harriet Lane,* and a boarding party stormed the federal frigate. The Union officers were killed almost immediately, and in the confusion that followed, the frigate's crew was overcome. When the men of the *Bayou City* turned the frigate's guns on the federal positions ashore, the 42nd Massachusetts surrendered, and the battle was won. Luck had been on Magruder's side. The victory was, in fact, nothing short of miraculous.

When I arrived in Galveston the following day, I was praying for another miracle. But when Otis opened the door, I knew in a glance that my worst fears were going to be realized. The old black man told me that the Yankees had come for his mistress the day before the battle. He broke down as he relayed to me the sad fact that she had greeted them with pistol in hand, and shot one of the bluecoats, wounding him gravely, before she was seized. They had then hanged her from the limb of a tree behind the house, without benefit of trial. The funeral was to take place later today, and Otis invited me to pay my last respects, as the remains of Lorelei James were lying in state in the sitting room. I went in only to confirm my suspicions—and after I saw that faint smile on her cold blue lips, I made a quick departure.

Chapter 7

WE TOOK GALVESTON back at the end of 1862. Six
months later the war was essentially lost, because the
Yankees captured Vicksburg—and took control of the
Mississippi River—while General Robert E. Lee's
Army of Northern Virginia, which many in the South
had come to believe was invincible, was beaten at a
place in Pennsylvania called Gettysburg. Of course, relatively few Southerners were going to admit defeat, but
the loss of Mississippi left the Confederacy divided,
with Texas and Louisiana isolated from the other
Southern states.

Following the victory at Galveston I returned to
Austin on furlough. There I discovered that my mother
had struck up a friendship with one Elizabeth Moore,
whose husband, Martin, was a very successful merchant in town. That was how I made the acquaintance
of Catherine, daughter of Martin and Elizabeth. It was
my mother's fervent desire that I marry—she hoped it
would settle me down and keep me out of trouble—
and in her opinion Catherine Moore was quite a catch.
I could tell she was prepared for stiff resistance from
me. But I surprised her by being agreeable to the
match.

You might expect that a prominent and well-to-do
businessman like Martin Moore—not to mention his
prim and proper wife—would have serious doubts
about the suitability of someone like me for the role of

son-in-law. I had a reputation, and it wasn't a good one. Austin remembered the Joe Smith business, and by this time word had spread concerning my misadventures in New Orleans as well as my stint as a gambler in San Antonio following my desertion from the army. All in all, not what you would describe as a sterling record.

Strangely, though, the Moores were also amenable to the idea of their daughter marrying me. "We face most uncertain times," Martin Moore told me. "I fear that the Confederacy may lose this struggle, in spite of the heroic efforts of all the brave men such as yourself."

I didn't bother clarifying that I had not made any heroic efforts on the behalf of the Confederate States of America.

"If I am right," he continued, "and the war is lost, Texas faces dark days ahead. There will be an army of occupation, and martial law. Many of those who supported the Confederacy will probably have their rights stripped away, their property confiscated. Slaves will be freed, and perhaps even persuaded to seek their vengeance against former masters."

"You paint a pretty bleak picture, sir."

"One must be prepared for the worst. If all this does come to pass, my daughter will need to be protected."

I understood then why Mr. Moore was willing to overlook the more shady aspects of my past.

"You could depend on me to do that, sir," I promised. "No harm would come to her. On that you have my word."

He nodded. "I have every confidence in you, Ben."

Now you might wonder in all this how Catherine and I felt about each other. She made it plain to everyone concerned that she had fallen in love with me at once. And I can safely say that I was fond of her. She was a bright and charming young woman, considerate and shy, and while not a beauty the way the late Lorelei James had been, she was not homely, either—a willowy, graceful girl with hair the color of cornsilk and big blue eyes and a smile that could melt the hardest heart. For someone raised on the frontier she had had a sheltered life; she was naïve about many things, and entirely too prone to giving strangers the benefit of the doubt. So I could understand why her father was concerned for her welfare. She was too much the trusting soul. Obviously, as she trusted me.

Did I love Catherine Moore? To be honest, I did not, though I professed that I did often enough to her. But I did feel the urge to be married, to be with someone who cared about me. I wanted to belong to someone. I needed an anchor in my life. And I thought it very likely that in time I would grow to love Catherine to the same extent that she loved me. And so, at the age of twenty, I was married.

Shortly after, I received a transfer that I had requested, and found myself posted to the Rio Grande and serving once more under the able Colonel Rip Ford. My younger brother, Billy, had come of age, and managed to get assigned to my company. For that I was grateful. I had always looked out for Billy, and he was one who needed a lot of looking after, as he somehow excelled even me where getting into trouble was concerned.

Fortunately, there wasn't much trouble to get into along the Rio Grande. Now that Cortinas had been banished to the mountains, the border was pretty quiet. For once I didn't mind the lack of adventure. One reason was that I wanted to keep Billy out of harm's way. Another was that I had lost my taste for war. All I could think about was getting out of the army alive and whole and embarking on a new and respectable life with my bride—though I admit I had some difficulty in figuring out what kind of respectable enterprise I was suited for.

Billy and I found a profitable way to sit out the war—gambling. In particular, the game of three-card monte. When the regiment was transferred to Laredo, I used seventy dollars in gold that Billy had brought with him from home as a grubstake and won a thousand dollars in a single night. The next day, Billy and I and a friend named Julius Brown crossed over into Mexico, where a Mexican regiment was stationed in and around the border town of Nuevo Laredo. Knowing that no Mexican worth his salt could resist a game of monte, we opened a game up for those soldiers in a cantina. While I dealt, Billy stood behind me watching the players, and Brown sat at a nearby table keeping an eye on the rest of the place. A border-town cantina was no place to let your guard down.

As it happened, the Mexican soldiers had little money between them, but as I heard that they would be paid in the next day or two, I was willing to come to some kind of arrangement with them. Since they were all armed to the teeth, we used their pistols as collateral, and by the end of the night we had won two dozen smokemakers. The Mexican soldiers took their bad luck in stride, vowing to return the following night with their pockets full of pesos, and confident that they would win their artillery back and then some.

The next night Billy and I again set up shop in the cantina. This time Julius Brown was unable to join us, having business of an entirely different nature to attend to. I cannot recall her name. But I wasn't worried. The Mexican soldiers seemed to be good sports.

With their hard-earned pay in their pockets, the soldiers came back for more that evening, and by midnight we were up nearly two thousand dollars, which meant that most of the *federales* had lost nearly all of their wages. By this time their mood had changed— and not for the better. Billy sensed this, too, and bent down to inform me that he was not heeled.

I gave him an angry look. "Why the hell not, Billy? What the hell is wrong with you, anyway? This is a fine time to tell me."

He shrugged, shamefaced. "I left my pistol in my saddlebags."

I swore under my breath, cursing him and myself for not noticing sooner that he was unarmed. My brother was like that sometimes. He could be awfully careless, and did some outright dumb things. But this, I thought, was the dumbest thing he had ever done.

"Well then go get it and hurry right back," I said tersely.

We had left our horses in a livery down the street, a business run by an American, because one did not leave his mount out in the open in this town. Not if he ever wanted to see it again.

Billy left the cantina and a few more hands were played—until I noticed one of the soldiers clumsily palming a card when I invited him to cut the deck. I promptly laid the pasteboards aside and swept all my winnings into a canvas sack, which I had used to carry the pistols that the soldiers had bought back earlier in the evening. Then I looked up to see one of the soldiers, an unusually tall, gaunt and mean-looking character by the name of Lieutenant Gonzales, looming over me, standing in front of the others.

"You cannot close the game, mister," he said.

"Watch me."

"Then you must give these men their money back."

I smiled at him. "I hope you're joking, Lieutenant. But if you aren't, I have but one thing to say to you. Go to hell."

Gonzales reached for his pistol. There were a couple of candles on the table and for some reason he took a swipe at them with the barrel of his gun, I assume in an attempt to plunge our corner of the cantina into darkness, though why he needed more an advantage than to have half a dozen of his *compadres* backing him I could not say. But that was his mistake, because in a gunfight one should use his hardware for one thing and one thing only—and knocking over candles isn't it.

One of the other soldiers, whose name was Miguel, I think, also drew his pistol, and he did so with a quickness that surprised me, especially since I had seen him down several glasses of *aguardiente,* which is as potent a libation as can be found the world over. Before I could bring my own pistol to bear, he had aimed at my chest and pulled the trigger. It was point-blank range, and all I could wonder at that instant was why I felt no pain. In the next instant I had put a bullet in Miguel's brain pan. I then turned my gun on Lieutenant Gonzales and plugged him in the chest. Sweeping the candles off the table, extinguishing them in the process, I tipped my chair over backwards, hitting the floor as some of the other soldiers started shooting.

For a moment the cantina was filled with the din of gunfire, the muzzle flashes, the acrid smoke. Lashing out with one leg, I knocked the table over and fired at the muzzle flashes. One of the soldiers gave a shout and suddenly the whole bunch of them were stampeding out the door. Taking only long enough to reload, I grabbed the canvas bag and went out right behind them, hoping that in the darkness and the confusion I might be able to slip away. I wasn't sure why they were running out of the cantina—perhaps the sight of Miguel's blood and brains emerging in a pink spray from a gaping hole in the back of his head had unnerved them. But I wasn't going to make the mistake of assuming that all the fight had gone out of them. I wasn't going to linger inside the cantina in the hopes that they would not find their courage, would not return to avenge the deaths of their comrades.

The cantina was located on the edge of town, hard by a canal, and I turned in that direction. I knew that if I followed the canal, it would bring me near the back wall of the livery where my horse was kept, and in that way I could avoid the streets of Nuevo Laredo altogether, which seemed advisable under the circumstances. But just as I reached the edge of the canal, one of the soldiers recognized me, and cut loose with a shotgun he had taken, I presume, from the saddle on his horse, which was tethered outside the cantina. I felt the shotgun's load tearing through the fabric of my coat as I hurled myself into the canal. Warm brackish water closed in over my head and I swam for the far bank. When I broke the surface and looked back, I could see none of the Mexican soldiers. I did, however, see Billy, running along the streets toward the cantina, and called out to him.

"Are you hurt, Ben?" he called back.

"No, I don't think so," I replied, with some amazement. Somehow Miguel had missed me. "Get back to the livery," I told him. "Don't wait for me. Get the hell across the river."

"I don't think I should leave you."

"Damn it, Billy, just do what I tell you. I'll be right along."

He could tell by my tone of voice that I was in no mood to brook any dissent, and with a jaunty salute, he turned and headed back in the direction of the livery.

I climbed up the steep bank of the canal, dragging the canvas bag along behind me. It was wet and heavy, and it had been no easy task to swim while clinging to it, but I wasn't going to part with that money. I had earned it, twice over. And I had it in mind that my share would be a good grubstake for Catherine and me when I got home. I could buy a house where she and I could set up shop. After all, it was a husband's duty to provide his bride with a home of her own. Mrs. Ben Thompson couldn't very well remain under her parent's roof forever.

As I reached the vicinity of the livery, I saw Billy riding hell-bent for leather away, and silently wished him all the best. I was about to attempt another crossing of the canal so that I could retrieve my own horse when several of the Mexican soldiers appeared. They didn't see me crouched in the darkness across the canal. I cursed softly but vehemently as they entered the livery. Billy had departed not a moment too soon. But I was a day late and a dollar short. I expected them to linger there in the hope that I would show up for my cayuse. So I proceeded on down the canal, knowing it would eventually bring me to the Rio Grande.

The river was three-quarters of a mile wide at this point. And it ran deep and strong. There was no way I could swim to the other side—not burdened as I was with the heavy canvas bag. I roamed the bank looking for something I could use—a log, a stout limb, a discarded board—anything that might support me in the water. But I had no luck in the search. So I resorted to pulling up some brush and, shedding my ruined coat, cutting it into long strips, which I used to bind the brush together. Then I stripped down to the skin, tied my pistol and boots in a bundle composed of trousers and shirt, tied that bundle to the brush raft, and set out. I kept a firm grip on the canvas sack, letting it ride on the brush, and clung to the raft with both arms, kicking to propel the raft and myself across the river. The current swept me more than two miles downriver before I finally reached the other side. Exhausted, I lay down in the wet sand to rest, and fell sound asleep.

The morning sun woke me and I immediately spotted horsemen coming along the river on the Mexican side. I dodged deeper into the chaparral, not knowing whether they were the same men I had crossed swords with the night before, and having no desire to find out. When they had passed on downriver and were out of sight, I got up and began walking westward, in the direction of Laredo. A couple of hours later a patrol from my regiment found me. They were looking for me, as Billy had spread word of my plight.

That afternoon I was summoned before Colonel Ford, who had established his headquarters in a small adobe house on the edge of town. He had declined the offer of much better accommodations made by several of Laredo's leading families. As I stood before his desk, he gave me a stern once-over and then shook his head.

"I don't know how you manage it, Thompson."

"Manage what, sir?"

"Getting into so much hot water. You have a God-given talent. There's some noise being made across the river. Colonel Benavides wants you handed over for the killing of two of his men, one of them an officer."

"I had to do it, Colonel. Self-defense."

"I expect that's true. You're just damned lucky that I believe you."

Chapter 8

I ACCOMPANIED JOHN Rapp back to Austin and there used some of the money I had won—and nearly died for—in Nuevo Laredo for a small but comfortable house into which Catherine and I settled. Rapp and I proceeded to round up recruits for the new company, the command of which went to Rapp, while I was commissioned lieutenant. I didn't want the rank, but there was no avoiding it. Finding men hardy enough for action against Comanche raiders was no easy task. After four years of war, most of the able-bodied men were either dead, crippled, or already in the army. Nonetheless, we eventually managed to fill the rolls, and a few weeks later I kissed my wife farewell and went with the company into camp near Waco. We were there, having not yet ventured out against the Comanches because Rapp, rightly so, thought the new recruits needed more drill, when word came of Lee's surrender at a place in Virginia called Appomattox Courthouse. The war was over. The Confederacy had been defeated.

Before long, federal troops commanded by a General Gordon Granger arrived in Texas by sea. Contingents marched immediately on Austin and San Antonio. Granger suspended all state authority, establishing martial law. His next act was to free all the slaves. The unit stationed in Austin was led by a colonel named Badger. One of his first orders was to issue a military warrant for my arrest. I was taken from my home in shackles and lodged in the town jail—my second stay in that establishment. I didn't like it any better this time around, especially considering that I had no idea why I was being singled out for such attention. My wife and family appealed to Badger to set bail so that I could be freed from that dark, reeking hole. But the colonel curtly refused. The Austin *Daily Statesman* ran a story speculating that my arrest had something to do with the ambush of several of Badger's men on the road south of town—an act that I'd had absolutely no part in, or knowledge of.

After a fortnight in jail I was visited by a pair of Mexican gentlemen. They were well-dressed, and obviously men of means. One of them, who introduced himself as Jorge Valiente, did all the talking. He began by informing me that the Emperor Maximilian was having some trouble with rebels in the provinces. His army had proven unreliable in dealing with the situation, as many of the conscripts sympathized with the insurrectionists. For that reason the emperor had dispatched agents to Texas.

"Our mission, señor," said Valiente, "is to recruit good, brave, experienced fighting men to serve the emperor by putting down the insurrection, and helping him retain the throne that is rightfully his."

"And how is that going?" I asked.

"It goes well. We have found that many Texans, most of whom served of late in the armies of the Confederate States, are highly discontented with the current state of affairs. They are denied what is necessary to work their farms and run their businesses. They chafe beneath the mailed fist of federal military rule. They find no justice in the military courts. Their rights are denied them at every turn. You, Señor Thompson, are a case in point."

"You're telling me."

"You were an officer in the Confederate army, is that not so?"

"A lieutenant."

"I am authorized, then, to offer you a commission in the army of the Emperor Maximilian."

"What's the pay like in that army?"

"You will be paid well, and in a timely fashion, I can assure you."

"That would be a pleasant change, after serving the Confederacy," I remarked wryly.

"Then you accept?"

"Well, I would, yes—except that, as you can see, I will have some difficulty in actually getting to Mexico at the present time."

"We can do nothing to help you there, I regret to say," said Valiente. "But rest assured that your commission awaits you in Matamoros."

I nodded. "I'll do my best to get there before your war is over."

It soon became apparent to me that as far as Colonel Badger was concerned, I could rot in jail. As there was no legal way to earn my freedom, my only recourse was to engineer an escape. I had Catherine bring me all the money that was left after the purchase of the house, and used it to bribe the jail guards. It was surprisingly easy to purchase their help. In fact, several of them expressed an interest in accompanying me to Mexico. Some of them had become addicted to war, and disliked this occupation duty. And a few even objected to the way the United States was mollycoddling the freed slaves while treating Southern whites with such contempt and harshness. Word was out that the men who fought for Maximilian were given license to loot, which meant one could come away from such a war with his pockets full.

In the end, two of my guards agreed, for a sum of money, to assist me. The day before we were to make our break, my wife and mother and Billy came to see me, and we said our farewells. Billy ached to go with me, but I told him that he had to stay and look out for the womenfolk. As there was no way of knowing when or even if I could return to Texas, I promised Catherine that when I could do so, I would send for her, and we would build a life together south of the border. I assured her that once the emperor had quelled the rebellious provinces, he would be very grateful to the men who had been instrumental in bringing that result about. It was said that Maximilian could be a very generous ruler. So I intended to be one of those men. I must admit, I felt a twinge of guilt where Catherine was concerned. We had been married for almost two years, and most of that time I had spent away from her side. But at least she had a home to call her own now—assuming the federals didn't confiscate it. My mother assured me that if they tried, or harassed Catherine in any way, she would take her in.

The next night my two accomplices were both on duty, and we got away clean. They had brought a horse around for me, and a pistol as well, and had brought along plenty of provisions. When we got across the Colorado River, we found five riders waiting for us, and that gave me a scare because they all wore the uniforms of the United States Army. But my two companions quickly set my mind to rest. These five, as it turned out, also wanted to desert and try their luck in Mexico.

"Well, damn it, I wish you had told me sooner that

we were going to have some company on this trip," I said crossly, putting away my pistol.

"We weren't sure you would like it, Ben," admitted one of them a little sheepishly.

"And I don't, because it means you boys were talking too much, and that could have scotched the whole deal, if you'd talked to the wrong man. I really don't have much choice but to go along with it now."

"No," said the other one, grinning. "I guess you don't, at that."

"Then let's keep moving. I want to be a long way from Austin by daybreak."

We rode hard all night, then found a place to while away the day, in a thick bosky of scrub oak, to rest the horses and to make sure no one was on our trail. No one seemed to be. Nevertheless, it was agreed that we would split up. I and two men—the guards who had helped me escape—would make up one group, the other five men the second. We would meet two days hence at a place called Seven Springs, about sixty miles south of San Antonio. Once we reached that point, the chances of our being apprehended would lessen considerably. There wasn't much between Seven Springs and the border except dust and cactus.

My accomplices and I reached Seven Springs without mishap. But the other group never made an appearance, though we waited an extra day for them. Had they been caught? Or had they had a change of heart? It was too risky to tarry longer, so the three of us rode south for Matamoros.

We crossed the Rio Grande several days later, and there I was first met by a Captain Jack Gilly, who was an aide to General Mejia. Valiente proved as good as his word. My commission as a lieutenant in the army of the Emperor Maximilian was waiting for me. I was placed, along with my two associates, in a company commanded by a Captain Frank Mullins, recently of the Confederate army.

The very day after my arrival in Matamoros, a rebel army commanded by Mariano Escobedo surrounded the city. Escobedo had a reputation as a butcher, a man who took no prisoners, and he outnumbered us by a three to one margin. But there was no panic in the ranks, and I soon found out why that was so. General Mejia had the complete loyalty of just about all the men who served in his command.

Mejia was a full-blooded Indio, of low birth, completely unlettered, but a man of tremendous cunning and daring whose many personal attributes—honesty, fairness, integrity, and compassion for his men—endeared him to the ranks. He wasn't much to look at—a short, stocky, and very homely man whose uniform consisted of a battered straw hat and a frayed green tunic. But he was intensely loyal to Maximilian, and, from what I could tell, was the emperor's most accomplished field commander. It was said that on one occasion his force was routed in battle, but Mejia placed himself at the head of a company of lancers and charged the enemy, stopping their advance and giving his subordinates a chance to rally his troops, who, inspired—and shamed—by the gallant charge of the lancers, counterattacked and won the day. With such an example as that from its leader, how could any army falter in its purpose?

Twenty-four hours later, Mejia led a sortie against Escobedo's besieging force. The fighting was fierce, but we inflicted heavy losses on the enemy. Our own losses were not light. More than twenty of the men in my company fell, among them one of the guards who had aided my escape from the Austin jail.

Mejia sent out sorties on an almost daily basis, and in this way kept open his lines of communication with the interior, where the imperialists still held sway. At the same time he kept Escobedo guessing and prevented the rebel leader from tightening the siege. I was involved in several of the forays, and earned a promotion during one of them, when I led a band of fifty hand-picked men to break through enemy lines and attacked a supply train that we had learned about from spies. We surprised the wagons, killing most of the rebels who accompanied it. After burning the wagons and the stores they contained—to try to get them back to Matamoros would slow us down and make us easy targets—we returned with the mule teams. The next day Mejia made me a captain, and I was given a company of my own, consisting almost entirely of Texans, most of whom were ex-Confederates. All modesty aside, we became the best cavalry Mejia had at his disposal.

In spite of our successes, Matamoros might well have fallen to the rebels, but for the fact that imperialist forces moved north to threaten Escobedo's rear, and he had to retire to Camargo. But then luck deserted our cause. An imperialist army was defeated at Saltillo. And then Mejia sent General Olvera south with over fifteen hundred men, with orders to rendezvous with another imperialist army at Charco Escondido. My company was assigned to Olvera, and he used us as an advanced guard. Which didn't do him much good because Escobedo came roaring out of Camargo with four thousand men and attacked the rear of Olvera's column. I led my men into the fray, and they fought with ferocity and courage, but the outcome was never in doubt. Escobedo won the day. When it was over, there were only eighteen men left in my command. Though

there were several bullet holes in my coat, I was untouched, and some of the men began to speculate that
I led a charmed life. I began to wonder the same thing,
remembering how that soldier in Nuevo Laredo had
fired at me, point blank, with no effect.

There were other battles lost, and by the end of the
year 1866 it appeared that Emperor Maximilian's days
were numbered. Men deserted the imperialist cause by
the hundreds. Even Mejia's army was weakened by
troops going over the hill. Maximilian left the comforts
of his palace and placed himself at the head of his army
and ordered all those still loyal to him to come to Queretaro, where the fate of the empire would be decided
in one final struggle. Mejia announced that he would
not order us to go with him. Seven hundred of us volunteered to go. Though things looked bleak, I felt I had
no choice in the matter. I had no place else to go.

We reached our destination after an arduous forced
march across the desert—just in time, too, for the rebels were converging from all points of the compass,
and before long, Queretaro was a besieged city. In spite
of this—or perhaps because of the near-certain doom
that confronted us—the gambling dens and fandango
halls did a thriving business. "It's eat, drink, and be
merry time," Jack Gilly told me. "Because tomorrow
we're going to die. And if it doesn't happen tomorrow,
then it will happen damned soon and that's an ironclad
fact."

I had to agree with his assessment, and in that ne'er-
do-well frame of mind he and I patronized the Queretaro dens of iniquity. We gambled a great deal and we
drank a lot—the difference being that Gilly couldn't
hold his liquor. So it happened that one night, as he
stumbled out of a fandango hall, he drew his pistol and
took some potshots at the moon. This noisy exuberance

attracted the attention of several constables, who disarmed Gilly and me and marched us in the direction of the city jail. Along the way a man in my company spotted us and ran off to alert his companions. One of the constables saw him and concluded that I had given some sort of secret sign to the soldier, when, in fact, I'd had no chance, and no need, to do so. The constable hit me twice in the throat with the barrel of his pistol, which thoroughly annoyed me. I was about to put up a fight—I did not relish the idea of visiting a Mexican jail—when about thirty men from my company arrived on the scene, guns brandished. The city police beat a hasty retreat.

It might have been so but for the fact that I visited the same fandango hall about a week later. As I danced with a pretty señorita, I noticed that the same constable who had struck me with his pistol was in the room. When the dance was over, I escorted my partner to her chair and, at her request, set off to find refreshments. The constable chose that moment to confront me.

"Gringo," he said, "you and I have some unfinished business."

"It will have to wait," I replied curtly. "I'm getting a lady a drink."

"You will step outside with me now."

"No, I'll deal with you later," I said, and tried to get past him. It was then that he drew a knife and lunged at me. I sidestepped him, took the pistol from under my frock coat, and shot him. As he went down, I shot him several more times as insurance against the possibility that he might get up again. I need not have worried on that score, but I didn't consider it a waste of ammunition under the circumstances, as I had a strong dislike for the bastard. In the confusion that followed, I slipped away into the darkness and went straight to General Mejia, to whom I gave a full and unvarnished report.

"None of that matters now," said the general grimly. He handed me a sack heavy with coins. I opened the sack and estimated its contents to be, roughly, a thousand dollars in gold pieces.

"What is this for, General? If I'd known you had a bounty on Queretaro constables, I would have done this sooner."

"I fear all is lost, Captain. I advise you to get out of Queretaro, and soon. Make your way to Vera Cruz and find passage on the next ship."

"What about you, sir?"

"I will stand by my emperor to the last breath."

I had to admire his loyalty. I felt a certain degree of allegiance to Mejia, myself. But not enough to stick around and face certain death if indeed, as the general seemed to think, all was lost.

The following night Jack Gilly and I slipped out of Queretaro, got through the enemy lines, and headed for the coast. At Vera Cruz I came down with a fever and spent a fortnight sweating it out, sometimes delirious and at others clear of head, in a seedy room above a waterfront mercantile. Gilly stuck by me. It was through him that I heard the news of Queretaro's fall. Traitors in the emperor's officer corps had conspired with the rebels, giving them access to the city, so that it fell with hardly a shot being fired. Maximilian was captured along with his most trusted generals, among them Mejia. Word was that though Mejia was given an opportunity to renounce the emperor and thereby save his own life, he refused to do so, and was taken the very next day to stand before a firing squad right alongside Maximilian.

Though my condition slowly improved, my spirits

remained low. I was a fugitive in Mexico as well as in my own country now. Gilly suggested that we travel to South America. The armies of the young republics down there, which had not too long ago thrown off the Spanish yoke, were always in need of soldiers of fortune. I could muster up little enthusiasm for his plan. I was weary of war. I missed my wife. I wanted to go home.

Once again Fortune smiled on me. A weeks-old copy of the New Orleans *Picayune* brought welcome news. Texas had reestablished a civilian government, ratified by the people. She was no longer under martial law. This did not mean, necessarily, that there was no risk involved in my returning home, but I was willing to take the chance.

Soon thereafter I was on a merchant brig sailing for Galveston. My friend Jack Gilly went to South America alone. I do not know what became of him, but I doubt that he survived long. Old age was something very few men like Gilly and I lived to experience.

Chapter 9

WE HUMANS HAVE a great knack for self-delusion. We believe what we want to believe. I suppose it was the fact that I had been on the losing side in two consecutive wars that made me so desperate for good news, and therefore so quick to accept as true the information I had gleaned from that New Orleans newspaper. By the time I discovered that it wasn't all that accurate, I was already in Texas. In Galveston, to be exact.

True, Texans had held a convention early in 1866, and produced a new state constitution that was ratified by the people that summer. They had even held elections and chosen a governor and lieutenant-governor. But by the time I had arrived on the scene, the United States Congress in its infinite wisdom had decided that Texas—as well as the other Southern states—wasn't ready for self-government just yet, and arbitrarily declared all constitutions and elections null and void. They had their hooks into us and they were not about to let us go so quickly.

Texas and Louisiana became the Fifth Military District, under the command of General Phil Sheridan. Sheridan made a tour of Texas, staying only long enough to remove the duly-elected governor, James Throckmorton, from office. Then he returned to his headquarters in New Orleans. Apparently he was none too impressed by what he had seen of the Lone Star State, for he was overheard to say that if he owned both hell and Texas, he would rent out Texas and live in hell. To be fair, Texans were not impressed with Sheridan, either, and most of us felt that his residing in hell was a circumstance devoutly to be wished.

Uncertain as to what lay in store for me, I decided to brave it out and go home to Austin. I took the precaution of slipping into town late one night and got into my house—and into Catherine's loving arms— without being spotted. She wept with joy to see me, as my last letter from Mexico had arrived many months earlier, and the news of Maximilian's fate had caused her to fear the worst where I was concerned. Then she told me that there remained an indictment against me for the killing of the soldiers, which I'd had nothing to do with, but which had given Colonel Badger the excuse he'd needed to lock me up. I told her not to fret, swept her up in my arms, and carried her off to bed. But I fretted, and was gone before daybreak, stealing away while she slept, to avoid a tearful parting. I left her a note assuring her that I would be nearby, and would come to see her when I was able, but to tell no one save my mother and Billy that I was alive and back in Texas.

I found a place to stay—out in the hills near Dripping Springs with some ex-Confederates who had taken up brush-popping maverick cattle out of the scrub. There were plenty of wild cattle to be found, as the war had disrupted the local livestock industry. My companions intended to round up about a thousand or so head of those mossbacks and drive them north to the railroad, where they would sell them to buyers who in turn would ship the beeves to eastern slaughter-houses.

Using some of the gold General Mejia had given me at Queretaro, I bought a handsome thoroughbred horse, a silver-studded saddle and bridle, and a sombrero with a band fashioned out of silver to resemble a rattlesnake. I could speak fluent Spanish and I was as dark as a Mexican, so figured to pass myself off as one. I tested that theory by riding into Austin in broad daylight, and was pleased to discover that everyone bought my disguise.

This ruse worked for a while, and I managed to see a good bit of Catherine, though always on the sly, as I did not think it would do for anyone to notice that she seemed to be entertaining some gentleman from south of the border. But eventually I came under suspicion, though I'm not sure what tipped the authorities off. And even while I was aware of the growing danger, I pressed my luck just to see Catherine a few more times.

Early one morning I left her and walked to a nearby livery where I had deposited my horse the night before with instructions that it be reshod. As I neared the place, I noticed a squad of soldiers loitering nearby. I had a hunch they were waiting for me. The sensible thing to do would have been to turn right around and walk quickly away. But I was fond of the thoroughbred, and not at all inclined to abandon the animal. It galled me to think that if I did, some bluecoat would appropriate the horse for himself. So I decided to brazen it out, and entered the livery to retrieve the thoroughbred.

As I led the animal out of the livery, the soldiers closed in—one, a sergeant, a little in front of the others.

"Hold on there, Mexico," he said. "What do you think you're doing?"

"What does it look like I am doing?" I asked, in Spanish.

"Speak English, you damned greaser."

"I said it was none of your business," I replied, in English this time.

"You can't take that horse."

"He belongs to me."

The sergeant grinned like a cat. "Can you prove that? I don't think any greaser could afford to buy a horse like that one. So that tells me that you must be a horse thief. Besides, I happen to know the identity of the owner of that animal. His name is Ben Thompson."

"Well, that would be me," I said.

"Then you're under arrest, you son of a bitch!" exclaimed the sergeant, reaching for the pistol at his side.

Before he could clear leather, I had my own pistol out, with the barrel pressed against the man's chest.

"Hand over that shooting iron or I'll have to put a hole in you," I said nicely. "Keep your hands empty, boys," I advised the rest of the soldiers, "or I'll send your sergeant to hell, and a couple of you just to keep him company until Phil Sheridan gets there."

"Do as he says," squawked the sergeant.

I thanked him for his cooperation, shoved his pistol under my gunbelt, and climbed into the saddle, keeping my smoke-maker trained on him. "Since you know who I am," I said, by way of a parting shot, "you know how dangerous it would be to come after me."

It was bald-faced bravado but I thought it might make an impression on the bluecoats. With that I whipped the thoroughbred into a gallop, riding low in the saddle. In a heartbeat I had turned a corner around the livery and was out of sight.

I rode hard about a mile out of town, then slowed the horse to a walk, fairly confident that the soldiers would choose not to pursue me. I thought it possible that the sergeant would not even mention the incident at the livery to his superiors. After all, I'd made a fool out of him.

Turned out I was wrong. A few miles further on, I heard horses on the run and looked over my shoulder to see about half a dozen soldiers coming up the road. I didn't waste time trying to discern whether they were the same ones I'd run into at the livery. I touched the thoroughbred with my big Chihuahuan spurs and veered off into a stand of trees. Beyond the trees was a fence, which the horse cleared effortlessly, delivering us into an open pasture. I was halfway across this when another band of soldiers erupted from the woods directly in front of me. I swung the horse toward the upper end of the pasture. The soldiers started shooting, trying to bring me or my mount down. But we escaped untouched, clearing the fence again and vanishing into the scrub. The two groups of soldiers joined forces and gave chase, but their horses were no match for mine, and they soon gave up.

It was a close call, and it forced me to sit down and assess the situation. There weren't many options available to me. I could go or I could stay. If I chose the former, where exactly would I go? And if I decided to leave, I would have to take Catherine with me, for I did not want to be apart from her. Yet this was her home. Her family was here. As was mine. Besides all that, I was heartily sick of being a fugitive. There was no future in a life on the run.

My decision, then, was to stay. To stand my ground. I had one thing going for me. Colonel Badger had been transferred. Perhaps I would find that a more reasonable man had taken his place.

I sent word to Joseph Glover, Old John's son. John had passed away during the war. His son had taken over the family law practice. Joseph was not a friend, as John had been, but he agreed to come out to meet me. He was the spitting image of his father. His beard hadn't turned white, and his paunch, though considerable, was not of the magnitude that John had acquired—not yet anyway. John Glover's adversaries in the courtroom had often made the mistake of underestimating him, of deeming him just a cheerful old fat gentleman. But John had been wily as a fox, and as remorseless as a wolf on the hunt when occasion demanded. I wondered if his son had those same attributes. After talking my situation over with him, I concluded that he did.

"I am familiar with the indictment against you," said Glover. "In my opinion they don't have a shred of real evidence against you. It is also my opinion that you should have fought them a long time ago."

"I didn't think I would get justice from a military court, especially before the dust had settled from the war."

"Perhaps not. But the indictment now rests in the hands of a state court."

"I'm not sure I would fare much better in a state court. The governor and all the judges have been handpicked by the military authorities."

"I happen to know the judge who would hear your case. I believe him to be a fair-minded man. Let me speak to him."

"Thank you, Joseph."

He smiled faintly. "Make no mistake, Ben. I am not doing this as a favor. I will expect to be paid, and paid well. I presume you have funds."

I told him that I did.

"Plenty of money, I should hope," he said. "Because, well, the judge may want to be paid for his trouble as well."

That startled me. "A bribe?"

Glover produced a pained expression. "I prefer to think of it as a consideration."

"I thought you said he was fair-minded. I presumed by that you thought I would stand a fair chance in his court."

Glover shrugged. "Probably. But why take unnecessary chances?"

I had to laugh. "Well, I'll be damned. Bribe the judge! Now why didn't I think of that?"

"Ben," said Glover, gazing at the sky, "I know a lot about your past. And based on what I know, I feel confident in predicting your future."

"Really? And what is your prediction?"

"I predict that this will be by no means the last time you need an attorney to save your hide."

"No, if I get out of this, I'm going to walk the line."

"Sure you will. My father was a good man, and a very good lawyer. But he wasn't much of a businessman, and made not much of a living, frankly. All too often he would take a case as a favor."

"And you don't do favors."

"No, I don't. I don't confuse business and friendship. I am, if I say so myself, a good lawyer, too. And I have connections. So if you are ever in need of my services, don't hesitate to call on me."

"Unless I'm broke."

Glover nodded. "I think we understand each other. Meet me back here in two days."

He didn't need to tell me not to come empty-handed, and I didn't, bringing all the funds I had left to my name. It wasn't enough, however. Apparently justice had its price—and a steep one. I had to borrow some money and sell the thoroughbred just to meet the price set by Glover and his friend the judge. But the indictment was dropped. Sure, it galled me that I hadn't even committed the crime in the first place, but I had already learned that life wasn't fair.

It was a relief to be free to move about openly, and to discard the disguise I'd been using so long. But I was destitute, and had to make some money quickly. Lady Luck was keeping an eye on me, because right about then Tom Bowles and Phil Coe opened a saloon in Austin. I knew Coe from my time in the Second Texas, and then later in Mexico, because like me Coe had gotten into some hot water with the regiment's officers and fled south of the border as a result, where he had served for a spell in the imperialist army. Smart fellow that he was, Coe had left long before the Queretaro debacle. He knew how successful I had been down there with the monte games, so when he and Tom opened The Palace, they offered me the gambling concession. They wanted twenty-five percent from the house, which was high, but I didn't balk. The Palace was the finest watering hole in Austin, and I knew it would be a great success from the start. And so it was. In a matter of months I had more money in my pocket than I'd ever had before. I usually manned the monte table, and as for the other games of chance, I just made sure The Palace employed the best—and most honest— dealers. If you gambled at The Palace, you were pretty sure to lose, but there would never be a doubt in your mind that you had lost fair and square.

Word about The Palace spread, and one day a fellow known as Big King dropped in to watch the monte game I was running. Big King was so called because of his size. He was the biggest man I had ever seen, standing over six feet six and weighing in at nearly three hundred pounds, more brawn than fat. He owned the Blue Wing Saloon in nearby Bryan, and he in-

formed me that he never lost at monte. I replied that
there was a first time for everything. With a grin Big
King recognized that for what it was—a challenge.

The game lasted through the night and all the next
day, and it became a part of Austin lore, not solely on
account of its length but also because when it was all
over, Big King had lost his money—and his saloon. I
had to hand it to Big King, though. He was a good
loser.

"You run a straight game, Thompson," he said in
his deep, rumbling voice. "So I have no quarrel with
the outcome. You won fair and square. This is the way
I won the Blue Wing three years ago, and I guess it
just makes sense that I would lose it the same way."

I gave him a couple of hundred dollars back, though
at first he would not take it. I knew I ran a risk, as
there are few ways better suited to turning a situation
ugly than to offend a Westerner by offering him charity.

"I'm not doing this for your sake," I told him, "but
for mine. In fact, I consider it an investment. I figure
with this kind of grubstake, you'll have a new business
up and running before too long. And when you do, I'm
hoping you'll come back here and let me win that one
off you, too."

Big King laughed. "We'll have at it again, Thompson, don't you fret. Only next time, the outcome will
be altogether different."

I wasted no time in riding over to Bryan and taking
a look at my new business. The Blue Wing was by no
means as ornate as Phil Coe and Tom Bowles had
made The Palace, but it wasn't a bucket-of-blood saloon, either. It did a brisk business and I intended to
keep it that way. I was beginning to think I'd found a
profession that would allow me to provide for Cathe-

rine—not to mention the family I hoped to have some-
day. The Blue Wing would provide me with a steady
source of income. True, the hours weren't as good as
a banker's, and many were the nights that my gambling
kept me away from home until daybreak. But Catherine
had never complained, not once, so I assumed she was
satisfied with the arrangement.

For a while I intended to continue running the tables
at The Palace—it was too lucrative a contract to give
up—while keeping an eye on the Blue Wing, visiting
at least once a week. Meanwhile I broached the subject
with Catherine of moving, eventually, to Bryan. She
wasn't overly enthusiastic about the idea. Austin had
always been her home, and her parents were there.
They were getting old, and both were in poor health.
But I was confident that I could persuade her. Catherine
was a dutiful wife above all else, one who accepted the
convention that a woman's place was at her husband's
side, and that her duty was to support me in all that I
did.

I ended up spending a lot more time at the Blue
Wing than I had expected to, because a gang of no-
accounts got it in their heads to put me out of business.
One of the barkeeps was of the opinion that Big King
was behind this. I found that hard to believe. These
toughs would come in during business hours to stir up
trouble, and when I put a stop to that, they broke into
the place after hours one night and wrecked the entire
saloon. I had to hire men as guards, and spent the better
part of a month there trying to resolve the situation.

It was during my absence that my brother, Billy,
killed a man in Austin.

Chapter 10

MY MOTHER HAD always feared that Billy would try to emulate me, and get into hot water as a consequence. She never judged me, but my pistols-and-pasteboards life caused her constant concern. She had reason to hope that I was smart enough—and mean enough when a situation called for it—to survive. But everyone, including her, knew that Billy wasn't all that bright, and that if he did get into serious trouble, he wouldn't be able to get out of it.

It all started when Billy and a soldier named Burke paid a visit to one of Austin's bordellos. How they had become acquainted, I never did know. Arriving at the place, they found another soldier lying naked and in a drunken stupor behind that house of ill repute. Billy laughed at the unconscious man's condition and, as a prank, started to take his clothes. Burke got angry when he saw this. He didn't appreciate the way Billy was treating one of his comrades in arms. Billy shrugged it off and left the man his clothes.

Later that night Burke busted into a room where Billy was being entertained by a soiled dove. The soldier reeked of cheap whiskey and leered at Billy's nakedness.

"I think I'll throw you out in the street just like you are," sneered Burke. "That was what you were aiming to do to my friend earlier."

"I didn't know he was your friend," Billy replied.

"Now go away. Can't you see I'm busy?"

But Burke didn't go away. He lunged at my brother, intent on carrying out his threat. They wrestled for a spell before Billy grabbed his pistol and shot Burke dead. Stunned by what he had done in the heat of the moment, Billy fled into the hills around Austin.

When I got back, I put out the word that I was looking for my brother, and he soon sent me a message regarding the whereabouts of his hideout. The problem was that the U.S. Army was also looking for Billy, and figured I might be just the one to lead them to him. Soldiers dogged my steps night and day. They were everywhere except under my bed, and even tried to deceive me by dressing in civilian garb. Several times I rode out of town, in hopes of eluding them, but to no avail. Meanwhile, patrols scoured the hills searching for Billy. I became frustrated, afraid that it was just a matter of time before they found my brother. And then—well, he would hang for sure. I tried not to let on to my mother how worried I was, since she was beside herself. Instead, I guaranteed to her that somehow I would get to Billy before the army did and spirit him away to the Indian Territory, where he would be reasonably safe.

Then one night at The Palace, Phil Coe came up and told me that he had overheard two officers talking about my brother, and how some Tonkawa scouts employed by the army had possibly located his hideout near Bee Springs. First thing in the morning a large detachment would ride out to capture him. Waiting until I had finished cussing a blue streak, Coe then asked if there was anything he could do to help.

Thinking fast, I nodded. "Phil, they're on the money. That's exactly where Billy is. And I've got to get to him before they do."

"Maybe now that they think they have him, they'll stop following you around."

I shook my head. "I doubt that. But tonight I must ride to Bee Springs. I assume they'll be on my trail. So that's why I need a few reliable men who know how to shoot."

"I know plenty such men, good Confederates all," said Coe, with a grin.

I told him what I had in mind. "And you know I will pay them well," I added.

"I doubt they will take your money, Ben, not for a chance to get back at the bluebellies like this."

"Just remember, Phil, I don't want anybody killed."

Coe nodded. "I'll relay that message. But in a situation like this, you won't be able to get any guarantees on that score. You know that."

"Yes, I know," I said grimly. "There are never any guarantees. About anything. I'll be back in an hour."

By the time I'd returned, Coe had found his men. I spoke to them about the plan and they were agreeable. When they left, I lingered at the bar long enough to have two stiff drinks and smoke a cigar before leaving as well. Coe wished me luck. I was going to need all the luck in the world.

As I left Austin, I didn't bother looking for the soldiers who I knew would be following me. Instead, I rode along at an easy pace, sticking to the main road north out of town, as though I were simply out for an enjoyable ride in the country. Except that it was very late at night. At one point the road squeezed through a pair of rocky slopes. About a mile further on I checked my horse and waited.

Less than a quarter of an hour later I heard gunfire coming from that narrow passage. I spun my horse around and rode like the hounds of hell were after me—leaving the road and striking out due north for Bee Springs and my brother's hideout. I knew right where to go. In a ridge above the sweetwater springs was a cave that Billy and I had discovered many years ago. As youngsters we had explored every inch of the country that lay twenty miles from Austin in any direction.

Reaching the cave, I roused Billy from a deep slumber. He was surprised to see me, to say the least.

"What are you doing here, Ben? What I heard, the soldiers were watching you so close, you couldn't get away from Austin."

I quickly explained how I had come to be here. The two men hand-picked by Phil Coe to aid me had set up shop on either side of the narrow passage. They had let me pass and then opened up on the soldiers who were trailing me. The idea was to force the soldiers to forget about me and seek cover to save themselves. I hoped none of them had been killed. Coe's men were to keep them pinned down for as long as possible before fading away into the night.

"I don't care if they did kill those bluecoats," said Billy angrily. "They don't belong here and they're nothing but trouble."

"Well, I care, because we're in deep enough as it is."

Billy turned remorseful. "I'm sorry, Ben. I didn't mean to drag you into this. In fact, you should have stayed out of it entirely."

"I wish I could have. But you're my little brother and it's my job to look out for you."

"So what do we do now?"

I informed him that, thanks to the Tonkawa scouts, the soldiers had learned that he was hiding in the vicinity of Bee Springs, and that they were coming for him in the morning.

"You've got to get out of this part of the country, Billy," I told him. "I figure the safest place for you right now is the Indian Territory. There's no law to speak of up there, and the army stays out to avoid any trouble with the Civilized Tribes."

"But what do I do once I get there?"

"Keep your head down and your nose clean. For God's sake, stay out of trouble. Don't send word where you are—the message might fall into the wrong hands. When the time comes that I think it's safe for you to come home, I'll find you."

Billy was silent for a moment, mulling it over. "And what if the time never comes?"

Unfortunately, I didn't have a good answer for him. Instead, I gave him a roll of paper money and a possibles bag filled with provisions—coffee, sugar, flour, some sidemeat. "This should help you get where you're going," I said.

"What about you, Ben? Won't you be in hot water for this?"

"I'll handle it."

"Maybe you should just ride with me."

I shook my head. "I thought about that. But someone needs to take care of our mother. And then there's Catherine. Don't worry, I'll be fine. Now you had better get a move on. Put as many miles behind you before daybreak as you can."

We shook hands, and I watched him saddle up and ride off into the night, wondering if I would ever see my little brother again.

I took a roundabout way back to Austin, avoiding the road that I had taken coming out, and got home without mishap. When I arrived, dawn was not far off.

Catherine was sleeping soundly, so I tried to be quiet as I brewed some coffee on the stove. Then I sat on the porch, drinking the java and waiting.

They came early, before the sun had risen—and before Catherine had risen, too. It was a detail of five, led by a young lieutenant who said the colonel in charge of things in Austin at the time wanted to see me at once. I assured them that I would go peacefully, and that I was unarmed. We got away without waking my wife.

The colonel's name was Reynolds, and I suppose he was an improvement over Badger—at least that was the word—but it was just a matter of degree. He was still the top dog of an army of occupation, which made him an enemy of every Texan.

"Mr. Thompson," he said gruffly, "I am a plain-spoken man, and I always try to get right to the point. Last night you left Austin and I want you to tell me where you went."

"I just needed some fresh air. Thought I would take a ride."

"The soldiers who followed you—and you know why they dog your steps, so let's not even get into that—rode straight into an ambush."

"Really," I said. "I did hear some shooting last night. But around here a wise man steers clear of gunplay, so I didn't investigate."

"I take it that you deny having anything to do with it."

"Of course I deny it. The roads are dangerous, night or day. A good many outlaws in the brush these days, you know. Ex-Confederates, mostly. Men who used to make an honest living but can't anymore because you won't let them."

"Two of my men were injured. One was shot, the

other broke an arm when his horse threw him."

"I'm just glad no one was killed."

Reynolds was skeptical, to say the least. "I don't think I believe you, Thompson. I think you rode out last night to warn your brother that we were closing in."

"I have no idea where my brother is, Colonel."

"Right. Well, I happen to know where he used to be. I've sent men out there this morning. If he's not there, I'll have to assume I am right about your activities last night. And then I am going to charge you as an accomplice to murder. Until then, you will be detained under guard."

And that is exactly what he did, which took me right back to my home away from home, the Austin jail. Reynolds was true to his word; when his soldiers came back empty-handed from Bee Springs, he had a state judge call up a grand jury, which was given the responsibility of producing an indictment against me. With the Reconstruction government in place, the military still called the shots. It just looked better this way.

I had regrets, sure, but I'd had no choice in what I had done. Billy was my flesh and blood, and I was obliged to help him. It made me feel better to know that he had gotten away, although it did bother me somewhat that he had to reside in the Indian Territory, which was a haven for bad men of every stripe, and so a very dangerous place to be. Sometimes, though, Fate just doesn't leave you with any good options.

When the indictment was handed down, Joseph Glover called on me and agreed to be my lawyer—after he had determined that I had the money to pay him. "But don't expect to get free of this with a bribe, like last time," he warned.

"Why not?"

"Well, for one thing, we're dealing with a different judge. And for another, the crime with which you have been charged has a great deal more, shall we say, currency."

"I don't understand."

"Colonel Reynolds is predisposed to make an object lesson out of you, Ben. Feelings run stronger than ever against the Reconstruction government. Texans feel as though they have suffered long enough, and that it is time the army departed the scene. Reynolds can't afford to let the killing of a soldier go unpunished. Now, he can't get his hands on the man who did the killing—thanks to you, I suspect. That means you are all that he has left. If he has his way, you will pay the price for the crime Billy committed."

"But why is it any different from the killing of those soldiers a few years ago?"

"Well, for one thing, that occurred at the tail end of the war, and some people saw it as just another skirmish rather than murder. Some people—not the United States Army, mind you. However, considerable time had passed, and passions cooled, Colonel Badger was replaced, and the military had other more important irons in the fire by the time we decided to resolve that issue."

"So what are my chances in this case?" I didn't ask Glover to be candid and not to sugarcoat. He wasn't the type to do that sort of thing anyway.

"From what I can see, they don't have much of a case against you. What evidence does exist is circumstantial. For instance, your leaving town the night those soldiers were ambushed. I don't think they can tie you to that, though it strikes me—as it will most others—a little too coincidental. Beyond that, I don't think they have any witnesses that can place you in the vicinity of Bee Springs. But don't fool yourself, Ben. I've seen men hanged on less evidence."

"Thanks, Joe," I said dryly. "That'll really help me sleep at night. Can you at least get me bailed out of here?"

"I'll see what I can do. But don't count on it."

I wasn't, figuring that the powers-that-be would be afraid I might bolt, as Billy had done, rather than pay the piper. But to my surprise I was released a few days later on a thousand-dollar bond that I was able to put up myself because I had just sold the Blue Wing Saloon back to Big King at a cut-rate price.

At Glover's suggestion I tried to lay low, mind my own business, and keep out of trouble. Then a detachment of soldiers on patrol north of Austin visited the farm of an Irishman by the name of McGuire. Now, McGuire was by all accounts a law-abiding citizen, but according to the report of the lieutenant in charge of the patrol, the farmer refused to come out of his house when called upon to do so. It was nighttime, and McGuire later explained that twice before he had been robbed by federal soldiers—or men masquerading as federal soldiers, anyway. At any rate, the lieutenant ordered his men to force the door, at which point gunfire issued from the farmhouse, and two troopers were mortally wounded. The lieutenant sent for reinforcements and laid siege. Eventually McGuire surrendered.

Amazingly—from my point of view, anyway—the lieutenant reported that he'd had reason to suspect that I had been in McGuire's company when the shooting started, and apparently had slipped away under cover of darkness, leaving McGuire to face the enemy alone, which made me not only a killer but a despicable coward as well. Joe Glover was of the opinion that the lieutenant was just trying to cover his backside—if he didn't throw me into the mix, he would have to admit that he and his command had been held at bay by a solitary plowpusher, and how would that look? In my opinion it was all part of a scheme by Reynolds and his subordinates to color me a cold-blooded killer.

Worst of all, they came to arrest me in the middle of the night, bursting into my house and dragging me from bed, scaring the life out of Catherine. It was bad enough that they had invaded my home, but to frighten and humiliate my wife was going too far. Naturally, I was released the next morning, since there was no evidence to sustain a decision to hold me.

To complicate matters, Catherine's brother, Jim, was causing problems. Some months earlier he had taken iron pots and skillets from the home of Catherine's parents and sold them for whiskey money. Because Jim was their son, the Moores did not press charges, but I confronted him and waved my pistol around enough to scare him right out of town. Now, though, he was back. At Glover's insistence, I tried to deal with Jim the "right" way, by going to a justice of the peace and requesting an injunction against him. The justice, W. D. Scott, refused. A week later, when Jim got into an altercation with Catherine and shoved her, I went looking for him. This time, instead of waving my pistol around, I put it to better use, inflicting a slight flesh wound, which was all I had intended to do. Had he not been Catherine's brother, and had my wife not made me promise to avoid killing him outright, I would have done much more damage.

That very day I got word that Justice Scott was drawing up a warrant to have me arrested. Furious, I went to his office and asked him what the hell he thought he was doing.

"Signing an affidavit against you for assault with the

intent to kill James Moore," replied Scott. He was leery of me, could see that I was beside myself with rage, and hastened to add, "Colonel Reynolds insisted that I do so."

"I see. You couldn't be bothered to draw up an injunction against that sorry bastard when I asked you to, but you can issue a warrant for my arrest after forcing me to deal with the matter myself. You dishonest old scoundrel, get out of my sight. If I ever see you again, I will shoot you down, even if I hang for it."

Those were words I was certain to regret, but I was madder than hell, and when I got that way, I just can't seem to hold my tongue.

Justice Scott was convinced that I meant business, and vacated the premises. As did I, since I saw no profit in lingering. Less than an hour later the soldiers once again came to my home to arrest me, as I had expected them to. That gave me enough time to say my good-byes to Catherine, and to give her money that I instructed her to pass on to Joe Glover, as obviously I was going to need his services yet again.

This time they didn't take me to the Austin jail, but rather to the regimental encampment on the eastern edge of town, where I was thrown into what was called a "bull pen" in army parlance. The bull pen was a twenty-by-twenty enclosure with high rock walls, open to the sky. A scaffold had been erected around the outside of the walls, so that heavily-armed guards could look over into the pen and keep the prisoners under constant watch. There were several of us incarcerated there, including the farmer McGuire. We were all shackled with leg irons. All one can do when bound in that way is move about in a slow, shuffling walk.

The other prisoners were owlhoots, suspected of various and sundry crimes. Colonel Reynolds had vowed to put an end to the crime spree running rampant in the vicinity. A few days later I discovered that Reynolds was convening a military tribunal that he had charged with trying all the men in his custody. That did not bode well for us. McGuire insisted that Reynolds had no right to do such a thing, since a state government was in place. He wanted to be tried by a state judge and a jury of twelve citizens—as did we all. But the farmer could rant and rave until he was blue in the face. It wasn't going to change anything.

A week later I was brought before the tribunal—in fact, it was my dubious distinction to be the first person tried by the colonel's kangaroo court. It was my first opportunity to talk to Glover—his requests to see me prior to my trial had been denied. And our talk was brief, to say the least.

"They won't allow me to represent you," he said. "This is a military court, and we can only hope they will offer you counsel."

I laughed bitterly. "You think that would do me any good?"

"This is why they let you bond out before," he said. "It makes more sense to me now. Reynolds had in mind even then to convene this tribunal, and he must have decided he would have a better chance of getting a conviction on you this way than to trust a state court to do it."

To my surprise, Joe Glover looked a little distressed. He knew, as did I, that my goose was cooked. I say it came as a surprise because I'd had no idea that he cared, personally, about what happened to me. In fact, he'd made it plain that he was only representing me because of the money.

"Don't worry about it," I told him. "Just do me a favor, Joe. Try your damnedest to make sure that they don't take my house and throw Catherine out into the street."

"Rest assured, I won't let that happen, Ben."

We shook hands on it.

The tribunal was presided over by Lieutenant Colonel Samuel Schwenk. The case against me was presented by the judge advocate, a Lieutenant Barton. Barton read the charge against me as I stood there holding nearly a hundred pounds of ball and chain they had attached to my leg irons.

"The warrant issued against you reads as follow: That you, Benjamin Thompson, on the second of September in the year 1868, did go to the office of W. D. Scott, justice of the peace in the city of Austin, state of Texas, and did threaten to kill Scott. The charge against you, therefore, reads assault with the intent to kill. You may request the assistance of counsel before entering a plea."

"Don't bother about the counsel. I plead not guilty."

It didn't take them long to find me otherwise, and I was sentenced to four years hard labor at the prison in Huntsville.

Chapter 11

THEY TRIED MCGUIRE once they were done with me, and his conviction carried a sentence of ten years. We were hauled off to Huntsville together, in the back of a wagon, under heavy guard, and we both were denied our fervent wish to see our loved ones one last time. Our "guard" consisted of fifty troopers, and I told McGuire that in my opinion that was a little excessive, considering that we wore leg irons and shackles on our wrists and were otherwise in a pretty sorry state, having survived on hardtack and water for the past couple of months.

"They're afraid of you, Ben," said McGuire.

"Yeah, sure, Mac."

"No, I'm serious. You have a reputation as a very dangerous hombre. They say you've killed a hundred men."

"Not even close."

"That you're quicker than a diamondback and never miss what you aim at."

"Not true. I missed Juan Cortinas once, and I had him dead in my sights."

"Besides all that, they're afraid you have a lot of friends just as mean as you are, and who might try to break you loose before we get to Huntsville."

"Not a chance of that, Mac."

"Well, then, I'm sorry to hear that, Ben."

"I'm sorry they're taking you to prison. It isn't right."

"Took me a while," said the Irishman pensively, "but I finally figured out that this has nothing to do with what's right. There's no such thing as justice, Ben. Not for the likes of us, anyway."

When we got to the prison, they put me away in solitary confinement for a spell. I suppose they were trying to get an early start on breaking my spirit, on the theory that once they had done that, I would not be much trouble for them. I will freely admit that it was touch and go there for a few weeks. Four years' confinement seemed like an eternity in hell. The only thing that kept me from breaking was stubborn pride. I just wasn't going to give them the satisfaction.

On the other hand, I was smart enough to know that if I fought them, they would win and I would die. That was no option, either. To die was to surrender, and I just wouldn't do that. So I survived. Did it one day at a time. And after a few months the prison guards changed in their attitude toward me. They came to respect me, I think, and I made sure they knew that I did not blame them for the situation I was in. They were just doing their jobs.

The weeks turned into months, and the months added up to years, and I took great consolation in knowing that there was no stopping time. In fact, time became my ally, because it moved me inexorably closer, minute by minute, hour by hour, day by day, to that moment when I would be free again. I was also consoled by the letters from my wife and mother. And finally there was McGuire. He and I became fast friends. When one of us began to falter, the other was always quick with the right word: "Courage!"

In 1870, a freely elected state government replaced

the Reconstruction government that had been in place
since shortly after the war's end. A few months later,
having served two years of my sentence, I was set free.
I promised Mac that I would look after his family until
he got out, and I returned to Austin.

They say prison changes a man. I wasn't aware of
any changes in myself, apart from the fact that I felt
twenty years older than when they had hauled me off
to Huntsville. But there was more. Catherine, I think,
noticed it right away, though for a long time she would
not speak of it. Actually, what Catherine saw were
merely symptoms of the affliction. I did not laugh
much anymore—and once I had been the life of any
party. I did not talk much, either. When I did, my
words were terse and to the point. Once upon a time I
had been a pretty talkative fellow. And I didn't talk
about the future at all, something I had often done before in Catherine's presence, because she never seemed
to tire of hearing all my grand schemes and big dreams.
No more of that, though, after Huntsville. Why?

They call it fatalism. By now I had learned my lesson. There was no point in making big plans for the
future. Big dreams were just a waste of time. I'd done
plenty of dreaming, and to what avail? Something always happened to set me back.

Once back in Austin I did the only thing I knew
how to do, the only thing I was good at—gambling.
Phil Coe let me run a table in The Palace, and in a few
months' time I had made enough money to take an
interest in a proposition Coe made me.

"I aim to go up the cattle trail to Abilene," he said,
"and open a business there. There's a lot of money to
be made off Texas cowboys who've just been paid their
wages for spending a hundred days pushing a herd of
ornery longhorns all the way from here to Kansas. I've

heard tell that about half a million head were pushed up the trail last year. This year it will probably be an even greater number. I'm also told that during the busiest part of the season they've got over five thousand cowboys roaming the Texas Side of Abilene, aching to find something to spend their hard-earned money on. If we leave in a week, we can be there in time to take full advantage of the busy season."

"What do you have in mind for me?"

"You and me, we'll be partners. Open up a saloon and split the proceeds right down the middle. You handle the gambling and I'll take care of rest of the business. Unless you think Catherine will object to you going."

"No," I said. "No, she won't. She never does."

And she sure wouldn't this time. My release from prison had made her smile. But since then, thanks to me, she'd had very little reason to smile. I wasn't the same man who had been hauled off to Huntsville two years earlier. Not by a long shot. No, she wouldn't raise an objection to my going off to Kansas for who knew how long. In fact, I figured she might even be relieved to see me go.

Phil Coe's plan made sense. The prospects were excellent. Of course, I knew that somewhere along the way something would happen to muddy up my water. Still, that was no reason not to go. So I told Phil I was in, and a week later we were headed up the trail for the wildest and woolliest town in the West—Abilene, Kansas.

On the way, we met up with plenty of herds being pushed north. On a single day I saw what I estimated to be at least thirty thousand longhorns. Most of the time we weren't made too welcome in the cow outfit camps. Oh, they were usually amenable to giving us

some coffee, but that was about it. The herd bosses
cast a suspicious eye on us, taking us for what we
were—predators. Not that the cowboys had much to
gamble away, but we seldom got a chance to win what
little they did have. If we traveled after sundown, we
were careful to give the bedded-down herds a wide
berth. The cow outfits were wary of rustlers. Cow
thieves would try to stir up a stampede, hoping to make
off with a few hundred head in the confusion that ensued. For that reason, Phil and I took care not to make
ourselves targets for some trigger-happy cowpoke.
Most of that breed were indifferent marksmen, but as
I told Phil, the only thing worse than getting killed was
getting killed by a rank amateur who made a lucky
shot.

It took drovers three months to push a herd from
Texas to Kansas. Ten miles a day was considered an
excellent pace. Phil and I made much better time,
reaching our destination in about three weeks. We
passed through the heart of the Indian Territory on the
way, and naturally, I wondered about my brother. I had
heard no news of Billy in over two years—had no idea
if he was even still alive. I had hopes of finding out
something about him before I returned to Texas.

Abilene turned out to be everything Phil Coe had
said it would be. On the Texas Side of town a cowpuncher could find just about anything his wild and
lonesome heart desired, from whiskey to women, card
games to dance halls, a new sombrero or a fancy set
of silver-studded spurs. A fellow by the name of James
Butler Hickok, also known as Wild Bill, was Abilene's
city marshal at the time. His job was to keep a lid on
things. That meant keeping all the rowdiness west of
First Street. The Texas Side was pretty much wide
open.

Phil and I looked things over, then bought a building on First Street and called it the Bull's Head Saloon. Phil had plenty of investment capital, and he spared no expense; as he had with The Palace in Austin, he wanted to own the finest saloon in Abilene. He figured his fellow Texans deserved that much—while he did them the favor of relieving them of all those wages burning holes in their pockets. The Bull's Head was an overnight success. We had an excellent location, honest gaming tables, good whiskey, pretty percentage girls. Best of all, the cowpokes liked patronizing a saloon run by a couple of fellow Texans.

Within a few months' time I had decided that Abilene was going to work out just fine, and since I wanted to remain there indefinitely, I wrote Catherine and asked if she wanted to join me there. She wrote back to say that she would come—but she wouldn't be coming alone. She had given birth to a son during my absence, and had named him Benjamin. Things were looking up again. So I had to wonder when the ax would fall.

It happened on the day Catherine and the baby arrived. I rented a buggy to transport them from the stage station to the Drover's Cottage, where I had been residing. On the way to the hotel I was so busy gazing at little Ben that I didn't see the pothole until it was too late. A wheel splintered, overturning the buggy. The leg I had broken during the war was fractured again. Catherine broke her arm. Worst of all, little Ben's foot was mangled. Fortunately, he healed up completely, and was none the worse for the experience. I healed, as well, though ever after I would experience pain and stiffness in that twice-broken leg when the weather turned cold and damp. But Catherine got the raw end of the deal. Her shattered arm became gangrenous, and had to be amputated.

I have to say she bore up better than I. It was difficult for me to come to terms with this tragedy because I felt that I was to blame. She tried her best to assure me that this was not the case. But the guilt was a constant ache in my heart. I regretted having married her—not for my sake, but for hers. Clearly she would have fared much better had she been wed to someone else. She deserved so much better. I made up my mind to take her and the baby back to Texas. There she could be among friends and family. About three months after their arrival in Abilene, we were embarked on the trek home.

We'd been in Austin less than two weeks when I read in the newspaper that Phil Coe had been killed in a shootout with Wild Bill Hickok. It was shocking news, for Phil had been a real friend to me—one of the few I'd ever had. But I wasn't surprised that he had died at Wild Bill's hand. The two had been at odds for some time.

Their first quarrel had erupted over something quite trivial. The red bull on the sign that decorated the front of the Bull's Head Saloon had been, according to some citizens, so realistically depicted, anatomically speaking, as to offend those burdened with tender sensibilities. Hickok had urged Phil and me to take the sign down. When we refused—thinking the whole thing was a tempest in a teapot—Wild Bill took it upon himself to have the sign repainted one night. Phil had been outraged by what he thought was outright vandalism, but I had managed to talk him out of rash action.

Then Phil had the great misfortune of meeting Jessie Hazel. Jessie was a pretty woman whose deceased husband had left her well provided for. Financially, anyway. But some people were beginning to question Jessie's moral fiber, because she seemed unable to do without the company of men. Of late her favorite beau had been none other than the city marshal himself, but rumor had it that his violent temper was putting her off, so that she was amenable to the vigorous courtship of Phil Coe. Much to the chagrin of Wild Bill, naturally. Knowing Hickok, it may be that Phil's fate was sealed at that moment.

I had to return to Abilene to attend to the business of the Bull's Head, but even before I left Austin, the speculations began to fly regarding my motives for going back. A reporter for the Austin newspaper accosted me on the day of my departure to ask me outright if it was true that my real reason was to avenge Phil Coe's death.

"It's my understanding," I said, trying to check my annoyance, "that the fight was a fair one."

"You mean you're not going to go gunning for Wild Bill Hickok?" He sounded extremely disappointed.

"No, I have no intention of calling Hickok out."

"That's a shame. Why, it would be a duel of historic proportions, Mr. Thompson. You and Wild Bill, *mano a mano,* perhaps the two foremost shootists in the country. It would be the stuff of legend, sir."

"I'm awfully sorry to disappoint you," I said dryly.

I figured that newspaper reporter wasn't the only one who would wonder if I had an ulterior motive for returning to Abilene, so I wasn't at all surprised to get a visit from Hickok himself my first day back in the cow town. I was in the Bull's Head with the head bartender, going over the ledgers, when the city marshal sauntered in. There were only a few patrons present at that hour, but when they saw Wild Bill, they made themselves scarce in a hurry, fearing that gunplay was imminent.

Hickok was a tall man, with long legs and a stocky torso. His face was broad and flat and sundark, so that to some he resembled a half-breed. His dark hair was worn shoulder-length. He sported a brace of Smith & Wesson pistols in cross-draw holsters under his frock coat. He had the look of a killer in his eyes. I'd seen that look before—in the eyes of Lieutenant Gonzales, the Mexican soldier who had challenged me over a game of monte in that Nuevo Laredo cantina some five years back. It is the look a man gets when he doesn't care whether he lives or dies. This cavalier attitude toward his own life is then combined with a similar indifference to the lives of others.

Wild Bill strolled up to the mahogany where the bartender and I stood, and a sardonic smile curled one corner of his mouth.

"Welcome back, Ben," he drawled. "I hear tell you have it in mind to come after me on account of I sent your friend and partner Phil Coe to boothill in a box."

"Are you calling me out?" I asked coldly.

Hickok blinked. I suppose he thought he could buffalo me with that gun-happy swagger of his, so that I would hasten to assure him that nothing was further from the truth. His bravado usually worked—even rough and rowdy Texas cowboys, men who were generally unafraid of anything—could be cowed by this man. It was reputation, mixed with attitude.

"I'm the city marshal," he said. "It's my job to keep the peace, not start a dustup."

"I take that to be a no, then."

He glared at me with hooded eyes. "I want to know your intentions. Why did you come back to Abilene?"

"Because I own this saloon now that Phil is dead."

"You aim to stay and run this place?"

"I'll let you know when I make up my mind."

Hickok exhaled sharply through his nostrils and leaned against the bar, one booted foot propped up on the brass rail. He was clearly exasperated. I took it that our confrontation was not going exactly as he had planned.

"If you have a quarrel with me, I hope you're man enough to try settling it with me face to face."

I bristled at that. "What are you trying to say?"

Hickok shrugged. "It's just that I've heard you once shot a man in the back."

That got my hackles up. "I won't back-shoot you, Bill, unless you lose your nerve and run away."

"Well then, we don't have a thing to worry about, because that's not something I would ever do."

"Then we don't have a problem. As long, that is, as your business with Phil was a straight-up fair fight."

"Oh, it was. Phil made the mistake of throwing in with a bunch of Texas rowdies who marched into the Applejack Saloon and commenced to messing with the other customers—forcing them to buy drinks all around, carrying them around on their shoulders when they didn't want to be manhandled that way, even stripping the clothes off of one fellow. By nine o'clock there were about fifty of them, Phil still among them, and all of them three sheets to the wind. I met them coming down First Street, told them I had no problem with them unless they started shooting up the real estate. They went one way and I went on my way.

"A minute later I heard a gunshot, then two more. I ran back to find Phil and his friends in the Alamo Saloon. Phil had his pistol in hand. I asked who had done the shooting, and Phil said he had been the one, that he'd been attacked by a dog in the street and had killed it. I ordered him to hand his pistol over, and reminded him of the city ordinance against discharging firearms.

He said he would not go defenseless around me, claimed I would shoot him down, and then he raised that pistol of his. We were maybe ten feet apart and we fired at the same time. He put a bullet through my coat. I put one in his gut. I'm afraid he took three days to die. That's what I regret most about the whole affair, really. I meant to aim higher. But he had the drop on me, and there just wasn't time."

I nodded sadly. "Phil wasn't much of a shot. And he had a hair-trigger temper, especially when he'd had too much to drink."

"They tell me you're quick and accurate. A real pistoleer."

"I am, Bill," I said, looking him straight in the eye—something else he wasn't accustomed to. "They say you are, too. We going to take their word for it, or do we have to find this out for ourselves?"

Hickok thought that over, making sure there wasn't a challenge in there somewhere, because if there was, he would be obliged to accept it. "Long as you toe the mark in Abilene, Ben, I won't be too curious." He glanced at the bottles of whiskey lined up on the back bar. "All this talking has sure made me one thirsty hombre."

The barkeep made a move to get one of the bottles.

"Hold on there," I said.

The barkeep froze. Hickok gave me a cold, hard look.

"Now, don't you think it would be bad form," I said, "to drink the whiskey of a man you shot dead?"

Hickok stared a moment—then threw back his head and laughed. "You're not the least bit afraid of me, are you, Ben? I must say that I admire you for that. And I reckon you have a valid point—that would be real bad manners, wouldn't it?"

"It's not something a gentleman would do."

Hickok paused, then had another good laugh. "I'll be seeing you around," he told me. Then he turned and walked out.

He was right. I wasn't afraid of Wild Bill Hickok. Not that I was sure I could take him. In fact, I figured Wild Bill and I were probably pretty evenly matched. But I really didn't care if I won or lost. I just didn't want to spend another day in jail. That was why I let Abilene's city marshal walk out of the Bull's Head Saloon.

Lots of folks in Abilene expected Hickok and me to clash at some point down the road. Most of the Texas boys who came up the trail and spent their money in my saloon were eager to see me try Wild Bill. In fact, a good many of them complained that they were being victimized by a gang of toughs who roamed Abilene with impunity, or so it seemed. Quite a few cowpunchers ended up facedown in the mud with their heads busted, victims of this pack of robbers. And rumor was that Hickok knew who these thieving bastards were and let them operate without interference from the law. All they had to do was give him a percentage of their ill-gotten gains. I never did find out if there was any truth behind this rumor. But the fact was that for some time now the uneasy relationship existing between Abilene and the Texas outfits had been deteriorating. The townfolk were sick and tired of the cowboys. And the cowboys were getting just as sick and tired of the animosity displayed toward them by the locals. As well as the marshal.

This was part and parcel of the gradual shift of the cattle trade from Abilene to Ellsworth. More and more of the merchants were moving—lock, stock, and barrel—to Ellsworth, following the money. So were the gamblers and the calico queens. I knew it was over in Abilene when they took down the Drover's Cottage, loaded all the pieces on flat cars, and hauled it to Ellsworth, where the hotel was put back together again. That was when I decided to move, too.

Chapter 12

THE WAY ELLSWORTH, Kansas, was set up, there were two main streets, one on either side of the railroad. The respectable side of town was along North Street and its tributaries. The Texas Side was south of the tracks. The cattle trade of 1872 had been good for Ellsworth, and the businessmen prepared for an even more prosperous second season. D. W. Powers opened up a bank on South Street to cater specifically to the cattle drovers. J. C. Veach opened a fine restaurant. The Grand Central Hotel on North was adorned with a sidewalk made of limestone, and twelve feet wide to boot. Oddly enough, that sidewalk became an object of immense pride for the residents of Ellsworth. They claimed that there wasn't a finer sidewalk west of the Mississippi. I thought they might be right. They also said it symbolized their commitment to making Ellsworth one of the great cities of the West. This town, they said, would be around for a long time. And it would prosper. I hoped they were right.

Over a dozen licenses for the sale of strong spirits were approved by the city council. One of them was in my name, as I had in mind opening up a new saloon in Ellsworth. The city hired Brocky Jack Norton as marshal. Brocky Jack had been one of Wild Bill's deputies back in Abilene, but he and I had always gotten along, so I figured I would have no trouble with the local law.

It's amazing just how wrong you can be about some things.

While trying to get a feel for the town and where best to put my saloon—keeping in mind that location had been crucial to the success of the Bull's Head—I set up some gaming tables in the back room of Joe Brennan's saloon. As always I went to great lengths to ensure that everyone who came to Ellsworth with a hankering to gamble knew that my "roost" was the place to come for a straight game. In no time at all I was making money hand over fist. Some of it I sent home to Catherine. The rest I kept in the Powers bank, intending to invest it in the new saloon, eventually. Things were going smoothly for me in those days, very smoothly. And that made me nervous. I fully expected something bad to happen.

Something happened, all right—something completely unexpected, but certainly not bad. Or at least, it didn't seem bad at the time. It seemed, in fact, more like a miracle.

That May, as the season opened, my brother, Billy, rode into town.

He came in with a cattle outfit, and looked me up in Brennan's saloon. I looked up from a monte game and just couldn't believe my eyes.

"God in heaven," I breathed. "Joe will let just anybody in here."

Billy laughed. "Just came by to make sure you were sitting with your back to the wall, brother."

I closed down the game and spent the rest of the night with Billy, telling him everything that had happened to me in the several years since I had last spoken to him, and finding out what he had been up to. After a few months of hiding out alone in the Indian Territory, Billy had made the acquaintance of a woman named Jennie Hoke, who could ride and shoot and cuss better than most men, or so he said. He immediately fell under her spell, as had several other hombres, who, as it turned out, made up her gang of horse thieves.

"Mostly we stole from the Indians," Billy told me. "Those tribal police gave us a rough time, let me tell you. I guess I knew we were going to get caught sooner or later, and I also knew what would happen to us when we did. A hundred times I tried to talk myself into leaving. But Jennie . . . well, she was hard to walk away from."

"Were you in love with her?" I asked.

He gave me a funny look. "Damned if I know, Ben. What is love, anyway? She could make a man feel like he was a giant—and then like a fool, when he found her under the blankets with one of the other boys in our little group. Maybe all of us loved her. She was smart, and she knew how to keep a man under her thumb."

"So what happened?"

"Well, I guess she wasn't smart enough. I was lucky, though—I had gone to a trading post to pick up some supplies when the Choctaw police rode in and rounded up all the others. They hanged them right then and there. I arrived just in time to watch them string Jennie up. I watched from a distance, and when she stopped kicking, I rode like hell away from there. Spent a winter holed up alone out in the Cache Creek badlands. When I came out in the open this spring, I heard that the Choctaws were still hunting for me, so I decided it was time to get out of the Indian Territory. So I hooked up with a cow outfit that had lost three men in a stampede and needed help bad enough to sign me on. I told the boss who I was, not sure if that was the right thing to do or not. Turned out to be the right thing. He's the one who told me about you. How you and Phil Coe had opened up a saloon in Abilene, and how after Phil got killed, you moved here to Ellsworth."

"We need to write home, Billy, and let our mother know you are still alive," I said.

"Sure. Of course. But we can do that tomorrow, right? Tonight we need to celebrate."

That we did—too much. We went from saloon to saloon and I bought drinks all around several times, so that by midnight we had picked up three or four rowdies whom I did not know for company. We tried to get into a dance hall at one point, but Brocky Jack was there to stop us at the door.

"You boys can't come in here tonight," said the city marshal.

"And why the hell not?" asked Billy, truculent.

"Because you've all had too much to drink and you're spoiling for a fight and nothing starts a fight quicker than a woman."

"We don't want a fight," protested Billy. "We just want to have a little fun is all."

Brocky Jack looked at me—and I nodded, understanding what it was that he wanted, namely for me to lasso my brother and keep the situation under control. I appreciated the chance he was giving me—before he came down hard on Billy.

"No, he's right," I told Billy. "They have a dance here every night. We'll come back some other time."

"Why come back when we're already here?"

"Because I said so. Some hombre won't let you cut in and you'll get all hot under the collar and start a dustup, and you know I'm right."

Billy stared at me. Then he grinned slowly. "Well, okay, Ben, if that's the way you want it, I'll play by your rules."

So we moved on, and as we drew near the Grand Central Hotel, I told Billy that I was tired, and of a mind to turn in, and advised him to do the same. He said he would be along shortly, and went on with the others, and I was still in the lobby of the hotel when I heard shooting up the street. Running out, I saw Billy and his cronies out in the middle of the street, taking potshots at the moon and yelling at the top of their lungs, yipping like coyotes. I looked the other way and saw Brocky Jack coming on the run. I got to Billy before the marshal did and jerked the pistol right out of his hand.

"You're a damned fool," I said angrily.

"Gimme back my smoke-maker, Ben," he muttered.

I gave it to Brocky Jack instead, as he arrived on the scene.

"Thanks," said the marshal. "I'd sure hate to have to shoot your brother, Ben."

"I'd hate for you to."

Brocky Jack disarmed the other men. One made as though to resist, but I put a stop to that before it even got started, throwing a punch that landed squarely on the man's chin. He was out cold before he hit the ground.

"You know," Brocky Jack told me, as he turned Billy and the others over to a pair of deputies who had come to assist, "you'd make a damned good lawman, Ben. You've got a cool head, steady nerves, and hard fists. And they say you can shoot the tail feathers off a sparrow in flight."

I laughed. "Thanks. But badge-toting just does not pay enough to suit me."

Billy spent the rest of the night in jail, and the following day was brought before Ellsworth's magistrate, Judge Osborne, an eminently reasonable man. He lev-

ied a twenty-five-dollar fine on Billy, which I paid.
Brocky Jack gave Billy his gun back and I accompanied my brother outside.

"You made a fool out of me last night," said Billy,
resentfully.

"You managed to do that all by yourself."

"Don't you ever try to take my gun away from me
again."

"Let's just put it all behind us, Billy."

"No. You might be quicker on the draw than I am,
Ben, but I ain't afraid of you. And if you pull a stunt
like that again . . . Well, just don't, that's all I have to
say."

With that he walked away. Dumbfounded, I watched
him go, reflecting on how his years on the run had
changed my brother. And it wasn't a change for the
better.

That night Cad Pierce came to my roost in the back
of Brennan's saloon, looking for a high-stakes game.
Cad was a Texas cattleman I knew from my days in
Abilene. In fact, Cad had made me a present of a fine
double-barreled shotgun with a silver butt-plate. That
was just Cad's way—when he liked you, he just
couldn't do enough for you. Cad got into a game of
monte with one Neil Cain, with Neil doing the dealing
and Cad the betting. Cad was a big-time gambler, and
soon wanted to bet bigger stakes, but Neil explained
that he could not cover such bets, so Cad asked me to
find someone who would make up the difference. I said
I would try and walked out into the saloon proper and
saw a fellow named John Sterling, a local businessman,
who I knew could not resist a big wager. When I told
Sterling the details, though, he hesitated.

"I don't know, Ben. Cad Pierce has a lot of money

to burn. He likes to throw it away, but sometimes he gets lucky."

"Tell you what," I said. "I'll be good for half of everything you might lose. But if you win, I'll want half of the winnings."

"Sure," said Sterling. "In that case, you can count me in."

When it was all said and done, Cad Pierce had lost a lot of money. The great thing about Cad, though— he wasn't a bad loser. In fact, you could never tell just by looking at him whether he had won a fortune or lost everything. Either way, his reaction was exactly the same. After the game was over, he offered to buy the rest of us a drink, which was, I think, all one needs to say about the kind of man Cad was. It wasn't until after we'd had that drink that anyone noticed Sterling's absence. Cad asked me if I knew where he was. I didn't, but fully intended to find out, because by my calculations Sterling had walked away with over a thousand dollars—and half of that was mine.

It took me until the following afternoon to find him—in a saloon owned by Nick Lentz. Nick was as crooked as a dog's hind leg. I didn't like him and he didn't like me, primarily because I was taking a lot of his business away. Seemed like the cowboys preferred to play at a straight table, and Nick's dealers were about as far from honest as you could get. I figured it was just bad luck that Sterling had holed up in Nick's saloon. I suppose I could have waited until he came out, but by then I was in no mood to be patient. So I marched right in and walked up to Sterling at the bar. Nick was on the other side of the mahogany and the two snakes had their heads together. When they saw me coming, Nick straightened up and backed away.

"Hello, John," I said to Sterling, pleasantly enough.

"I guess you've been looking for me, haven't you?"

"What? Looking for you? Why would I be looking for you?"

"You know. To give me my share of last night's winnings. I decided to save you the trouble of finding me, so here I am."

"I don't know what you're talking about."

"We had a deal, John. You owe me five hundred dollars, at least. I'll take the money now."

Sterling remained hunched over the bar, one hand wrapped around a shot glass. He knocked the whiskey back and reached for a bottle—to pour himself another dose of liquid bravemaker, or so I thought.

"Don't press your luck with me, John," I warned, trying to keep a tight rein on my temper. "It's not the money so much as that I just cannot abide a man who goes back on his word."

Sterling hurled the bottle at me. I ducked, and he missed, and when I straightened up, I had a pistol in my hand. Sterling was backing up along the bar, grasping for his own shooting iron, and I would have killed him before he could clear the leather. Would have, except that Nick had a scattergun leveled about ten inches away from my left ear, so that I could very clearly hear the sounds both hammers made as they were being cocked.

"Stay out of this, Nick," I said coldly. "It's none of your business."

"You so much as blink, Thompson, and I'll be mopping your brains up off my floor."

I knew he wasn't bluffing. I had a knack for spotting men who had killed before. It changes a man in subtle ways. And after the first time, it does get easier. The look in his eyes, the tone of his voice, the steadiness of his hand—they all made very clear the fact that Nick Lentz would find it easy to kill me.

Of course, he was making one big mistake.

"Now you get out of my place, Thompson," said Lentz. "John here is a friend of mine, and you're not. I don't mind his company, but I can't stand yours."

"How much is he paying for your friendship, Nick?"

"Get the hell out of here."

Moving very slowly, I holstered my smoke-maker and walked out.

Nick's mistake, of course, was that he let me.

Chapter 13

ON THE WAY back to Brennan's saloon I made up my mind that I was going to have to kill Nick Lentz and John Sterling. It wasn't about the five hundred dollars, mind you. I could make four or five times that much in a good week at the tables. No, I was going to have to kill them because before long Nick and John would realize their mistake—and when they did, they would set out to remedy the situation. So I didn't even have to worry about when and where I would do the deed. They would come looking for me. And the first place they would look was Brennan's. All I had to do was make sure they found me. I made one quick stop: the Grand Central Hotel, in order to retrieve my Winchester repeating rifle from my room. I made sure it was fully loaded—sixteen rounds.

Billy was bellied up to the bar at Brennan's when I got there.

"You still mad at me?" I asked him.

"Yeah, and I got every right to be, too."

I nodded. "Possibly. Well, pretty soon there will be two men coming in here looking to kill me. They could probably use your help."

He stared at me, and I held that gaze for a few seconds before walking to the back room to check the action at my tables.

About an hour later Nick Lentz and John Sterling showed up. The came striding through the bat-wing

doors and stood just inside, shoulder to shoulder, Nick
with his scattergun and John with pistols in both hands,
and the patrons of Brennan's saloon took one look at
them and got very still, very quiet, in a big hurry.

That was what I was listening for—that telltale silence—and came out of the back room.

"Get your guns, Thompson," rasped Nick. "Then
come out onto the street and fight, you son of a bitch."

With the challenge issued, they backed out of the
saloon. I went to the bar where Billy and Brennan were
standing. Brennan poured me a drink—I didn't have to
ask.

"Two to one," muttered the saloonkeeper. "Hardly
seems fair."

Some of the cowboys in the place had moved to the
windows so that they could jostle for a view of the
street. Others seemed to gather around me—wanting, I
suppose, to see how I would react to these develop-
ments.

"What are you saying, Joe?" I asked. "Should I give
them some time to round up a few more men?"

The cowboys who heard this silly bit of bravado
laughed. Brennan grimaced. He considered himself a
friend of mine and was taking all of this very seriously.
Therefore, he was concerned that I didn't seem to be
doing the same.

"I don't know much about Sterling," he said, "but I
do know that Nick Lentz is not one to trifle with."

"Don't worry, Joe. I don't intend to trifle with him."

I started for the door but Billy grabbed me by the
arm.

"Hold up," he said. "Joe, hand me the shotgun."

Brennan reached under the bar and came up with
the shotgun that Cad Pierce had given me. He checked

to make sure both barrels were loaded before handing it over to Billy.

"Stay out of this," I told my brother.

"Stop treating me like a kid," he said crossly.

"This is my dance. You aren't invited."

"You're my brother, so that makes this my fight, too. Would you let me walk out there all by myself if the shoe was on the other foot? Hell no, you would not."

He had a point. Still, I hesitated. Billy had heart, but he was no shootist, and I wasn't too sure about his nerve, either, though I would never say such a thing.

"You know our mother would never forgive me if I just stood by while you went out and got yourself shot to hell," he said.

"And she would never forgive me if I let you take a bullet."

"Then I guess we can't let either thing happen, can we?"

I smiled. "No, I guess not."

We stepped outside into the bright sunlight, and I paused on the boardwalk in front of Brennan's place to look up and down the street, trying to locate Sterling and Lentz. I saw them down at the north end, near the railroad tracks.

"There they are," I said.

I guess Billy's finger twitched, because right when I said that, he whirled and the shotgun went off, discharging one barrel, and the buckshot clipped the tail of my frock coat and then shattered a plank in the boardwalk right behind me.

Cursing, I snatched the shotgun away from Billy. He was as white as a sheet.

"Goddamn it," I rasped. "What's wrong with you?"

"I—I guess I'm just a little nervous, Ben, that's all."

"Yeah, well, so am I—now more than ever. You could have killed me."

"I'm sorry," he said, abashed.

My anger ebbed as quickly as it had come. "Forget it," I said, and tossed him the shotgun. "Just, whatever you do, don't point that thing in my direction again."

"I won't, Ben." He reloaded the shotgun.

"Least now I know my luck's still holding. Now if it will just hold a little while longer."

I mean, how many times do you have to get shot at with no ill effects before you start to wonder?

As we started down the street, the city marshal, Brocky Jack Norton, quartered over to intercept us.

"Now boys," he said, "let's all cool down."

"We're cool enough," I replied, and pointed down the street at Sterling and Lentz. "Go talk to them."

"I know what this is all about," he said. "Is five hundred dollars worth shedding blood over, Ben?"

"It's not about the five hundred, Jack. They stormed into Brennan's and called me out. I'm not here because I want to be, and you know that."

"I know. You've gone out of your way to steer clear of trouble while you've been in Ellsworth. Don't think I haven't noticed."

"And how long do you think I would last in Ellsworth if I backed down from those two?"

"Just put up your guns. Go back to Brennan's, and let me go talk to Nick and Sterling."

I thought it over—and nodded. "Okay, that suits me. But if they come marching down here with guns, I'll finish what they started. Come on, Billy."

We walked back to Brennan's but didn't go in, standing in the shade of the boardwalk, instead. For some reason, going inside smacked of turning away from a fight, and I wouldn't do that. In my line of work

I couldn't be seen as one who could be buffaloed. I would be challenged every time a drunken cowboy lost his poke at one of my tables.

From where we stood we could clearly see Brocky Jack at the end of the street talking to Lentz and Sterling. Then a fourth man joined them.

"Who the hell is that?" asked Billy.

"It's Whitney," I said. "The county sheriff. He and Lentz are pards."

"Oh, well, that's just great."

The four men were engaged in a heated discussion— that was obvious even at this distance because of all the gesturing. I figured the longer the conversation lasted, the less likely this would all be settled amicably. And then, abruptly, after about ten minutes of jawing, Lentz and Sterling, followed by Whitney, started down the street. Brocky Jack took a few steps as though to go after them, then stopped.

"Why doesn't the marshal arrest them if he's so worried about bloodshed?" asked Billy skeptically.

"He knows now that wouldn't settle anything. Only postpone it. He will just wait and arrest whoever is left standing after the smoke clears. Are you ready?"

Billy nodded. "I'm tired of waiting."

"Me, too. Let's go."

We returned to the middle of the street and started toward the trio coming at us. I noticed that Sheriff Whitney was falling behind the other two. A case of cold feet, perhaps?

And then, when we were about thirty feet apart, Sterling raised one of his pistols and fired. The bullet went wide. Sterling dodged into the doorway of a general store. At the same time Nick Lentz broke in the other direction, crouching as he triggered the scattergun he was carrying. The buckshot kicked up dust just a few feet in front of Billy and me. Hoping to hit Sterling before he could reach cover, I fired at him, but he got lucky, stumbling as he crossed the boardwalk, and falling as he reached the doorway, so that my bullet splintered the wood behind him. Billy weighed in with one barrel's worth of buckshot, hitting Whitney. It was not the target I would have chosen—the sheriff hadn't yet drawn his gun. Lentz and Sterling, to my mind, were the greater threats. But Whitney *had* sided with those two, and he was a tempting target. The buckshot struck him in arm and chest, and the impact sent him spinning into a fall. Lentz fired the second barrel of his shotgun but he made the mistake of doing so while on the run. I snapped off a shot at him and knocked him down, then quickly turned my attention back to the doorway concealing Sterling, who was lining up another shot around the corner. I put a bullet into the wood inches from his face and he gave up the fight and dove into the store.

I checked Lentz, and was disappointed to see that I had only winged him, for he was limping into an alley and out of sight and I didn't have the time to try for him again. Running into the general store where Sterling had sought sanctuary, I was informed by an understandably jittery desk clerk that my quarry had bolted out the back way. Cursing under my breath, I went back out into the street. Several men were congregating around the form of the fallen sheriff. Billy walked over to me.

"That was easy," he said, vastly relieved. "I didn't figure they would lose their nerve and run."

"Me neither," I said, darkly. "Damn it, I wanted to settle this business once and for all."

One of the men over near Whitney shouted that he would fetch a doctor, and ran off, which I presumed to indicate the sheriff was still alive. But I didn't like the way some of the other good citizens in that ever-growing bunch were looking at us. And, beyond that throng, I saw Brocky Jack heading our way.

"Come on," I told Billy tersely, and set off with long strides for Brennan's saloon. Once there I asked Joe to give me my cash box, which he kept behind the bar. I took out two hundred dollars and handed this to Billy.

"Get your horse and ride out of town," I said. "And don't come back until we hear whether Whitney is going to live."

Billy was slow to understand. "But why run, Ben? It was a fair fight. They called you out."

"Just do it."

"He's right, Billy," said Joe. "You both need to go, or you'll be shot down in cold blood. Whitney had a lot of friends among the citizens of Ellsworth."

One of the Texans who had watched the shootout from the saloon's windows came forward.

"Us Texans have got to stick together," he drawled. "We'll stand with you, Thompson. If those Yankee shop clerks want a fight, then by God we'll oblige them."

I shook my head emphatically. "I appreciate the offer, but the last thing we need is another war between the states breaking out right here. No, I'll handle this. Billy, why are you still here?"

"Why aren't you coming with me?"

"I'll be leaving, too. But it's better if we split up."

"Look here," said the cowpuncher. "Me and my pards will ride back to our camp, and your brother can come with us."

"That's a good idea," I said. "Go with them, Billy. I'll get word to you when the coast is clear."

Billy didn't like it, that was plain, but he didn't ar-

gue, and departed Brennan's with half a dozen cowboys. I figured he was in good hands. Those drovers
would not let him come to harm.

"You aren't leaving, Ben," said Brennan, with a
smirk. "You just said that to get Billy out of town."

He was right. I went out the back way and made it
to the Grand Central Hotel. I had been in my room but
ten minutes or so when there came a knock on the door.
It was Cad Pierce.

"A bunch of townsmen formed themselves into a
posse, of all things, and set out after Billy," he told
me. "Brocky Jack tried to talk some sense into them
but they wouldn't listen. I went to Brennan's and offered the Texans in there one thousand dollars if they
would ride out and round up those yahoos and bring
'em back to town where they belong."

"Christ," I muttered. "We'll be lucky to get through
the day without somebody getting killed."

"Somebody already did," drawled Cad. "Sheriff
Whitney is no longer above snakes."

I stared at him for a moment as this news sank it.
"Well, that's just fine. Means there will be a warrant
issued for Billy's arrest on a charge of murder, I'd bet."

"It wasn't murder. It was a fair fight. There were
plenty of witnesses."

"I don't know if you noticed, but Whitney hadn't
drawn his gun. And those are Texas witnesses. They
don't count for much in Kansas, you know."

"Well, he was out there, so if he hadn't, that just
goes to show he was dumber than a fence post."

I went to the window. Some of the townsmen were
gathering in the street in front of the Grand Central,
and most of them were armed.

"Don't worry about them," said Cad, looking over

my shoulder at the street. "Some of my boys are on their way."

"You're a good friend, Cad, but I need for you to help me keep this from turning into a war."

"You can't ask us to just stand by and watch a fellow Texan get railroaded."

"Just do me a favor and find Brocky Jack and send him here."

"What for?"

"So I can turn myself in."

Cad Pierce shook his head. "You must be in a hurry to die, hoss."

"You want to help me, then just do what I ask."

Cad shrugged, nodded, and left the room. He was back a few minutes later with not only the town marshal but the mayor, James Miller, as well.

"The marshal has told me what happened," said Miller. "He saw the whole thing. And he says Whitney told him that this was as good a time as any to get rid of the Thompson boys. Were those his words as you remember them, Jack?"

Brocky Jack Norton nodded. "Whitney would have liked to drive every Texan out of Ellsworth."

"But the fact remains there will need to be a grand jury called," continued Miller. "It's the only way to resolve this. You have to give up your guns, Mr. Thompson, and allow yourself to be taken into custody."

"That was my intention," I replied. "But first I want to tell you, Brocky Jack, that I won't let a lynch mob have me. You let that happen, and you know what will follow."

"If he doesn't know, I'll enlighten him," said Cad Pierce. "You'll have so many dead bodies lying around here, you'll have to open up a brand-new bone orchard just to plant 'em all."

Norton grimaced. "I know what's at stake. But we need Billy, too, Ben."

"I know. Let tempers cool down, and I'll talk him into giving himself up. But you know as well as I do that they'd have hanged him had he not made dust."

"Fair enough. As for Lentz and Sterling, I've got my deputies hunting for them. They'll be arrested, too."

"You're a fair man," I said, handing over my pistol and Winchester. "I hope you can handle this."

"I guess you'll just have to trust me."

He was right. I didn't have any other choice.

Chapter 14

MAYOR MILLER AND Brocky Jack both agreed that I should not remain incarcerated for long, so on the very next day an inquest was held, and the judge presiding determined that all accounts of the shootout concurred to the extent that clearly I had not fired the shot that resulted in the death of Sheriff Whitney. Therefore, all I could be charged with was the attempted murder of Nick Lentz and John Sterling. But no one was going to even try to make such a charge stick. Sterling had fired first, which made my shooting at him and his cohort a clear-cut case of self-defense. And besides, both Sterling and Lentz had left town. So no one appeared to testify against me and after I had told my side of the story, and it was all taken down for the record, the judge dismissed the charge and informed me that I was a free man. Miller and Brocky Jack seemed as happy with the outcome as I.

You might wonder, then, why they had been so insistent that I surrender to authority on the day before. It was all for show, an attempt to defuse the crisis. I'd had that very thing in mind as the best case scenario, and for a change it had all worked in my favor. Miller and Brocky Jack were hoping that tempers would cool once at least one of the participants in the shootout had been taken into custody and judged in a court of law. And it also demonstrated that the authorities had the situation well in hand. They were hoping to discourage

vigilantism. The gang that had set out after Billy returned empty-handed; it was rumored that when they
found out that an even bigger gang of Texans had come
after them, intending to collect Cad Pierce's offer of
one thousand dollars, the unofficial posse had lost all
enthusiasm for the task they had set out to perform.
The mayor and the marshal hoped to prevent anything
else like that from happening. In fact, the mayor made
a statement, published in the Ellsworth newspaper, to
the effect that he had every confidence in Brocky Jack
where bringing Billy Thompson to justice was concerned. After all, they'd brought the older—and more
dangerous—Thompson brother to court, hadn't they?

   And for a while at least it looked like the situation
had been defused. Of course, we were all still sitting
on a powder keg and knew it. My brother still faced a
murder charge. And I kept looking over my shoulder,
wondering when Lentz or Sterling or both would slip
back into Ellsworth and try to finish what they started.
I figured that sooner or later one of them would, and
that the odds were it would be Lentz. For one thing he
owned a business here, and didn't strike me as the type
who would just walk away from something like that.
But, more than that, I had winged him, spilled his
blood—and he sure wasn't the type to let that kind of
thing go.

   But instead of Lentz or Sterling, it was Billy, of all
people, who showed back up in town.

   A theater had opened recently in Ellsworth, and one
night I was in attendance there, watching a perfor-
mance of Shakespeare by an itinerant troupe, when an
acquaintance sought me out to say that my brother was
waiting for me in an alley behind the Grand Central
Hotel. I tried to appear casual as I left the theater, but

once I was sure nobody was paying me any attention, I made haste to the alley.

"What the hell are you doing here?" I asked Billy. "I said I would send for you when the coast was clear."

"I know, Ben. But I had to come, just in case you didn't know."

"Didn't know about what?"

He handed me a folded piece of paper. I unfolded it and read by the light of a match that Billy struck and held up so that it illuminated the letter.

It was a notice, type-set, which led me to believe that it had been reproduced in quantity, sent to one of the Texans in the bunch that had escorted Billy out to their cow camp in the wake of the shooting. And at the bottom, in bold letters, were the words "Ellsworth Vigilance Committee."

Consider yourself warned! This affidavit, approved by all members of the committee, is to inform you that you have been deemed an undesirable presence in Ellsworth. If you are seen in town after this, you will forfeit your life. The good name of Ellsworth and its decent citizens will be defended at all costs. As the elected officials who represent the law have proven themselves inadequate to that task, we take it upon ourselves to dispense justice. This will be your one and only warning. Enter Ellsworth again at your own risk.

"Who else has gotten one of these?" I asked.

"A few other men in the outfit I'm with, and several in another outfit, too, that I know of. You mean you haven't gotten one?"

"No. In fact, I didn't know anything about this."

"You better get out of town, Ben."

I nodded. "Maybe so. You get back to that camp, Billy. When time comes for those boys to head back down to Texas, you ride with them if you haven't heard from me before."

"Where are you going to go?"

"I'm not sure. Can I keep this?"

"Be my guest."

After seeing Billy off, I went to the marshal's office and showed the affidavit to Brocky Jack.

"I had no idea," he said solemnly, after reading the notice. "I wonder just how many men are members of this vigilance committee."

"No telling. But I know this: I'm not calling my brother in until you've handled this problem."

"You said you would, Ben."

"And I will—when you've done your job, Jack."

He gave me a long look, then nodded. "Can't say that I blame you. I'd probably do the same were I in your place."

"I'm going to pay a visit to Kansas City. Will be on the next train out. When you've cleaned these vigilantes out, send me a wire and I'll come back."

"Fair enough."

My next step was Brennan's. I showed the affidavit to Joe and asked if he had seen Cad Pierce lately.

"He was here earlier tonight. Left a couple of hours ago, though, and I have no idea where he went."

"Well, in case I don't find him, and you can see him, tell him about this. I figure if he hasn't received one of these already, he's bound to."

Brennan said I could count on him, and I knew that was so. I spent another hour looking for Cad, but had

no luck, before boarding the train bound for Kansas
City.

Looking back, I regret not having made more of an
effort to find Cad. Not that I could have talked him
into leaving Ellsworth, at least temporarily—because if
there was one thing you could count on where Pierce
was concerned was that his pride would never permit
him to run. No, I regret it because I never got to say
so long to him.

I was in Kansas City for only two days before I
heard that Cad Pierce had been gunned down.

Along with a couple of other Texas boys named
John Good and Neil Cain, Cad had found out about
the vigilance committee's affidavits that had been issued on all three of them. After sharing a few drinks
the trio decided to find someone they could confront
about the affidavits, and began to prowl the streets of
Ellsworth. This brought them into contact with the new
sheriff, Jack Hogue—Whitney's replacement—who
was standing in front of a mercantile chewing the
breeze with his deputy, Ed Crawford. As both Hogue
and Crawford were well-known for their antipathy toward the Texas crowd, Cad figured they had to know
all about the vigilantes—if they weren't themselves
members of the committee.

"Well, Jack," said Cad, approaching Sheriff Hogue,
"I hear you have an affidavit with my name on it."

Hogue denied that this was so, or that he knew anything about any affidavit, which Cad knew was a lie.

"I think you and me need to go have a private talk,"
said Cad.

"I'm not going anywhere with you, Pierce. And
there's been too much talk around here lately."

That was when Crawford stepped out into the street.
"Yeah, entirely too much talk. In fact, I hear you

bragged about how it was a shotgun you bought for Ben Thompson that killed Whitney, and you thought the hundred dollars you paid for it was money well-spent. Now, that's what I call bad talk, and you ought to be held accountable because of it."

"You reckon you're man enough to do that?" asked Cad, letting the whiskey do the talking for him.

"Let's find out," replied Crawford, drawing his pistol. Cad went for his six-shooter too, but he was no pistoleer, like Crawford was, and before he could get off a shot, the deputy sheriff had put a couple of bullets into him. Cad stumbled into the mercantile, but Crawford followed, and finished him off. John Good and Neil Cain found themselves under Hogue's gun and had to stand by helplessly.

A few hours later a band of at least twenty Texans rode into Ellsworth, mad as hornets, and making known their feeling that the town should be burned right down to the ground. Instead of turning thought into action, they collected Cad's body and escorted it out of town. It would be sent home to Austin, Texas.

Many of the townsmen armed themselves and went before Mayor Miller, saying that they were ready, willing, and able to defend Ellsworth against the Texans, who everyone assumed would return with malice in mind. A meeting was convened, with all concerned citizens invited. It was decided that several emergency measures needed to be taken. First, no Texan would be permitted to go about town armed with a firearm. If one was caught, any citizen had the right to arrest him. Second, the saloons and gambling halls would be shut down early each night, in keeping with a new curfew. And third, twenty townsmen would form a nightly detail to patrol the streets. In effect, they had as much authority as Marshal Norton or Sheriff Hogue to deal with any cowboy they considered a hazard to the community.

The Texans were not going to roll over, especially after a dozen of them were arrested for carrying firearms in the city limits—and most of the arrests were violent ones. When the rest made belligerent noises, Mayor Miller reluctantly requested help from the governor of Kansas, who responded by sending troops. The Texans knew when they were whipped, and the cow outfits departed. So did many of the gamblers and percentage girls. The brief and violent reign of Ellsworth as queen of the cattle towns was over. I for one wasn't sorry.

When the Kansas governor issued a bounty of five hundred dollars for the arrest of my brother, I realized it was time for me to leave the state for good, which I did, in the company of Neil Cain. I had known Cain for some time. He lived north of Austin on a small spread, and had been one of the first to realize that in the aftermath of the war, there was a future in rounding up maverick beef and selling it to northern markets.

Since Billy was still wanted for the killing of Sergeant Burke, he had to remain in hiding back home in Texas, and when Neil and I got to Austin, we arranged for him to stay at the Cain place. I was of the opinion that he would be as safe there as anywhere. As it turned out, I was wrong.

A couple of months later, Cain and Ed Stewart and a few other cowboys moved about a hundred head of cattle to the new railhead at Rockdale. Billy went along as one of the drovers. When allegations arose that some if not all of the cattle had been stolen in Llano and Blanco counties, a company of Texas Rangers rode out to serve a warrant.

When the Rangers showed up, Cain and Stewart

took to the brush. The former escaped. Stewart wasn't so lucky. Billy's luck was—as it had always been—consistently bad. He had no idea that any of the beeves were stolen, so he didn't run. The Rangers weren't interested in hearing his side of the story. They put him in shackles and hauled him off to Austin.

I went at once to Joseph Glover, explained the situation to him, and gave him a thousand dollars—money I had won of late at the Austin gaming tables.

"What we must do," I told the portly attorney, "is whatever's necessary to stop them from sending Billy back to Kansas. In my opinion he's as good as dead if they send him back there."

Glover nodded. "I agree. The charge against him for the killing of that man Burke is eight years old and I doubt they could find a jury in the state that would convict him for it now. As for this rustling business, it is my understanding that Cain and Stewart bought the cattle from a gang running irons out in Blanco County, knowing that the beeves were stolen. There is no evidence that I am aware of to indicate that Billy had so much as an inkling of what was really going on."

I sighed. "All too often that's so true. But, evidence or not, I've seen men railroaded before. How well do you know the judges these days, Joe?"

Glover smiled. "I know them all quite well. And that's another reason to keep your brother out of a Kansas courtroom. How much can you afford?"

"Whatever it takes," I replied.

Billy was brought before a county judge named Smith first, for the purpose of revisiting the charge of murder against him that related to the Burke shooting. Judge Smith reviewed the case, then dismissed it for lack of evidence. As soon as he was free of that charge, Billy was hauled before Justice Fritz Tegener on the charge of cattle rustling. There was another hearing, after which Tegener dismissed the case. When Billy left Tegener's court, he was arrested on a warrant issued by a district court judge that charged him with the murder of Sheriff Whitney in Ellsworth. This time the Texas Rangers got involved. A Captain Sparks took Billy into custody because the local authorities were clearly reluctant to keep shunting my brother back and forth between jailhouse and courthouse. In a desperate ploy to keep my brother in Texas, Joe Glover arranged for a warrant from Aransas County charging Billy with being an accomplice to a murder down there. He wasn't, of course—the charge was completely fraudulent. Billy had never been to that county, and there wasn't even a murder. But it forced the district court to determine the issue of custody.

A week later the court, pressed by the governor to do so, decided that the Kansas charge should take precedence. A few days later, Captain Sparks and two other Rangers escorted Billy to the railhead and took him off to Kansas. Sparks was worried that an attempt might be made to hijack the train and free Billy, and he figured I was the one behind that conspiracy. In fact, while the plan had been suggested to me, I refused to permit it. I was more concerned that Billy might fall into the hands of a lynch mob once he got to Kansas. So I hopped the next train to Ellsworth.

I was surprised to find that Billy's case had received a lot of press in Kansas. In fact, it became part and parcel of a political battle between two factions in the state, those who understood that the economic well-being of Kansas depended, at least for now, on the Texas trade, and those who thought that the only way to guarantee the state's long-term prosperity was to get rid of the Texans. The former were inclined to cut us a lot of slack; the latter thought we were vermin. Generally, the former thought Billy had acted within his rights in shooting Whitney; the latter declared him a cold-blooded killer. Hang him, they said, and show his kind what happens to gun-happy scum who don't walk the straight and narrow.

They took Billy first to Salina, but by the time I got there, the Rangers had handed him over to a United States marshal who had deemed the Salina jail unsatisfactory, and transferred my brother elsewhere. I didn't know where, and they refused to tell me, the general consensus being that my true intent was to break Billy out of jail. I had no such plan—not at the moment, anyway. I didn't really have any kind of plan at all. I did have a goal—to keep the hangman's noose from around my brother's neck.

Then an acquaintance from my days in Abilene handed me an edition of the Leavenworth *Times*, in which an editorial discussed Billy's situation and expressed the point of view that I was up to no good.

It is known that Billy Thompson's notorious brother, Ben, has followed him to Kansas. The matter has become so serious that a strong guard had to be kept around the Salina jail night and day, not only to prevent a rescue but also to save the prisoner from the due vengeance of lynch law. Finding it no longer safe to keep him in Salina, the United States marshal, along with the sheriffs of two counties, agreed that he should be lodged in the penitentiary here until the time for his trial—in the March term of court—arrives. Thompson is described as a powerful man and a willing slave to the worst passions. His guards not only had him heavily ironed while conveying him here, but kept him constantly covered with shotguns. He is now in a place where he is not likely to receive anything in the shape of assistance.

So Billy ended up in the federal penitentiary at Leavenworth. The editorial was right about one thing— there would be no breaking him out of there.

My intention was to be present for Billy's trial, and I made arrangements to have him ably represented by two lawyers by the names of Case and Pendleton. But, as good as they were, they could not prevent a postponement asked for by the prosecutor, who complained that witnesses were scattered from Texas to Canada to California. He needed time to locate and summon them. The judge postponed the trial until September.

As I could do nothing more for Billy, I went home to Texas. I felt bad doing it, knowing my brother was wasting away in that Leavenworth hellhole. And all because he'd felt obliged to back me up in a quarrel that had started over five hundred dollars. If I'd had it all to do over again, I would never have gone hunting for John Sterling to get my share of those monte winnings.

When the trial came up in September, I took the advice of Billy's attorneys and stayed in Texas. They argued that my presence would do nothing to favor Billy and, considering my reputation, might in fact do him harm to his cause. I answered in writing two long lists of questions, one from the defense, one from the prosecution, and swore to the truth of what I wrote before a justice of the peace.

All I could do then was wait for word, and try to comfort my mother, who was beside herself with worry.

Some of my friends told me over drinks that if Billy was convicted, there would be a move afoot to gather one hundred or even two hundred men and ride to Kansas and set the whole state ablaze. The honor of Texas was at stake, after all. And of course, I was expected to lead this army of gun-crazy cowboys. I knew how such an excursion would end, but I was pretty bitter at the time, and didn't close the door on the possibility of wreaking vengeance if my brother was hanged.

Fortunately, we didn't have to ride to Kansas—I say fortunately because I was fairly certain that few of us would have come back alive. To my amazement, at the conclusion of a week-long trial, Billy was found not guilty. The attorneys I had hired were able to convince the jury that Sheriff Whitney had exceeded his authority by siding with Lentz and Sterling, and that in a gunfight Billy could not be expected to wait until an adversary had drawn and fired his gun before reacting.

Once freed, Billy wasted no time getting home, as he had been cleared of both the old charge against him—for the shooting of Burke—as well as the one stemming from Neil Cain's cattle-rustling venture. And so I was able to close the book on my Kansas adventures once and for all. Taken as a whole, they could only be described as a complete disaster.

Chapter 15

I SPENT THE next year in Austin. After that bad business in Kansas, I'd had it in mind to stay there for good, to spend the rest of my days with Catherine and my son, whom I had missed terribly while away. Then, too, my mother was ailing. My father's death a few years earlier had seemed to take a lot of the zest for life right out of her, and while all of us had expected her to recover, given time, she never did.

It was my hope to make her last years, or months, on earth as pleasant and easy as possible. She and Catherine had become very close, and, in fact, it was my wife who suggested that she move in with us. I had bought a new and larger home, so there was plenty of room. And even though Catherine had proven entirely capable of taking care of herself and our son in spite of the loss of her arm, my mother's presence under our roof provided me with an excuse to hire some help in the person of a Mexican woman who quickly made herself indispensable. She became intensely loyal to every member of my family—with the exception, ironically, of her employer. She took the liberty of chastising me on a regular basis for spending too much time in the gambling dens and not enough with my loved ones. I countered by pointing out that I had a great many expenses, of which she was one. She scoffed at that, for she knew that wasn't the real reason I spent all those long hours away from home. Of course, she was quite right. As much as I loved Catherine, I could not set eyes on her without being overwhelmed by guilt.

I fared reasonably well, professionally, in Austin during this period. But then, in 1876, word came that silver had been discovered near the source of the Arkansas River, in the mountains of Colorado. Extremely rich deposits of silver. It didn't really compare in richness to the great gold strikes in California thirty years before, but still a good many people flocked to Colorado in hopes of striking it rich—not a few of them from Texas. I resisted the temptation—for a while. But I had never been very good at resisting temptations for long. In early 1879 I let a friend by the name of Frank Cotton talk me into going up to a see a boomtown called Leadville.

"I'm telling you, Ben," said Cotton, "I've heard from several reliable sources and they all say that Leadville right now is the richest damned town in the nation."

"I'm not going to dig around in the ground for a nugget of silver," I replied. "My hands will not fit around the handle of a pickax or a shovel."

Cotton laughed, and gave me the once-over. As was my habit, I was dressed to the nines. I wore the best broadcloth frock coat and trousers to be had in Austin, along with my best and snowy-white muslin shirt, and a derby hat to top it off. I cut a fine figure according to all who chose to comment on my appearance. The only flaw was the pistol I wore in a holster beneath the coat. But I never went anywhere without being heeled.

"Anyone who saw you would know that," said Cotton.

"Frank, you once said I looked like a dandy, and I

let you get away with that because you're a friend of mine. But don't press your luck."

Cotton knew I was kidding. "Don't give me that. You don't give a damn what people call you—which is a good thing."

I laughed. "No, you're right, I don't care what they say. Maybe that's my problem. But as long as they don't start throwing lead at me, I'm okay."

"I am not suggesting we go into prospecting, for Christ's sakes. Look, you made a decent living off the cowpunchers who went up the cattle trails to Kansas. I swear, Ben, you would make a fortune off the Leadville prospectors. All I'm asking is that you run up there with me and take a look around. If you don't like what you see or if for any reason it doesn't pan out, what have you lost?"

"I'll go, on one condition. That you stop making fun of the way I dress."

"I'll never laugh at you again. I'll swear it on a stack of Bibles."

"Well," I said, "I'll give it a go. It couldn't turn out any worse than Kansas."

Which goes to show you that some people just never learn.

In order to avoid Kansas, Frank and I traveled by horse through the Panhandle country, until recently the domain of fierce Comanches. A determined military campaign against this tribe, culminating in a battle at Palo Duro Canyon that crushed the Comanches in their favorite lair, had by and large removed the Indian threat—one that had plagued the Texas frontier since even before my arrival from England nearly thirty years ago.

Though we met up with mustangers and wolfers and

even hidehunters—the latter pursuing what remained of the once great southern herd of buffalo—we had no trouble with any of them. It struck me how greatly the West had changed just in the handful of years since the end of the Civil War. One by one, the Indian tribes were being subdued. More and more pioneers were settling down, until it seemed as though nearly every nook and cranny hosted a newly erected cabin and corral. Where once there had been nothing but hundreds of miles of uncharted terrain, there were now towns springing up all over—with stage routes and railroads connecting them to one another. The dream of a transcontinental railroad had been realized a decade ago, and I suppose that single event, more than any other, marked the beginning of the end of the wild frontier.

Many was the Westerner who lamented the taming of the West—my traveling companion among them. Unlike Frank Cotton, I didn't mind the coming of civilization at all. I could appreciate the value of a lonely camp under the stars where peace of mind and freedom were concerned. I had lived in the wild places. But I preferred town life, and the amenities that progress afforded such a life—good food, well-made clothes, an expensive cigar, bonded whiskey. And, most importantly, the opportunity to ply my trade as a gambler. As I told Frank, it would be a sorry state of affairs if the only takers we could find for a game of five-card draw or three-card monte were buckskin-clad trappers with plews to wager.

Of course, Frank wasn't convinced. He grumbled constantly about the signs of civilization he saw during our journey north. "I came out here as a youngster because I wanted elbow room," he said. "And I didn't like living where there were so many rules. People always telling you what you could do and not do, where you could go and not go." He shook his head morosely. "The more people you have all pushed together in one place, the more rules you get."

"Without rules they would just wind up killing one another."

He gave me a wry look. "You're a funny one to be defending rules, Ben," he said. "Since when have you played by them?"

"All rumors to the contrary, I haven't killed a single man since I served in Mexico with the Imperialists. I try to play by the rules all the time, Frank. I have to. I have a family to provide for."

"That makes me wonder, then, why you never pinned on a tin star. Lord knows you've got all the attributes that a Wyatt Earp or a Bat Masterson has. You've got ice water in your veins. You're a crack shot. You don't buckle under pressure."

I shook my head emphatically. "No, thanks. I do not want to be a lawman. The pay is miserable. I've made more in one good night at the tables than some lawmen can make in a year."

Frank grinned. "So it's just the money?"

"Just the money?" I laughed. "Well, what else is there?"

When we reached Denver, we lay over there for a few days, making arrangements for the last, over-mountain leg of the journey to Leadville. Denver represented everything about the changing West that Frank deplored—but which I found exciting. In less than twenty years it had grown from a trading post to a bonafide city, bustling with activity and commerce, a genuine entrepôt of the high plains. It even boasted an opera house. And there were plenty of high-stakes games of chance to be found. Unfortunately, I had a run of bad luck while there, losing a good bit of money.

But I didn't let this setback worry me. As every gambler knows, the cards will sometimes run cold. The measure of a true professional is how well he sustains himself during a dry spell, and how quickly he bounces back. Winning is easy. To deal with a bad streak and keep it from turning into a disaster—that's the hard part. A lot of men get rattled. They try to force Lady Luck to come back to them by putting everything on the line. I never tempted fate like that, not where a card game was concerned.

To get to Leadville from Denver we rode the Denver & South Park Railroad seventy miles to a town called Webster, where we transferred to a stage. On our way through the mountains we were hit by a heavy snow. We crossed the Continental Divide at noon on the second day, and as we began the descent, the driver nearly lost control of the wagon, and we came perilously close to hurtling over a cliff that was at least a thousand feet high. During the journey we were several times compelled to get out and walk, as the team of mules could not pull a fully-loaded stage up certain steep grades, and I learned just how exhausting the slightest exertion could be above the timberline, where the air was so thin. Especially for a flatlander like me.

I was surprised by the size of Leadville. It had over ten thousand inhabitants. Cut off from the rest of the world by formidable mountain ranges, the town was remarkably civilized, with an efficient waterworks, and plans were afoot for a gas works and street trolley. There were churches, schools, theaters, an opera house, and half a dozen first-rate (by hotel standards) hotels. It seemed like nearly every other home was a boarding house—and why not, when a resident could let out a small room for sixty dollars or better a month. There were plenty of saloons and dance halls and gambling

dens, too. A shot of whiskey cost two bits, and a whole
bottle five dollars. High prices all around, but it was
not more than the market would bear. The miners and
prospectors were taking a lot of silver out of the mountains, so they could afford to pay top dollar for their
pleasures.

Where there was money, there were the predators—
the cardsharps, confidence men, and percentage girls—
and I knew some of them from my days in Kansas,
when these same people had endeavored to relieve
Texas drovers of the wages paid them after three
months of pushing cattle up the trails. They knew me,
too. In spite of this, a crooked outfit cheated me of
several thousand dollars at faro. I made a ruckus, shooting up the saloon and warning those characters that it
would be hazardous to their health if they lingered
much longer in Leadville. Then I crossed the street to
another saloon and had a drink and waited for the town
marshal to show up. He had also heard of me, and
cordially apologized for having to place me under arrest. I paid him a bond in cash and promised to appear
in court the following day—an arrangement that he
readily accepted. And I did appear, pleading guilty to
the charge of disturbing the peace, paying a fine as well
as damages. I considered these out-of-pocket expenses
to be an investment, and, as I had hoped, I had no
further difficulties at the tables during my sojourn in
Leadville. Needless to say, I quickly recouped my
losses. It was important, I felt, to firmly establish that
no one interested in a long and happy life should attempt to cheat or con Ben Thompson.

That's not to say that I did not have other difficulties
in Colorado, or that a reputation like mine is necessarily an asset.

I had heard of Bat Masterson. We had been in Kansas at about the same time, but we had never met, as he'd pinned on a badge in Dodge City while I was in Ellsworth. He had made a name for himself as a fearless lawbringer. Then one day he walked into a Leadville saloon where I was engaged in a profitable game of poker, looking for me.

"I've heard a lot about you, Ben," he said, after we had introduced ourselves. "I would be honored if you allowed me to buy you a drink. In exchange, I'd like for you to listen to a business proposition I've got."

"I'm always open to a business proposition," I replied. "Not to mention a free drink."

Masterson laughed. He was a solidly-built, dark-complected man with brown eyes that reminded me of a hound dog's, and a thick, drooping mustache—of which, I learned, he was exceedingly vain. He was an educated and urbane man, eastern-born and city-bred, who had come west to satisfy an unquenchable appetite for adventure. He dressed well—as well, I must admit, as I did, right down to the derby hat. It was immediately clear that he and I had a lot in common.

"I suppose," he said, as we bellied up to the bar and downed whiskey shots, "that you are familiar with the railroad situation in these parts."

I shrugged. "My understanding of it is that there are two iron roads competing to finish a spur into these mountains. There is the Denver and Rio Grande on one hand and the Atchison, Topeka, and Santa Fe on the other. Whoever completes an extension to Leadville first will prosper because of all the ore that will be shipped out of here—and all of the goods shipped in."

"That's about it in a nutshell. Thing is, there's only one viable route into Leadville, and that is by way of Royal Gorge. Now, I have not yet seen this passage with my own eyes, but I'm told there is only room for one line through it."

"Now that I think of it," I said, "I remember hearing something about the Denver and Rio Grande suffering financial losses, and recently settling with its rival, allowing the Santa Fe to have access to the gorge."

"It's a little more complicated than that." Masterson signaled for the bartender, who filled our glasses and then moved discreetly away. "Both roads were poised to build into the gorge. Both got court injunctions prohibiting the other from proceeding. The Rio Grande had already invested so much money into the spur that it soon got into a financial bind. That's why General Palmer, the man who owns the Rio Grande, capitulated. But then the good people of Denver dealt themselves a hand in the game. You see, they feel as though the Santa Fe is a Kansas road, while the Rio Grande is a Colorado one—so there's an element of pride involved. More than that, however, is the fact that the owners of the Santa Fe plan to make Kansas City the center of their operation. That means Denver will lose out. So they came up with money to loan Palmer so he can complete his spur. And now Palmer has broken his agreement with the Santa Fe."

I nodded. "Yes, this all sounds familiar to me. And I think both companies have built forts to protect their roads through the gorge. But I confess I haven't paid much attention to this whole affair. It has nothing to do with me. I don't care which road reaches Leadville first, frankly."

"I'm here to change your mind about that," said Masterson, smiling. "The Santa Fe has hired me to round up fifty professionals to defend the crews working on their road."

"Defend them from what?"

"It seems men with rifles have been taking potshots at the Santa Fe crews. And someone has used dynamite to blow up new sections of track on three different occasions. I'm told that the Rio Grande is recruiting its own gunmen."

"And you want me to sign on."

"That's right. I've got about thirty men with me now. Your name alone will make it that much easier for me to recruit more. It might also save lives in the long run."

"How do you figure?"

Masterson chuckled. "Don't be so modest, Ben. Most men would think at least twice before going up against you."

"How much does this piece of work pay, anyway?"

"The Santa Fe has offered a hundred dollars a month."

Now it was my turn to chuckle. "But I just made a hundred dollars in the last hour at that poker game you interrupted."

"I realize that. But I can promise you that the Santa Fe will make it worth your while, Ben. You will be my lieutenant, and the company will give us both a handsome bonus once the job is completed."

I thought it over. My first impulse was to decline the offer. My days of hunting for adventure simply for adventure's sake were over. And there was no telling how much money I would lose if I spent weeks in a cold mountain camp instead of at the tables in Leadville. It didn't make a bit of sense, even with the promise of a bonus.

"Why are you doing this anyway, Bat?" I asked.

Masterson summoned the bartender again and waited until our third shot of whiskey had been poured and the apron had moved out of earshot before responding.

"Because," he said, "it will pay big dividends to be on the good side with a company like the Santa Fe, that's why. The men who own that company are very powerful. Very wealthy. They have a lot of influence. I'm just looking ahead, Ben."

"But what if they lose this fight?"

Masterson glanced at me. His warm brown eyes had suddenly turned glassy and cold. I knew that look. I had seen it in Wild Bill Hickok and a few others—and in my own reflection.

"I'm here to see that they don't," he said.

And that pretty much guaranteed, I thought, that the Atchison, Topeka, and Santa Fe would not lose.

"Okay," I said. "Count me in. For a while, anyway."

He raised his glass in a toast. "To long life and prosperity."

I touched his glass with mine. "I'll settle for prosperity."

Chapter 16

I RODE WITH Masterson to Canon City, one of the Santa Fe's depots, and there we were joined by thirty-three gunfighters Bat had recruited in Kansas. A few of them I knew by reputation, but had never met any of them. They were a rough-looking bunch. Most gunmen are loners, outcasts, men who don't fit in and who don't play by the rules. The vast majority had broken the law on at least one occasion, because generally they did not respect any authority except the kind you could dispense through the barrel of a six-shooter. And they lived hard, because they knew that in their line of work, you usually didn't get to grow old gracefully. So they were not inclined to postpone gratification, wherever they derived it, be it from whiskey or women or games of chance. This meant that the camp near one end of Royal Gorge that Masterson set up for his crew was one rough and rowdy place. They called it "Dodge City" or "Little Dodge," I suppose because Masterson and at least half of the gunhawks he had brought to Colorado had come from the vicinity of the Kansas town by that name.

Our job was to make sure that the crews working on the Santa Fe line through the gorge were not set upon by the gunmen that the rival Rio Grande company had employed—and for several weeks we had no trouble to speak of. But then the courts got into the act again, and brought things to a head. First the Supreme

Court ruled that the Rio Grande had what they called a "prior right" to the gorge. Nobody knew for certain what that really meant, so we didn't worry about it. Then the Attorney General filed a suit in state court asking for an injunction against the Santa Fe that, if granted, would prohibit the company from running railroads anywhere in Colorado. The case was brought before a judge named Bowen, who presided over the fourth judicial district. Everyone knew that Bowen was biased in favor of the Rio Grande. Some suggested he had been bought by General Palmer, but I don't know that there is any truth in that. The Santa Fe's lawyers asked for a change of venue, but failed in that effort, and by suggesting that Bowen was not capable of making an impartial judgment in the case virtually guaranteed that, indeed, he would not. And he didn't. He issued a writ enjoining the Santa Fe from operating within the state. The writ also gave the owners of the property upon which the company had bought right of way the restoration of their property—including any "improvements" made upon it. Those improvements, naturally, consisted of Santa Fe rail and, in some cases, rolling stock.

This was a blatantly illegal confiscation of a company's property, and everyone knew it. Masterson informed me that I was to ride to Pueblo with a dozen men and hold the Santa Fe roundhouse there until a United States marshal arrived to take possession of the place and all the equipment it contained.

"The company is pretty sure that Judge Hallet up in Denver will overturn Bowen's ruling," said Masterson. "Hallett is an incorruptible judge."

"Well, for once, I'm glad to hear there is one."

"The U.S. marshals will be on our side in this, too. The problem is that most of the local sheriffs along the line are not. They are the ones you will have to watch out for, Ben."

"Not a problem. I've been watching out for sheriffs all my life. Now, just how far do you want me to go to protect the company's property?"

"Do whatever you have to do," said Masterson grimly.

"You know, I've managed thus far to avoid killing anyone who wore a tin star, Bat."

"Do you want out?"

I shook my head. "No, I guess not. I like to see things through to their end."

Masterson nodded. "Good. I'm headed for Denver to defend the Santa Fe's property there. Good luck to you."

I wished him good luck as well and picked my men from the outfit populating Little Dodge. When I was done, nine of the twelve men I chose to ride with me were from Texas. All I can say is that I felt better being accompanied by my own kind.

When we rode into Pueblo two days later, the round-house engineer, a man named McKenney, informed me that all hell was breaking loose elsewhere, and was just about to here.

"I've gotten several telegrams in the past forty-eight hours," said the burly Irishman. "And the news is all bad."

"I'm not surprised," I said. "So what's happened?"

"A sheriff's posse seized the roundhouse in Denver before Masterson and his men could get there. And Palmer has put about one hundred armed men on a train and has them rolling through the state, on *our* lines, grabbing up every depot and mogul and supply yard along the way. They will be here before too much longer."

"A hundred men. Are you sure about that?"

"Masterson sent the wire himself, so what do you think?"

"He tends to tell it like it is," I sighed.

"So just what are we supposed to do now?"

"Well, I don't know what you're going to do. But I'm going to do what Bat sent me here for."

I relayed the bad news to the men who had come with me, and gave them the option of standing with me or calling it quits. It looked now like we had backed the wrong horse in the Santa Fe. Two men decided it was all over, and headed for the tall timber. The others chose to stick—including, of course, every last one of the Texans. One of these told me he would consider it an honor to go down fighting alongside the famous Ben Thompson. I thought that was a foolish way to look at things, but didn't tell him so.

The roundhouse and adjacent company office were made of stone, as timber was as rare as a high-bred woman in this arid section of the country. Being a place where locomotives and cars were turned around on a revolving section of rail, the roundhouse was a circular structure with two wide arches through which the rolling stock passed. These we barricaded, using anything we could find that would stop a bullet. Not that I actually thought that ten men could long hold this place against a hundred. Our only advantage was that there wasn't much cover for the enemy as he approached our position. If the Rio Grande outfit wanted to storm the roundhouse they would have to cross a good deal of open ground to do it. So we could make them pay dearly.

We spent a sleepless night, keeping our eyes peeled and our guns handy, but nothing happened until early the next morning, when two men approached the roundhouse under the protection of a white flag.

"Hey, look, Ben," said one of the Texans with me. "They heard we were here and decided to surrender!"

The others laughed, which I took to be a good sign. These men knew their situation was grim, but they weren't going to let it get them down. Such men are the ones you want at your side when the shooting starts.

"That's Sheriff Price," McKenney told me. "And the man carrying the truce flag is Williams. He's with the Rio Grande."

I let the duo come to within twenty yards of the barricade before advising them that they were close enough. Price introduced himself and Williams before asking me who I was. I told him.

"I've heard about you," said Price. "You're that killer from down Texas way."

"I haven't killed anyone in a while," I replied. "I'm a little rusty in that department. But then, that could change any minute now, couldn't it?"

Price looked suddenly very uncomfortable. He gestured at the white flag—actually just a strip of white linen tied to one end of a walking stick that Williams was holding aloft.

"We're not heeled, either one of us," he said. "We have just come here to talk."

"Then do what you came to do."

Price produced a piece of paper. "I have here a copy of Judge Bowen's writ. According to this, that roundhouse and everything in it no longer belongs to the Santa Fe. Which means you've got no business being in there. In fact, you're trespassers, the whole lot of you."

"You've come to arrest us, then."

"I've come to give you the opportunity to ride out of here unmolested. You won't be arrested. You won't be fired upon. All you have to do is leave, and don't come back."

"We'll leave—when the United States marshal gets here. Until then, we're going to stay right here and do our jobs. Which is to make sure you thieving scoundrels don't get your hands on what rightfully belongs to the Santa Fe."

Price brandished the paper overhead. "This writ says otherwise."

"You'll need more than that to take this roundhouse," I told him.

Price scowled. He was a man full of his own importance, and he didn't appreciate it that I was challenging his authority. Clearly he wasn't accustomed to such intransigence.

"You've got one hour to change your mind, Thompson. That's all. I'll be back in one hour and you will either hand over that roundhouse or I'll take it from you."

"Okay," I said pleasantly. "But here's a little advice. When you come back, leave that writ at home and bring a gun instead. Because you'll need one."

Price was punctual. Exactly one hour later he came marching back up the street from Pueblo. This time there was no flag of truce. And this time he had about eighty men with him. Some of them looked like railroad workers, others like cowboys, and still others like store clerks. But in one respect they were all alike. They were all armed to the teeth.

"I have sent a telegram to the governor," Price told me—though he had to shout it because I had ordered him to stop fifty yards away this time. "I informed him that I had served the writ, but that an armed mob retained possession of the roundhouse in open defiance of the law."

"Looks to me like you're the one with the armed mob, Sheriff."

"Every last one of these men has been deputized. Now, are you going to give way, Thompson? This is your last chance."

I glanced at my Texas comrades. One look was all I needed to confirm that they were ready for a fight.

"Come and take it," I called to Price.

The sheriff hesitated. But one of his deputies did not. A shot rang out. Then another. One of my men let loose with his Winchester. Then everyone was shooting. In seconds the mob was largely obliterated from view by a cloud of gunsmoke. Though we could not pick our targets, we continued to sling lead, firing as fast as we were able. The four men stationed at the opposite entrance to the roundhouse began to shoot, too—apparently some of Price's deputies had tried to slip in the back way. The din of gunfire was deafening. I had not heard the likes since my days with Mejia down in Mexico, fighting for the Emperor Maximilian. Price's boys were doing their fair share of contributing to the noise; their bullets slamming into our barricade sounded like a hailstorm hammering against a tin roof. At least for a few minutes. And then the noise diminished significantly—and a moment later I called out to the Texans to cease firing.

An eerie silence descended on the scene. The smoke gradually thinned. I saw several bodies lying very still in the dust where I had last seen Price's gang of "deputies" standing.

"What the hell," muttered one of the Texans. "Where in the blazes did they run off to?"

"Reckon they went home," said another. "And that badge-toter was probably leading the pack." He let out a triumphant rebel yell and a few of the others responded in kind.

"Don't start celebrating just yet," I advised them. "It's not over by a long shot."

One of my men had been hit, but the bullet had passed clean through his shoulder. We had built a fire in the roundhouse, and left some iron tongs in the blaze. These I took up and slapped the red-hot iron against the bullet hole to cauterize it. The wounded man cursed like the devil but he didn't pass out, and I gave him a drink from my whiskey flask. After a long pull he smacked his lips and sighed contentedly.

"Now that's worth getting shot for," he said.

It was a shame, I thought, that such brave men had to die.

McKenney came up to me. He was clearly shaken. I knew he had not participated in the shootout—having taken shelter in one of the locomotives inside the roundhouse instead—but I didn't hold that against him. He was an engineer, not a shootist. He wasn't paid to do this kind of work.

"You think they'll give up now?" he asked, hopefully.

"There's no telling," I replied. "They might wait until that trainload of gunmen gets here. We'll just have to sit tight and see."

That's what we did—all through the long day. As the shadows of evening lengthened, a young boy, about age ten, scampered across the open space and over the barricade, which I thought was either a very courageous act or a very foolish one, considering the circumstances. But McKenney knew him—I found out later that the boy was the son of a widow whom the Santa Fe engineer had been seeing socially—and he had come to warn McKenney (he called him Mac) that

Sheriff Price had gotten his hands on some dynamite and was talking about blowing up the roundhouse, with us in it. He was being advised against this by the local judge as well as by Williams, the representative of the Rio Grande, who, I presumed, didn't care about the damage that dynamite would do to me or my men but rather its effect on the Santa Fe property his company wanted to get its hands on. But apparently Price was taking his setback earlier in the day very personally, and the boy wasn't sure the sheriff was going to listen to the others.

I told McKenney that he might try to slip away to safety under cover of darkness. Price had posted some lookouts to keep an eye on the roundhouse, but they were located at a safe distance from the Texans' rifles, and were keeping their heads down, so I thought it was entirely likely that McKenney could successfully effect an escape. He asked me if he thought Price would actually use the dynamite, and I said I didn't know, but that if he did, this was the last place anybody interested in living ought to linger. I also shared the boy's unwelcome news with the Texans, and again gave them an opportunity to make a break for the tall timber. They had fought well, I told them. They had earned their pay. And no discredit would attach itself to them if they chose now to go. But none of them would leave. Not so long as I was staying. And I fully intended to stay. Not because I was eager to die to protect the Santa Fe's property. But simply rather because I wasn't in the mood to run.

McKenney and the boy left the roundhouse late that night. When daybreak came, I expected Sheriff Price to make his play. Instead, another man approached under another flag of truce. This turned out to be a United

States marshal by the name of Lane. He instructed me to hand the roundhouse over to him.

"I'll be happy to," I told him. "Those were my orders, after all. But first I need some sort of guarantee that my men will be allowed to ride out of Pueblo without being shot by Sheriff Price and his so-called deputies."

Lane nodded. "That's been taken care of. I've already had a talk with Price. There's just one hitch. Men died yesterday. For that reason I'm going to have to arrest you, Thompson. But your men can go free."

I was skeptical. "You're going to put me in the Pueblo jail? In the sheriff's keeping? How long do you figure I would last?"

"No, you'll be in my custody. Price won't get his hands on you. You have my word on that."

"Just how many men did you bring with you, Marshal?"

"Two deputy marshals."

The Texans with me, to a man, scoffed at the notion. "They'll hang you for sure, Ben," one of them said. "I say we just make our last stand right here." The others concurred.

But I didn't agree, and shook my head. As grim as my own prospects seemed, this looked to be the only way the others would have a chance to get out of this alive. So I agreed to Lane's terms, thus ending what would come to be called The Battle of the Roundhouse.

As it turned out, Lane was as good as his word. I was incarcerated in the Pueblo jail, guarded by a pair of deputy U.S. marshals, until the following day, when Lane released me and gave me safe escort out of town.

"The Santa Fe company made your bail," he told me. "Now I suggest you get out of Colorado and not come back."

"Looks like I was on the losing side in yet another war," I said wryly.

Lane nodded. "Looks that way. Most of the Santa Fe rail and rolling stock in the state is now in the hands of the Rio Grande's people. Except for the line running east out of Pueblo. I suggest you follow it."

Which is exactly what I did, ending up eventually on a train bound for Dodge City, where I was reunited with Bat Masterson and what was left of his gunslinger army. Bat told me that I would be paid well, and I was—the Santa Fe company gave me five thousand dollars and a letter of appreciation for my services. Our fight for the Pueblo roundhouse had been the company's one and only victory in the War of the Railroads. That war now progressed to the courts, where it would be waged for years. The Rio Grande would lose its monopoly on Colorado's iron roads, but that took a while.

Still, the rightness of the Santa Fe's cause was no consolation as I made my way back to Texas by rail via Kansas City and St. Louis. The five thousand dollars didn't help much either. I'd had a lucrative future in Leadville. Now I was persona non grata in Colorado. And I had backed the losing horse in the feud between the Santa Fe and the Rio Grande. I was a bitter man when I got home to Austin, wondering why it was that Ben Thompson never caught an even break.

Chapter 17

BACK IN TEXAS I used the money that the Atchison, Topeka, and Santa Fe had paid me to open up a few gambling rooms in several towns, principal among them being a faro establishment in the Iron Front Saloon in Austin. The owners of these watering holes were eager to get into business with me. They knew I ran straight games, and to top it off, my reputation as a pistoleer was security against any trouble.

From the beginning these arrangements proved very profitable—to the extent that I was able to move my wife, son, and mother into a larger home at the corner of San Antonio and Linden streets. I furnished the house with expensive furniture imported from England. I provided Catherine with a carriage and a matching team of horses so that she could go about in style, and hired a driver who helped our Mexican house servant with other chores as well. All along, Catherine protested that she was perfectly content to live without such trappings. And while I knew that this was so, I insisted that she have them anyway. She understood—as I came to understand eventually—that I bought these things not for her but for me. Or, to be more precise, to assuage my guilty conscience. Though she would never have agreed with my assessment, I knew I had been a poor husband to her, and a less than exemplary father for our son. I had rarely been at home, having run off to Kansas and then Colorado seeking financial success. And that still held true, for I spent most of my time looking out for my investments in the red-light district of Austin and elsewhere. Ironically, it didn't seem to matter how much I spent on nice furniture or fancy carriages—I couldn't shed the guilt. The one thing that seemed to help was liquor. Strong spirits dulled the pain, at least temporarily, and if I drank enough, I was unable to dwell on all the bad things I had done in my life.

It came to my attention that a keno operation in which I was partners with a fellow named Solomon Simon was acquiring the reputation for being crooked. Whether that was true or not I never discovered. I resolved the issue by marching in one night and pulling my pistol, blasting the "goose"—the globe in which the game's ivory balls were contained—into pieces. To make sure my point got across, I also shot out the expensive chandelier that provided the room with illumination. The patrons scattered like quail. The only person remaining in the room when I was done was Simon, sitting at a table puffing on a cigar, outwardly calm.

"That wasn't very good for business, Ben," he said.

"On the contrary," I replied. "This will put all the rumors to rest. I'm just hoping that's all they were, too."

"This is—or was—an honest game. I told you that."

"That's likely so. But facts are one thing and perceptions another entirely. Just buy a new goose and a new chandelier. I'll pay for them. And trust me, business will be better than ever after this."

The following day I went to a local judge, pled guilty to disturbing the peace, and paid my fine. Outside the courthouse Joe Glover pulled me aside and handed me the most recent edition of the *Daily States-*

man, hot off the press, urging me to read the editorial, which I did. It read, in part:

> Last night, Ben Thompson single-handedly effected what the authorities of the city and the county have for so long failed to accomplish. He demolished a keno game that by all accounts was crooked. That put an end to the game, and for that we are glad; glad for the young men who nightly spend their hard earnings at the fascinating game; glad for the wives and children of the husbands who put their dollars in the game when the money should go to buy food and clothing for their families; glad, in short, that the game, so enticing yet so ruinous and demoralizing, has been abolished.
>
> Still, we are not persuaded that the conduct of Ben Thompson is excusable. The future of our city depends on the establishment of law and order. But it seems that Thompson is his own law. He has all the officers bulldozed. When it is known that he is in one of his defiant, reckless moods, the officers invariably give him a wide berth. They avoid him and act like craven cowards. Thompson knows they are a disgrace and must hold them in supreme contempt. If, however, we had men of nerve and courage on duty, men who knew no such word as fear, Ben Thompson would soon cease his lawless acts.

I swore under my breath, and told Glover I was of a mind to pay a call on the newspaper's editor, Frank Stillman.

Glover sighed and shook his head. "I thought that would be your first reaction. I suppose it's too much to hope that you would ever act with some restraint. Ben, it's your mastery with the gun that has made you this way. Made you the kind of man that you are."

"And what kind of man is that?" I asked, belligerently.

Glover snatched the newspaper from my hand and brandished it. "As Stillman writes, a lawless man. You think you can get away with just about anything because no one can surpass you when it comes to the gun. But don't you see, Ben? The future is spelled out for you right here in this editorial. And it bodes ill for you."

"The future always has," I said.

"It doesn't have to. All you have to do is open your eyes, change your ways. Austin isn't the same town that it was thirty years ago, when you first came here. Times are changing and you must change with them, if you hope to survive."

"So you want me to hang up my gun and become— what? A store clerk?"

"Hang up your guns, yes. You've made a lot of money in your time, Ben. You're an astute businessman. Except for one thing—you picked the wrong business."

"Gambling is all I know."

"Because you chose to have it that way. Invest in other kinds of business. Put away the gun. Most of the money you've made you had to spend to get you out of trouble. Become a respectable member of the community."

I laughed. "Respectable member of the community! There's only one reason I get any respect around here, Joe." I put my hand on the pistol holstered on my hip.

Glover shook his head. "No. You're confusing fear with respect. People fear you. Even the authorities, as this editorial notes. Sooner or later people will get around to doing away with what they're afraid of. Look, I know why you think the way you do. My father knew, as well. You were different when you came here from England. Too different. Your accent was one thing. The way you dressed another. And you were well-educated. They made fun of you. They never accepted you, or your father. But then you found out you had a talent—a talent that made them fear you. Your mistake was to think they accepted you, too. But they never have. And, as you have just read, they never will. You can't change them. The only person you can change is yourself."

"Are you going to charge me a consulting fee for this, Joe?"

Glover smiled, pensively, and shook his head. "You're not a bad man, Ben. You just have picked up some really bad habits. And no, this advice is free of charge. Just don't tell anybody that."

Upon reflection, I came to the conclusion that Joe Glover was right—not only about me but also about what the good people of Austin would have to do about me, eventually. For the moment, though, they still needed men like me, as evident by a situation that arose a few weeks later.

By this time the Comanche threat to the Texas frontier had been pretty much eradicated, with all five of the tribes making up the Comanche Nation being driven off their lands and relocated in the western portion of the Indian Territories with their Kiowa cousins. However, near the end of 1879 a large war party of Comanche and Kiowa braves struck deep into Texas, so deeply, in fact, that some feared their goal was Austin itself. It seemed the Indians were motivated by nothing more or less than revenge. They wanted to make the whites pay for taking their homelands. They weren't after horses or loot. They knew they could not win back their land. All they wanted was blood. And they spilled plenty of that.

Though the raiders veered away from Austin and headed west into the still largely uncharted expanse of the Llano Estacado—the Staked Plains—the governor called for volunteers who would be willing to organize into a company and set out after the hostiles. While it seemed the raid was over—most of us figured the Indians were making a big circle westward with the intent of turning north for home—that didn't matter to the governor. Or, for that matter, to most of the men who grabbed their horses, strapped on their guns, and volunteered. No, it was once again about vengeance. Good Old-Testament vengeance—an eye for an eye. The Indians had killed some of ours and now we were obliged to kill some of them.

I went along on this punitive expedition because its leader, Ed Burleson, son of the Colonel Burleson who had led the Texans against General Cos and a Mexican force occupying San Antonio, personally asked me to do so. Both Burleson father and son were famous Indian fighters. I had never met the former but knew the latter well and could not say no. So it was that I struck out into the wild country with Burleson's Rangers, as we called ourselves. We chased those Indians past the headwaters of the Brazos River, through the Sand Hills, and into the arid mountains along the Pecos. The hostiles just kept fading away from us, always barely out of reach. It was infuriating, not to mention grueling. There was precious little water along the route we had to take, and men and horses suffered terribly. We pushed on, though, as long as we could. But it was to no avail, and finally Burleson called a halt to the pursuit.

We made camp at the head of the North Fork of the Concho River. Burleson announced that he intended for us to remain here for at least a week to rest and recuperate before beginning the long trek homeward. There was water here, and good graze for the horses. We found game, and had fresh meat to roast over our cookfires. It bothered us some to think that the Indians were getting away—bothered Burleson most of all, I think—even though we knew our commander had made the right decision. He knew it, too; had we pushed on another few days, men would have started dying.

Little did we know that the hostiles weren't getting away. On the contrary.

On the second day of our journey home Burleson pulled his horse alongside mine.

"I've been fighting Injuns my whole life," he told me. "Most of the time you don't even see them until it's just about too late. That's why you tend to develop a feeling."

"What kind of feeling, Ed?"

"Well, with me it's kind of like little critters crawling up and down my spine. Like as not, when I get that feeling, turns out Injuns are close by."

"You've got that feeling now, do you?"

"Yep, I sure as hell do."

I pointed to a knoll about two miles to the north. "Why don't I go on up there and take a look around."

"Good idea. But pick a man to go with you."

"Okay. I'll take Buckskin Sam."

Burleson nodded. "Catch up with us by nightfall."

"You can count on it."

Buckskin Sam was a bearded, rawboned hombre of indeterminate age who had spent his whole life—how-

ever long that might have been—on the frontier. He
was short on social graces, to put it mildly, and no
conversationalist by a long shot, but he was as good a
man as any to have at your back in a scrape. From
what I knew of his past, he had been engaged in the
Santa Fe trade in the forties, spent the fifties in Mexico,
fought Apaches in the sixties, and scouted for the army
against the Comanches in the seventies. I figured that
a man who could do all that and live to tell about it
was damned near indestructible.

We reached that knoll and, leaving our horses at its
base, climbed up nearly to the top, carrying our rifles.
From that vantage point we had a commanding view
of the plains for at least ten miles in all directions. We
spent an hour up there with our eyes peeled and didn't
see a thing. Just as we were about to depart, Sam spotted some dust way off to the west.

"No way of telling what's making it," I said.

Sam grunted agreement. "Could be buffalo. Or mus-
tangs."

"Or Indians."

We watched that dust a while longer, until we could
ascertain that it was headed, more or less, in our direction.

"Well," I sighed, "I don't want to be up here like a
sitting duck if those are Indians."

"Me neither," said Buckskin Sam.

"So I guess we better go take a look."

"Yep," he agreed.

We went down to our horses, mounted up, and rode
west, toward the dust.

About half an hour later we topped a rise and spotted
a small herd of buffalo. The shaggies were producing
most of the dust we had seen, but not all of it. About
fifteen braves—Comanches and Kiowas, by the looks

of them—were in hot pursuit. Before we could get out of sight, the Indians spotted us. They forgot all about the shaggies and went after us.

I had no doubt that these warriors were a portion of the raiding party that we had been chasing. But where were the rest of them? I didn't know and didn't want to find out. Fifteen Comanche and Kiowa bucks were more than enough to have to deal with.

We gave them a good run, but after several miles of stretched-out galloping it became clear that we were not going to outrun our pursuers. The Comanches were the best horsemen the world has ever seen and I suppose the Kiowas were just about as good.

"Let's try to slow them down!" I yelled at Sam.

We checked our lathered horses, spun them around, brought rifles to shoulder—I had my Winchester '73 and Sam carried a Henry—and fired. The range was long, but not too long; we each brought a warrior down. The others halted, began to scatter, thinking that we had turned to put up a fight. They couldn't have been more wrong. Sam and I turned our horses east again and spurred them into a gallop. That tactic gained us some ground. We rode another mile or so, and since it looked like the Indians had closed the distance some, we decided on an encore. Once again we stopped, turned, took aim, and fired. This time Sam missed his mark while I accounted for another brave. The Indians stopped and returned fire. They were all armed with rifles. As we spun our horses around to again take flight, my mount was hit. Killed instantly, it fell like a stone. I managed to jump clear, hanging on to my rifle. Buckskin Sam looked back and I waved him on. But he nimbly executed a running dismount, sent his horse packing with a slap on the rump with the barrel of his

Henry, and joined me as I took cover behind the carcass of my cayuse.

"You're such a damned fool, Sam," I said.

"Yep."

We started shooting at the Indians charging at us, firing as fast as we could, and clearing four more saddles. The eight remaining braves fell back to regroup and hash things over. One of them then rode off to the west.

"I guess he must be going to fetch the rest," I said.

Sam was squinting at the sun, which was high in the afternoon sky. "Reckon about four hours afore dark," he muttered.

I knew what he was thinking. In the darkness we might stand a slim chance of slipping away. But if the rest of the raiding party arrived before sundown—there were about sixty braves in the bunch—then our goose was cooked for sure.

The Indians kept us pinned down for about an hour—and then we heard the thunder of many hooves, distant at first but steadily getting louder. Where was that sound coming from? It took us a moment—the longest moment of my life—to figure out that it came from behind us.

Burleson and his men came charging into view a few minutes later. The Indians made a run for it. While the rangers gave chase, Burleson got down off his horse and shook our hands.

"Glad to see that you two are still above snakes," he said.

"What brings you, Ed?" I asked.

He grinned. "Oh, you know me. Just had another one of those feelings."

Chapter 18

FOR THE NEXT couple of years I plied my trade as a gambler in Austin without much trouble to speak of. There was that evening, as I left the Iron Front Saloon, that I had a small problem with a couple of drunken cowboys from over San Saba way. As was my custom, I was dressed to the nines, wearing a Prince Albert coat and derby hat, with Middleton half-boots polished to a high sheen on my feet, and a staghorn walking cane in hand. The cane was not entirely for show; the old leg wound I had suffered during the war—when my horse had fallen on it and broken the bone—would often give me a limp, particularly when the days were cold or damp.

As I emerged from the Iron Front, the two cowboys loitering on the boardwalk gave me a once-over and began to snicker.

"Hold on there," said one as I began to turn and walk away. "Where do you come from?"

It was obvious that they had mistaken me for some greenhorn dude from back east. "Were you speaking to me?" I asked.

"Why, yes, darlin', I am speaking to you," he said, and they both dissolved into laughter.

Smiling, I stepped closer. "I've come out west for my health. I have an affected lung, or so the physicians tell me."

"Affected? Well, this country ain't healthy for a man

like you," said the second cowboy. "I think you better go back where you come from."

"On the contrary," I said, "the climate here has improved my condition quite a bit, and in a very short period of time. This country is actually very healthy."

"So you're calling me a liar," sneered the second cowboy. And then he reached out and knocked the hat off my head.

I looked at him, at the hat, back at him—and then stooped to retrieve the derby. Dusting it off, I said, "I hope you two gentlemen do not intend to mistreat a stranger. And an ill one, at that."

"Oh, no," said the cowboy. "I won't mistreat you, I promise." And he knocked the hat out of my hand. This time he bent to pick it up—to do, I suppose, further damage to it. That's when I slipped the revolver from under my coat and laid the barrel, forcefully, across the back of his skull. As he collapsed, the first cowboy dodged for cover around the corner of the saloon.

"You damned coward," I rasped.

At the corner he whirled, pistol in hand, and snapped off a shot. It went wide, confirming my impression that there weren't a dozen cowboys in Texas who could really shoot worth a damn. The man tried to duck out of sight but I could still see the side of his head as he crouched there, and I presumed he was about to have another go at me, so I raised my revolver and, taking quick aim, shot his ear off.

He took off running down the alley, howling like a wounded cat. After relieving the unconscious man sprawled at my feet of his six-shooter, I put my derby on—and stepped purposefully on the cowboy's hat as I walked away. As usual, I presented myself before the local magistrate the next day and pled guilty to disturbing the peace.

A few months later—early in 1880, to be exact—
the Texas Livestock Association convened its second
annual convention in Austin. Cattle kings from all over
the state congregated. These included Seth Mabry, John
Simpson of the Continental Land and Cattle Company,
and the towering and colorful Shanghai Pierce. They
met and palavered for four days. For myself, their presence was of no particular interest, beyond the possibility of snaring one or two of them onto the losing
end of a poker game, and I assumed they had even less
use for me. Which is why I was surprised when a committee of five, including Mabry and Pierce, called on
me one day at my home on Linden Street.

We settled down on the long porch in front of the
house to enjoy the coolness of the evening drinking
coffee or whiskey depending on individual preference,
or, as in my case, both at once. For a while the conversation wandered over various topics irrelevant to the
business of raising cattle, during which time I tried my
best to appear at least politely interested. The cattle
kings discussed the new herd law being considered by
the state legislature. It was tied in with their belief that
the days of the free range were over, and good rid-
dance.

"Free range just doesn't make sense anymore," said
Mabry, addressing me, and I could tell the others
agreed with him. "Sure, twenty years ago it did. We
went out and popped all those wild cattle out of the
brush, slapped a brand on them, and then pushed 'em
north to the railhead. It's how a lot of Texans survived
following the war. Hell, it's how some of us got our
start in the business. But these days there aren't many
wild cattle left. And yet we've still got hombres who
believe the range should be open to everyone and that
an unbranded maverick is anybody's property. But

that's no longer true. When that unbranded calf drops out of my branded she-stuff it belongs to me."

"I can't argue with that," I said. "But with some, old habits die hard, if at all."

"The open range encourages rustling. You know yourself, Ben, that we've had a lot of trouble with men who are running irons. Your own brother got caught up in just such an affair, I believe."

"He was innocent of those charges," I reminded Mabry.

"Yes, of course."

"How is your brother, Ben?" asked Shanghai Pierce. "Haven't heard anything about him for a while."

I smiled. "No news is good news in this case. He's become a shiftless no-account." We all laughed, and I added, "He can't seem to settle down or figure out what he wants to do with his life."

"Well, you appear to have done pretty well for yourself."

I nodded. "I've got some money stashed away now, so we're doing okay."

"They say you've killed twenty men, not counting Indians, or any killing you had to do during the war," said Mabry. "Is that true?"

"Not even close. The number is much less."

"But when you did have to, it was always in self-defense, wasn't it?"

"I always make it a rule to let the other fellow shoot first. If he wants a fight and I have the chance, I try to reason with him. Make him see how foolish it would be to draw down on me. But if he doesn't listen, I let him have the first crack. That way I've got the self-defense verdict in my pocket."

"But if you let the other man fire first," said Pierce, "how is it that you have never been hit?"

"Because the other man is always in too much of a hurry. I never miss because I take my time."

"That's where nerve comes in," said Mabry, nodding his approval.

"Right," I said. "I am a crack shot, but not a quick one. If I miss, it's because I'm rushed for some other reason." As an example I described in some detail the Ellsworth shootout with Nick Lentz and John Sterling. "I only managed to wing both of them because they were in such a big hurry to get off the street. Had they stood their ground, I would have killed them both."

"Some people say you lead a charmed life," said Mabry. "Because you've never been shot, not once in all those instances where people were throwing lead at you."

I laughed. "Well, other people say I wear a steel vest, and that's why. In fact, I took a trip to Galveston last year and several newspaper reporters cornered me and asked me if that was true. To convince them that it wasn't, I stripped for them."

Pierce laughed. Being a big, rough-hewn man, his laugh was an explosive bellow that could shake the rafters.

"But I'm not the superstitious sort," I said. "I don't really believe I lead a charmed life. The only time I wondered was when a Mexican soldier down in Nuevo Laredo fired at me at point-blank range. There was simply no way he could have missed me. I can only conclude that there was something faulty in the cartridge. I was just damned lucky that night. No, the reason I've never been shot is what I mentioned earlier. My reputation is such that when men face me, they get edgy, and they tend to rush their shots and miss me as a result. I used to think a reputation was a bad thing to have. I don't think that way anymore. It's my reputation that keeps me out of trouble these days because nine times out of ten a hombre will decide to steer clear of me."

The cattle kings exchanged glances.

"Okay, boys," I said. "So when is someone going to tell me the real reason for this visit?"

Shanghai Pierce grinned. "Why, you don't think we're just paying you a social call?"

"Nope. No offense, but you would have nothing to do with the likes of me unless you wanted something."

"No pulling the wool over your eyes, is there, Ben," said Mabry. "Go ahead, Shanghai. We're caught red-handed. Might as well tell him."

"There's an election for city marshal of Austin coming up in a few months, Ben," said Pierce. "We would like to see you run for the job. You're the right man for it in our book."

"I'm not lawman material," I said. "Do you know how many times I've been hauled into a court of law? How many times I've been thrown in jail right here in Austin?"

"Are you trying to tell us that you have no respect for the law?" asked Pierce.

"I respect it when it's right. But I've learned that sometimes the law and what's right are two different things."

"Do you think stealing cattle and robbing banks is right?"

"Of course not. And I've never done either."

"Then that's all that matters. Look, Ben, the hills around here are still chock-full of outlaws. We need men like you to bring law and order to this country. We've got herds to protect, and we have money in the banks. We're businessmen, and we're just trying to make a living. Rustlers and bank robbers are making it hard for us to do that."

"I see. But a lawman's pay . . ." I shook my head. "It just isn't enough, boys. I try to provide the very best for my family. I can't do that on a hundred dollars a month. And you know how folks are. They won't take kindly to their marshal running a faro table in the Iron Front even if it's just to make ends meet."

"Here's a proposition for you," said Mabry. "Just try it for a year. During that time we'll make it worth your while."

The offer caught me by surprise. "Let me get this straight. You will pay me extra, over and above the salary I would get from the city, to be marshal."

Mabry nodded. "That's right."

"We figure in a year's time you could clean out all the riffraff in Austin," said Pierce.

"There are a lot of folks here that never have liked me," I said. "They consider me part of that riffraff."

"But they will probably still vote for you," predicted Mabry.

"What makes you think so?"

Mabry settled back in his chair. "I know a rancher up near the Palo Duro. For years when he was first starting out he had a lot of trouble with wolves killing his cattle. He knew why they were doing it. We had wiped out the buffalo so the wolves had to turn to livestock to survive. He battled those lobos for years but never could clean them out. They are smart creatures. Then he found a litter of wolf pups and instead of killing them he decided to raise them, and then bred them with Scottish hounds. What he got was a wolf-dog, a whole pack of them. They were as fast and smart and dangerous as wolves. But they didn't kill cows. He made sure they had no taste for beef."

"How did he manage that?" I asked.

"He raised them on mutton. Kept a whole herd of sheep just for that purpose. A wolf pup raised on mutton won't eat anything else as long as mutton is available."

"I see. Now isn't that clever."

"Yep. My friend, he outsmarted those wolves. His wolf-dogs ran all the wild ones off—the ones they didn't kill, anyway."

I nodded. "So you figure the good folks of Austin will hire themselves a wolf to get rid of the other wolves."

Mabry grinned. "I can almost guarantee that they would, yes."

I told them I would give their proposition a lot of thought, and let them know my decision in a couple of days. They didn't want to wait that long, but they had no choice in the matter.

It might not make much sense, but I entertained the notion for Catherine's sake. I had taken Joe Glover's words to heart. How much longer would the people of Austin tolerate a man like me? I belonged to the past, not to the future. All one had to do was look around to see that the frontier had been tamed. Except for a few loose ends. Namely men like me. The animosity was growing. And the antipathy was spreading, until it included my wife and son. For myself I didn't really care. But I hated to see them treated with contempt on my account.

The last few years had been profitable ones. As I had told the cattle barons, I had a handsome sum of money saved up. So financially I could do it. Especially if Mabry and Pierce and that bunch sweetened the pot. And it wouldn't hurt to be on the good side of men such as these. The big cattle kings pretty much ran things in Texas these days. There were a number of good reasons for running for the job of city marshal. There was only one reason not to—wearing a tin star was still a dangerous business. But I wasn't worried about that. My reputation would keep most from trying me. For the rest—well, I knew I was better.

The next day I'd made up my mind to take the offer. But before I'd had a chance to tell the cattle kings, I got a visit early in the evening from Joe Glover. He found me in the Iron Front, which had become my home away from home, and he was fuming as he joined me at the bar.

"I've never seen you this mad before, Joe," I said. "Not that I can recall, anyway. You don't usually let anything get under your skin."

"Well, something did tonight," growled Glover. "I've never been so humiliated in all my life."

"What happened?"

"Those damned cattlemen. Ride in here and act like they own the whole city. I went over to Simon's restaurant for dinner, and they threw me out. Said they were having a private party and no one else was allowed in. Especially a lawyer."

"Is that right," I said. Finishing my whiskey, I turned for the door. "Come along, Joe."

He followed me outside. Suddenly he seemed more worried than mad.

"What are you planning to do, Ben?" he asked.

"You're a friend of mine, and nobody is going to treat a friend of mine like that."

"Just forget it. I'll go somewhere else to eat. It isn't that important."

I smiled wryly. "It sure seemed important to you a minute ago."

"You have a quick temper, Ben. Too quick for your

own good. I don't want you to get into trouble, especially on my account."

"Sure you do," I said. "That way I'll have to pay you a king's ransom to get me out of it." I laughed at the expression on his face.

"That isn't funny, in my opinion," he said.

I shrugged. "You don't have to come along if you don't want to. But I'm going over to Simon's."

He followed me to the restaurant, which was located on Congress Avenue. I walked right in on the festivities. They had put tables end to end and laden them with good and drink, and by the looks of things, the feasting and carousing had been going on for quite some time. Everybody seemed to be talking at once. One man, whom I did not know by name, was in the process of climbing up on his chair in an effort, I presume, to capture the attention of the others.

I got their attention first—by drawing my six-shooter and putting a hole in the ceiling. That shut everybody up.

"I'm looking for the dirty scoundrel who says my friend Joe Glover isn't good enough to come in here."

For a moment no one spoke. Then a fellow at one end of the table, whose name was Lee Hall, said in a calm and quiet voice, "I guess that would be me. This is a private party. We rented out this restaurant for the night. And I'm afraid your friend wasn't invited. It isn't anything personal."

"I'm taking it personally," I said, advancing on Hall. "And I'm inviting him."

"But you're not invited either, Thompson," said Hall, and there was steel beneath his cordiality.

I hadn't expected him to back down. These cattle kings were hard men—had to be to accomplish what they had accomplished. So I wasn't trying to intimidate him. I was looking for a fight, and it appeared that Hall was just the man to give it to me.

A fellow I didn't know suddenly got to his feet and placed himself between me and Hall. He was short and slight, but one look and you could see he was tough as old leather. Only a fool would judge another's ability by size. This man had a steely gaze, and he also had a six-shooter under his coat. I knew this because he wasted no time in showing it to me.

"This is none of your business," I told him.

"Sure it is. Lee Hall is a good friend of mine."

"And who might you be?"

"John Lucy's the name."

Shanghai Pierce decided then to intervene. "John's an ex-Texas Ranger, Ben, a captain, and he won't back down. Now, I know you won't, either. So why don't we just call a truce and have a drink together like civilized men."

"Makes you wonder just how civilized we are," I said.

"You must be Ben Thompson," said Captain Lucy. He looked me over from heel to hat brim—and nodded. "I hope you will run for the city marshal's job. We could use a man who will stand up for his friends."

"If I do, are you going to vote for me."

He chuckled. "I reckon I must."

I holstered my smoke-maker. "Then I guess I can't shoot you, Captain. I'll need all the votes I can get."

He put his pistol away, too—and stuck out a hand. "Then you won't shoot my friend here, either, as I believe he intends to cast his vote for you, as well."

Chapter 19

THE ELECTIONS IN Austin were held every other year on the first day of November. The candidates for the various offices were expected to launch their campaigns by stating their case formally in a letter published in the newspaper. I labored hard and long on my letter, and produced the following:

To the good people of Austin:

I have been asked by a number of citizens to become a candidate for the office of city marshal. No man from the highest to the humblest can successfully charge me with dishonor or dishonesty. I can truthfully say without boasting that I have always been a friend of the defenseless, and most of the difficulties attending the independent life I have led were incurred by love of fair play and impulse to protect the innocent and the weak. I am thoroughly acquainted with the character of Austin and the magnanimity of her citizens. Like so many others, I have a family for whose welfare and happiness in society I have an abiding solicitude. I now repeat in this public manner the promise I have made to my friends in private, that if honored with the confidence of the people in their selection for the important post to which I aspire, my whole time and attention shall be given to the discharge of the official duties that pertain to it, and no good and

law-abiding citizen will have reason to regret the
choice, provided it shall be within the compass of
my ability or fidelity to the high and delicate trust
to prevent it. Upon these terms and conditions I in-
voke the support and suffrage of all my fellow cit-
izens.

> *Your obedient servant,*
> *Ben Thompson*

Flowery language, but such, I was told, was expected in such matters—even from a shootist.

To my surprise, the *Daily Statesman* heartily en-
dorsed my candidacy, pointing out that no one was
better qualified to deal with the lawless element that
still plagued Austin, and noting that in my announcement I had implicitly forsaken my profession of gambler with the remark that promised my "whole time and
attention" to the task of enforcing the laws. The *Daily
Statesman*'s editor, Frank Stillman, had never shied
away from criticizing my activities in the past. We
were certainly not friends. So I could only surmise that
one or more of the cattle barons who were behind my
run for office had prevailed upon him to support me.

My opponent, the incumbent marshal, was Ed
Creary. He wasn't much of a lawman, but he was an
excellent politician and crafty campaigner. He dredged
up all the dirt on me that he could, and tried to make
the case that I was in fact a member of that very lawless
element the good people of Austin were sick and tired
of having to deal with. The only reason I wasn't behind
bars, according to Creary, was because I had bought
my way out of the charges against me. He reminded
the voters that I had shot my first man at the tender
age of sixteen, had deserted from the Confederate
army, had been wanted for several killings south of the

border, had been involved in the murder of a law officer in Kansas, was a denizen of the red-light district,
and was known to drink too much. I was informed that
he even toyed with the idea of bringing my wayward
brother and long-dead father into the picture—but his
friends talked him out of it, for fear that I would react
unfavorably. On the theory that it would avail him
nothing to win the office he sought posthumously,
Creary decided not to press his luck.

I could not argue with the facts—and most of what
Creary said about me was true enough. But what I
could do was bring to everyone's attention the fact that
Creary was in cahoots with some of the thieves and
cutthroats that infested this country. As luck would
have it, Seth Mabry's cowboys corralled a gang of rustlers and hanged all but one, sparing his life on the
condition that he publicly state that every criminal
knew Creary would turn a blind eye and bend the rules
if the price was right. Now I doubt this cattle thief had
ever even met Creary, nor could I deny that he probably would have tried to implicate Jesus Christ if he
thought it would save him from the noose—but it finished Creary. I won the election by a handsome margin.

The problem, where the ranchers were concerned,
was that the men who ran irons on their range were
suspected of finding safe haven in Austin, where the
county sheriff had no jurisdiction. What men like Mabry and Pierce wanted from me was to make these
outlaws feel unwelcome in town. There was usually no
way of knowing for certain whether a particular individual was in fact a member of a rustling outfit. But
there were plenty of suspicious characters. Many of
them took special care not to muddy up their own water
by violating city ordinances. After all, this was their
sanctuary, the place they liked to come to blow off

steam. With Creary in charge they'd never had to
worry. With me it was another matter entirely. If I had
reason to believe that a particular hombre was someone
who was running irons out on the range, I ran him out
of town whether he broke the law or not. Many protested, some made threats, and a few resisted. The latter
I pistol-whipped, took to jail, and then had them hauled
before a magistrate so that they would have to pay a
steep fine. Then I ran *them* out of town, too. A minority
of the good citizens of Austin were concerned about
the way I rode roughshod over these men, arguing that
usually a person had to commit a crime before being
treated like a criminal. But for the most part the Austinites gave me a free hand. They had elected me to
clean up the town, after all, and as long as I didn't start
shooting old men and small children on the streets, they
were willing to provide me with a lot of discretion.

As for my gambling days—well, they were over. I
sold all my interests in the faro, keno, and monte op-
erations located in several saloons in Austin as well as
a few adjacent towns. During the campaign I had as
much as said I would do so, and the people needed to
know they could take me at my word. That way I could
pursue a campaign to make certain all the gaming tables in town were honest without giving anyone the
opportunity to suggest I was playing favorites by shut-
ting down games other than my own. The citizens were
very happy with my activities in this department. The
other gamblers and the saloonkeepers, however, many
of whom had counted me as their friend in years past,
weren't so happy.

Solomon Simon, one of my former business partners, confronted me one day with his conclusion that I
was a turncoat.

"You've turned your back on your own kind," he

said bluntly. "Trying to make yourself respectable at our expense. My hunch is that you aim to shut us all down eventually, Ben."

"I have no problem with honest games being operated in the city limits," I replied. "Just keep them straight, Solomon, and you can keep them running as long as you want."

Unconvinced, he shook his head. "No, you intend to sell us all down the river. I can see it coming."

"You're wrong and I'm sorry you feel that way."

"It doesn't matter how hard you try," said Simon. "You'll never be someone that you're not."

I had capable help in the person of a deputy by the name of Johnny Chenneville. Johnny was a young man who was as brave as a lion and a little on the brash side, as young men tend to be, especially when they are handy with their fists and good with a gun. I could always count on Johnny because he demonstrated a nose for sniffing out trouble and the ability to deal with it before it got out of hand. The only two things about Johnny that troubled me some was that he had an eye for the ladies, and he seemed to think I walked on water. In addition to Chenneville, I had several other deputies on whom I could call when I felt I needed some extra help. They were all reliable men and did a good job, and I made sure they were handsomely rewarded by the city council for their efforts.

By the end of my first year in office, I was able to report to the council that criminal activity in Austin was down. There had not been a single killing, assault with intent to kill, or robbery that took place. The people of Austin were thrilled. I could see a radical change in their attitude toward me and—more importantly— toward my family. The cattle kings were well-satisfied, too. They had busted up several rustling rings, hanged

about a dozen owlhoots, and seen their stock losses
reduced substantially. While they cleaned up the countryside, I cleaned up the streets. It looked like everyone
was going to be able to live happily ever after.

Yes—I should have known better.

In the summer of 1882 I received a letter from a detective agency about a man named Bill Reglin on
whose head was a thousand-dollar reward. A wanted
poster was included. Reglin was suspected of killing a
Pennsylvania businessman and his wife. After robbing
them, Reglin had fled westward. The agency had been
tipped off that a man fitting Reglin's description and
habits was currently residing in San Antonio, and asked
me if I would go ascertain if that was the case. There
would be a fee involved if I assisted in the apprehen-
sion of Reglin. It occurred to both my wife and Johnny
Chenneville to wonder why the agency had not seen
fit to make this request of the authorities in San Antonio. I explained that it was because the agency was
closely affiliated with the Atchison, Topeka, and Santa
Fe Railroad. As Bat Masterson had told me up in Leadville, it paid off being on the right side of powerful
men. The offer came at an opportune time, as I had
been planning to take Catherine and our son, Ben,
down to San Antonio to visit the family of one of my
wife's dearest friends. I saw no reason why I couldn't
mix business with pleasure and, besides, it cut against
my grain to turn down a chance to make some easy
money.

We hopped the train to San Antonio, and on my
second evening there I headed for the red-light district.
Reglin's bad habits included gambling and loose
women, so that seemed to be the place to start looking.
I located the place I was looking for, the Vaudeville

Theater and Saloon on Commerce Street. The Vaudeville was a notorious establishment. It put on the most popular shows in town, performed by the most beautiful singers and dancers in the West. Wealthy men flocked to see these shows and to throw their money around, some I suppose hoping to entice some winsome nightingale to go away with him. Of course, where there was a lot of money and beautiful women, there were predators, and predators spawned trouble. The Vaudeville had been the scene of considerable bloodshed—several notable gunfights, the murder of the beautiful Georgia Lake, and the sensational suicide of the scion of one of the state's leading families, who had climbed on top of a table and blown his brains out, reportedly after being spurned by a lovely singer.

One would have been surprised to learn of the Vaudeville's reputation if all he had to go on was the appearance of the place. Phil Coe's old Palace in Austin paled in comparison when it came to opulence. The saloon was located on the ground floor of a two-story building, accessible from the street by two pairs of doors at either front corner. The theater was in a large room behind the saloon. Staircases in a narrow hallway separating the theater from the saloon led to the gambling rooms upstairs. In the saloon was an immense, crescent-shaped bar where only the very best liquor was served.

I went upstairs to the gambling hall because I knew that a dealer named Hopkins—a man who had once worked in one of my Austin roosts—was now employed at the Vaudeville, or at least that had been the last news I'd had of him. I was pleasantly surprised to see him working one of the tables, and stood off to one side until he happened to look up and recognize me.

His reaction was not at all what I'd expected, though. He looked alarmed.

"Ben? This is the last place you should be."

He was busy and could say no more at the moment, so I got a drink and moved off into a corner of the crowded room and put my back to the wall. Sipping the whiskey, I watched the activity and wondered why Hopkins had reacted to my presence that way. It made me uneasy, and put me on my guard.

Half an hour later Hopkins joined me. "What are you doing here, Ben?"

"Just dropped by to say hello."

He peered at me. "You don't know, do you?"

"What don't I know?'

"Jack Harris owns this place. Well, him and Joe Foster and Billy Simms. But Harris is the real honcho."

"So what's your point?"

He stared at me like I was crazy, then laughed nervously. "I'll be damned. You don't even remember, do you?"

"I know Billy Simms. He and I used to be friends. In fact, I taught him a few tricks of the gambling trade."

Hopkins shook his head. "No, it's Harris who's the problem for you. Two years ago you had a quarrel with him."

I shook my head. "Maybe if I saw his face it would come back to me. I've had a lot of quarrels. What was this one concerning?"

"Harris was dealing poker in The Gilded Lily up in Austin and you dropped by and bought into his game. When it was all over, you'd lost a few hundred dollars. You got up to leave, but Harris said you needed to pay the bank before you did."

"Ah, yes," I said softly. "It's coming back to me now."

"Everyone knew you were good for it. That you needed to leave so you could go get the money and bring it back to pay what you owed. In fact, someone else who was there at the time explained all this to Harris, because obviously he didn't know you. But he wouldn't apologize, and when you turned to go . . ."

I nodded. "He pulled a pistol."

"Right," said Hopkins. "But you were quicker, and got the drop on him, and I'm surprised you didn't shoot him dead on the spot."

I smiled. "If I shot every man I ever had a quarrel with, there would hardly be anyone left in this part of Texas. So I see that Harris has done well for himself."

"Yes, I reckon he has. But he hasn't forgotten. He still talks about you, Ben, and he doesn't say nice things, either. His temper is a bad one. Worse than yours, even."

I laughed. "Now that's saying something. Don't worry about him, though. I'm looking for someone. A fellow by the name of Reglin. He's a cold-blooded killer. The word is that he's here in San Antonio."

"Well, if he is, he's probably been here. Nearly everyone comes here sooner or later. What does he look like?"

I showed him the wanted poster that the detective agency had included with the letter they'd sent me. Hopkins studied it closely—but then shrugged and shook his head.

"I don't think he has ever been to my table," he said.

I believed him. A good dealer has an excellent memory—for faces as well as pasteboards—and Hopkins was a very good dealer.

"Well, I guess I'll just have to keep looking," I said.

"If you do happen to see him, wire me in Austin. There will be something in it for you."

Hopkins nodded. At that moment I glanced beyond him and saw Billy Simms, in the same instant that Simms, who had just entered the room, saw me. Wearing a quizzical smile, he sauntered over, a slender, black-haired young man with a long, pale face. I didn't know that much about him, except that he had come to Texas from Louisiana to try his hand at cowboy work. But that didn't suit him, so he'd fashioned himself into a gambler. I'd heard he was a cardsharp, and used a marked deck or shaved cards whenever he could get away with it. If that were so, he had not learned the lessons I had tried to teach him some years back, when he was just starting out. I thought it entirely possible that the rumors were true; Simms was one of those men who always took shortcuts if given the chance.

"Well, I'll be," he said, with his slow Southern drawl very pronounced. "If it isn't the one and only Ben Thompson. I heard they made you city marshal up in Austin. I couldn't believe it. Not you!"

I nodded. "Yes, it's true."

Simms laughed. "That must be a pretty sweet deal for you, then."

"Just what do you mean by that, Billy?"

"Just that if it was me, I would make sure I got a percentage of every table in town. That would be the cost of doing business in my town."

"I see. Well, the thing is, Austin isn't my town. It doesn't belong to me. I just try to keep the peace."

He cocked his head to one side, and that quizzical smile was still in place. "I never thought I'd live to see the day that you pinned on a badge."

"Times change. So do people."

"I guess so." Simms glanced at Hopkins. "Don't you have something to do?"

Hopkins grimaced. "I sure do. So long, Ben."

"See you around, Hop."

"You know," said Simms, "you're a lucky son of a bitch, Ben. Jack Harris isn't here tonight. Or were you looking for him? Is that why you showed up here?"

"No, I have no business with Harris."

"To hear him talk, he thinks he has some unfinished business with you."

I showed him the wanted poster. "Seen this hombre?"

Simms glanced at the likeness of Reglin and I saw no glimmer of recognition in his eyes when he said no, so I decided he was telling the truth, bade him farewell, and left the Vaudeville.

Around noon the following day I paid a visit to the city marshal's office to inquire there if anyone had seen Reglin. When I introduced myself, the marshal really sat up and took notice.

"So you're Ben Thompson. Did you know that Jack Harris was looking for you?"

I sighed. It looked like Harris was an annoyance that just would not go away. "And when was this?"

"My deputy saw him prowling the streets this morning with a shotgun. He was asking around trying to find out where you were. The deputy told him to go home and put the scattergun away. As far as I know that's what he did. Why is there bad blood between you and Harris, anyway?"

"Just a little misunderstanding, Marshal, that's all. I'm not looking for trouble. Just looking for this man."

The marshal studied the wanted poster. "A murderer, I see. No, can't say that I've ever seen him in San Antonio. But I'll keep an eye out, just the same."

"Fine." I folded the poster up and put it in my pocket.

"So how long you going to be in town?"

I looked him squarely in the eye and said, "I am here with my family visiting some friends. It is my intention to take the train back to Austin tomorrow. I hope that's soon enough to suit you."

"Sure, sure. I'm just trying to keep a lid on any trouble."

"There won't be any." And on that note I took my leave.

I was beginning to think that Billy Reglin had never been in San Antonio, but I checked some of the hotels anyway, and dropped in at least half a dozen saloons. No one recognized the man in the wanted poster, or the name. Of course, it was possible that Reglin was using an alias, and that the drawing on the poster didn't at all resemble him. Where wanted posters were concerned, that was sometimes the case.

As for Harris, I can't deny that the thought of someone who had a grudge against me wandering around town with a shotgun under his arm bothered me. There had been a time when I would have set out to find the man and have it out with him. But I had a feeling that if I did, I would end up having to kill him, and then some would say I had gone out of my way to hunt him down and take his life, and I was trying hard to put an end to that kind of talk about me. So I exercised restraint and steered clear of the Vaudeville, figuring I could make the afternoon train tomorrow without having any more to do with Mr. Harris.

Naturally, I was wrong.

Chapter 20

THAT EVENING I took my wife out to dinner and then to the opera house. As we left the latter establishment, I heard someone call my name, and turned to see Hopkins hurrying across the street. I handed Catherine up into the hack I had hired for the evening, and then stepped out to meet the dealer so that whatever passed between us was out of my wife's earshot. She didn't know about Jack Harris, and I was hoping I could keep it that way.

"I'm glad I found you, Ben," he said. "Billy Simms has been stirring up a hornet's nest."

"I can't say that I'm surprised."

"Did you know that Harris was looking for you?"

"Yes, I've already been informed."

"Well, it was Simms who told him you were in town and had dropped by the Vaudeville. Said he figured it was just a stroke of good fortune for Harris that he wasn't there when you did. Implying that Harris didn't stand a chance against you."

"Now why would Billy Simms want to do something like that?" I asked. "I thought he and Harris were partners."

"Business partners. But not friends. Figure it out for yourself. Harris gets planted and there are only two owners left. Simms and Joe Foster."

I nodded. "So it's like that, is it?"

"You bet," said Hopkins emphatically. "Anyway, after he couldn't find you, and got a warning from the local law, Harris gave up the search. But he let it be known that you were not welcome at the Vaudeville. That if you ever stepped foot in there again, they would carry you out in a box."

I put a tight rein on my anger. No man likes to be told where he can and cannot go, and what he can and cannot do. Clearly Harris was hoping I would take the bait, that I was too prideful to let a challenge like that go unheeded. And if I showed up at the Vaudeville, he could say I had come to kill him, and plead self-defense. Harris was no fool.

"Well, this is easy enough to deal with," I said, with a taut smile. "I'll just stay away from the Vaudeville."

Hopkins looked surprised. "You mean you're going to let him get away with that?"

"It's his place. He can say who's welcome and who isn't."

"But they'll go to calling you a coward if you don't call his bluff, Ben."

I peered at the dealer. "Who said he was bluffing? I'm beginning to wonder about you, Hop. Whose side are you really on?"

"I'm your friend, Ben, you know that."

"Seems to me that a friend would not try to talk me into going anywhere near the Vaudeville under these circumstances."

"I'm not trying to do that, honest," protested Hopkins.

I have learned that when people feel they have to tell me that they're being honest, they usually aren't being anything of the sort. It was possible that Simms had informed Harris that he'd seen Hopkins talking to me, and that Harris had pressured the dealer into acting as a messenger. The question was, how? Had he threatened Hop's job? Or offered him money? Had I been concerned about Hopkins or his friendship, it would have made a difference. I could let it go if Hopkins felt he had no choice. If he'd taken money to betray me, that was something else. But I didn't care. So I didn't ask.

"Thanks for the warning," I told him. "I'll be leaving San Antonio tomorrow. And you don't have to worry. I'm not going to respond to your employer's challenge. So long, Hop."

I thought for sure that would be the end of it. But the next day, shortly before noon, I went to the train depot to purchase tickets for the afternoon express to Austin. When I mentioned my name to the ticket agent, he looked up at me and then over my shoulder at someone else, and I discreetly laid my hand on the pistol under my coat as I turned. The man approaching me wore a tin star on his coat and I relaxed . . . a little.

"Mr. Thompson?" asked the deputy, pleasantly enough.

I nodded. "I'm Thompson, unless you're here to arrest me, in which case my name is Jones."

He laughed. "No, sir, I'm not here for that reason. You think I would come alone if that was my aim?"

I smiled. "I'll take that as a compliment."

"Yes, sir. The marshal has had me down here all day, hoping to catch you before you left town. He wants to see you. Says it's important. Something to do with that man you came here looking for."

I accompanied the deputy to the marshal's office, without paying for the tickets, thinking that if Reglin really was in town, my departure would probably be delayed.

The marshal greeted me amiably and said that late last night a bartender from the Vaudeville had come to

see him with word that the man Ben Thompson was
looking for had shown up in that establishment.

I stared at him in disbelief. "You've got to be kidding me."

He looked me straight in the eye and said he was
just relaying a message.

I realized then that I was neck-deep in a nest of
vipers. I didn't believe for a moment that anyone had
seen Reglin. It was a ploy, a ruse to get me into the
Vaudeville. This meant that even the city marshal was
playing the role of accomplice for Jack Harris. Maybe
Harris had paid him off. This time I could not contain
my anger. Planting my knuckles on the marshal's desk,
I leaned over so that the San Antonio lawman and I
were face to face. It was gratifying to see that he suddenly looked nervous.

"You know exactly what's going on here," I told
him. "Or else you're dumber than a fence post. Jack
Harris has been gunning for me ever since he found
out I was in town. So why are you just sitting here,
marshal? Why isn't he behind bars?" He opened his
mouth to utter a protest of innocence, but I wasn't interested and stopped him by holding up a hand and
saying, "Don't bother. I know why. Well, I've been
trying to walk this long enough. Now I'm going over
to the Vaudeville—and if you know what's good for
you, you won't interfere."

"I don't cotton to being threatened," he said.

"That wasn't a threat. Consider it professional cour-
tesy. One lawman to another. Stay out of my way."

Leaving the marshal's office, I went straight to the
Vaudeville, perfectly aware that in all likelihood I was
walking into an ambush. But I didn't care. I had done
all the backing up I was going to do. Jack Harris
wanted a fight so badly that he would eventually track

me down, and if that happened, my family might be put in harm's way. Reaching the Vaudeville, I marched straight in and went to the crescent-shaped bar. A bartender came up to take my order. I asked for his name and he said it was Barney Mitchell.

"Mine is Ben Thompson," I said.

I could tell by his expression that he knew about me, and could figure out why I was here.

"I hear your boss has been looking for me," I said. "Well, you go tell him that I'm here."

"He's—he's not here right now."

"Then where is he?"

"He usually doesn't show up here until after dark. That's when we start getting busy. I—I don't know for sure where he is at the moment. Maybe at home."

"Then you go to his home and tell him I'm waiting."

"Yes, sir." Mitchell removed his apron and hastily exited the saloon.

I motioned for the other barkeep and he approached with some hesitation—and then seemed much relieved when all I asked of him was a shot of the best whiskey he could lay his hands on. As he poured, I carefully scanned the saloon. There were about twenty customers at the bar and scattered among the tables, along with a few of the ladies who worked as percentage girls when they weren't performing in the theater. Two of them came up to me. They appeared to be identical twins, both small, slender, raven-haired, with somewhat Oriental features.

"Hello," said one of them, with a saucy smile. "I'm Kate Mauri. This is my sister May. And you are?"

"Married," I said coldly, and turned away.

It was a good thing that I did, because Billy Simms had been trying to come up behind me. As soon as he realized he'd been discovered, he burst into a smile—

and brought his hand out from under the coat he was wearing.

"Hello, Ben, how are you doing today?"

"Things are shaping up nicely, thanks. Oh, and if I see that smoke-maker you've got stashed under your coat, I'll kill you where you stand."

Simms held up both hands. "Take it easy, Ben. I'm not a threat to you."

"No, you're not. You just can't decide what you want. You think about trying me yourself, which would make Harris beholden to you. But that might get you killed. Or you can stand off to one side and let me kill him."

"I don't know why you have such a poor opinion of me."

"Maybe it's because I'm such a good judge of character." I downed the whiskey and gestured for the barkeep. He eased over and refilled my glass. I put four bits on the mahogany.

"The drinks are on the house," Simms told the bartender.

"No. Take the money," I said.

The hapless man looked at Simms, then at me, and then at the money—before gingerly picking up the coins.

"You're in a lousy mood, I see," said Simms.

"I sent a man to fetch your partner. Harris is a shotgun man, isn't he? I advise you not to be standing too close to me when he shows up."

Simms gave me a long look, a smile frozen on his lips. Then, with a curt nod, he walked away, into the hallway that separated the saloon from the theater.

Finishing the second whiskey, I went outside to stand on the boardwalk in front of the Vaudeville, midway between the entrances at either corner. An older

gentleman stood nearby reading a newspaper by the
light of a storm lantern. He glanced at me, returned to
his reading, then gave me a longer appraisal.

"I know you," he said. "You're Ben Thompson. I
lost money at your monte table in Austin a couple of
years ago."

"That happens," I said, keeping my attention focused on the street, looking for Harris.

"I've heard that Jack Harris has said he will kill you
if you step foot in the Vaudeville."

"I've heard that, too. That's why I'm here."

"My name is Biencourt. Harris happens to be a
friend of mine."

I took a closer look at him then, just to make sure
he wasn't heeled. He wasn't. Even if a man wears his
pistol under a coat, I can usually tell it's there.

"Then I'm sure you'll want to attend his funeral, Mr.
Biencourt," I said.

"That's pretty rough talk," he replied, disapprov-
ingly. "What if you're the one who ends up dead?"

I smiled. "You're invited to my funeral."

"You're a bold one. Thanks for the invitation. I may
just be there." He touched his hat brim, slipped the
folded newspaper under his arm, and walked away with
purposeful strides, quartering across the street. I had a
hunch he was going to warn Harris that I was out for
blood.

A few minutes later the bartender, Mitchell, reap-
peared, coming along the boardwalk. I expected him to
go into the saloon without saying a word to me. Instead, he threw a cautious look around before joining
me in front of the Vaudeville.

"He's coming," he said. "But you should know that
there is a back way into this place."

I thanked him for that information and with a curt

nod he went on inside. Having been told all sorts of things by all kinds of people I naturally wondered what Mitchell's motives might have been for telling me about the back door. Was he trying to tell me that Harris had no intention of meeting me on the street? That he intended to slip into the saloon and lay in wait for me there? But why would Mitchell want to help me? Maybe it was as simple as that he didn't like his employer. Or maybe he was deceiving me. Others had been trying to, so why not him? Maybe Harris wanted to make sure I was inside the Vaudeville when the trouble started.

I fired a cigar and stood there, my back to the wall, keeping an eye on the street as I smoked. While I stood there, at least a dozen men left the Vaudeville. Nearly every one of them glanced at me and hurried away. They knew something was brewing and wanted no part of it. The cigar half-smoked, I flicked it away and went back inside.

Mitchell and the other barkeep were behind the mahogany. Billy Simms was on this side of the bar. Most of the customers who had been in the saloon earlier were gone. The big room was virtually empty. Seeing me, Billy came forward.

"Why don't you just let this go, Ben," he said.

"You don't really want that. There is going to be some hell here tonight, Billy. Are you planning to buy into it?"

"Nope, not me." He backed away, hands well away from his sides, and he moved past me as though headed for the exit, and I half turned to watch him go, not trusting him at all—until it occurred to me that I was putting my back to the room, and so I turned back, just in time to see movement in the doorway that led to the hall.

Realizing he had been spotted, Harris came out of hiding. A broad, bearded man, his bulk filled the doorway. I had not seen him in nearly two years, but recognized him instantly.

"Come on, you bastard," he shouted. "I'm ready for you."

Raising the shotgun he carried, Harris triggered one barrel. I made a running leap for the bar, and the buckshot whistled overhead as I hit the floor, sliding about ten feet and fetching up against the brass rail that encircled the base of the mahogany. I pulled the revolver from under my coat.

"Stand up and fight, Thompson, damn you," roared Harris, and I could tell that he had moved closer, to the other end of the bar, about ten feet from the doorway where he had stationed himself to wait for my entrance. Taking off my derby hat, I sent it skidding across the top of the bar. As I had hoped, Harris took the bait, reacting by triggering the second barrel of buckshot, which demolished my hat. I stood up, took quick aim, and shot Harris through the chest.

He fell backwards, spinning away and dropping the shotgun, disappearing from my view as he dropped to the floor. I moved to my right, out among the saloon's tables, until the bar no longer obstructed my view and I could see him. He was still alive, dragging himself through the doorway into the hallway. I checked the saloon, looking particularly for Simms, but he was nowhere to be found. The barkeeps had sought cover behind the bar.

I went through the doorway into the hall, aware that Harris might be carrying a pistol, but doubting he was in any shape to resort to it. There was no question in my mind that the wound he had suffered would prove to be a mortal one. I found him sprawled on the stairs, half conscious, his breathing ragged, his eyes lacking focus, and a pink froth staining his blue lips, which indicated that the bullet I had fired had passed through his lungs. I considered finishing him with another shot, but decided not to. It would have been an act of mercy on my part—but no one else would see it that way. So I put my revolver away, turned my back on him, and walked out of the Vaudeville.

A number of citizens had gathered outside the saloon to await the outcome. They gave me a wide berth. I didn't see Simms, but Biencourt was present and accounted for.

"Did you kill him?" he asked coldly.

I nodded. "He won't last long. If you want to say good-bye, you'd better hurry."

"Damn you, Thompson."

I nodded again and walked away.

Not wanting to go to the house where Catherine and I had been staying, I bent my steps instead to the Menger Hotel. In the saloon adjacent to the lobby I ordered a whiskey. To my surprise, two acquaintances—Dick Scrayhorn and Charlie Bennett—walked in and joined me. Scrayhorn was a cattleman and Bennett was a troubleshooter for the railroad.

"We've been looking for you, Ben," said Scrayhorn. "Heard that Jack Harris was gunning for you, so we thought we'd offer you some assistance."

"Thanks, boys. But I just killed Harris over at the Vaudeville not half an hour ago."

They exchanged looks of surprise. Then Bennett said, "Mind if we have a drink or two with you, then?"

I told him I didn't mind at all, and was grateful for the company. And I was. I knew why they wanted to stick close. Like me, they thought there was a good chance more gunplay was in the offing before the night was done. This was why I had decided to stay away from Catherine, at least until I knew that one or more of Jack Harris's friends weren't going to come looking for me in order to settle the score.

Scrayhorn, Bennett, and I spent a couple of hours in the saloon, and then at Scrayhorn's suggestion we rented a room, where we spent the rest of the night polishing off a couple of bottles of good Kentucky bourbon and talking over old times. All the while keeping our pistols in our laps. But if anyone knew where I was, they didn't come for me, and when morning arrived, we trooped downstairs and had a hearty breakfast. When we were done with that, I consulted my stem-winder and told them it was about time for me to turn myself in.

"You sure you want to do that?" asked Bennett. "I know Shardeen, the marshal, and I'm not sure he's one to be trusted."

"I have no choice in the matter," I said. "If I leave town, they can brand me a fugitive from justice. I want to thank you both. Your friendship means a lot to me, and I owe you."

"You would do the same for either of us," said Scrayhorn.

"Is there anything else we can do to help?" asked Bennett.

"Yes. Go to Catherine. Tell her everything that has happened. And see her and my son safely back to Austin."

Bennett nodded. "You can count on us, Ben."

I told them where to find my family—and that I would be forever in their debt. Then I headed for the city marshal's office. Shardeen and his deputy were there with a third man I later learned was the county sheriff, T. P. McCall.

Shardeen took one look at me and said, "Jack Harris is dead—and you're under arrest, Thompson."

I held my coat open and invited the deputy to relieve me of my six-shooter.

"It was a fair fight," I remarked. "And he fired both barrels of his shotgun before I killed him."

"I'm not sure that going up against you can be considered a fair fight under any circumstances," said Shardeen.

I shrugged. "As you may recall, it was Harris himself who pressed the issue."

"That will be for a jury to decide."

The coroner's inquest determined only that I had shot and killed Harris, and a grand jury convened a fortnight later decided there was sufficient cause to issue an indictment against me. The trial was scheduled for two months later. During this time I was held in the San Antonio jail. They treated me well. Scrayhorn and Bennett visited me often, and much to my surprise Shardeen allowed them to bring me whiskey and cigars and books and a deck of cards. Joe Glover came down from Austin and said he would represent me. I gave him a letter that I asked to be delivered to the Austin city council. He asked me what the letter contained.

"It's my resignation, Joe."

He shook his head. "I'll see that it gets delivered if that's what you want. But I will tell you right here and now that they won't accept your resignation. The people are behind you all the way, Ben. They know the truth of what happened. Everyone does. There shouldn't even be a trial, in my opinion."

"The people are behind me?"

Glover chuckled. "Never thought you'd live to see the day, did you?"

"No. No, I sure didn't."

"To be frank, neither did I."

Glover was right—the Austin city council refused to accept my tendered resignation, and appointed Johnny Chenneville acting marshal until such time as I could resume my duties.

Since Harris had many friends in San Antonio, Glover didn't think I could get a fair trial there, and prevailed upon the judge for a change of venue, which was denied. I was tried in the courthouse on Soledad Street and it only lasted two days. The prosecution argued that I had gone to the Vaudeville looking for a fight, and for that reason was not justified in claiming that I was only defending myself. But Glover persuaded the jury that any reasonable man would have confronted Harris. Not to do so could have placed my family in grave danger, as sooner or later Harris would have found me. Under the circumstances I'd had no choice but to force the issue. The jury agreed, voting not guilty by a nine to three margin.

Accompanied by my wife and Joe Glover, I returned to a cheering crowd that had gathered at the Austin train station. A brass band, a welcoming committee, and even a church choir was on hand to sing hallelujahs for my safe return. A carriage festooned with bunting transported Catherine and me to our home, and the people made a parade of it. They took us all the way down Congress Avenue, and the street was lined with citizens who waved and applauded. I was completely overwhelmed, so that when we did finally arrive home, and I was called upon to make a speech to the assembled throng from my front porch, I was only able to admit that I was at a loss for words. The people just cheered more loudly.

Chapter 21

ALTHOUGH THE AUSTIN city council had refused to accept my resignation, it soon became clear to me that the good people of that town, while immensely supportive of me during my recent legal struggle in San Antonio, were ambivalent about having for a city marshal a man who had spent as much time as I had in jail with a charge of murder hanging over my head. Johnny Chenneville was doing an exemplary job as acting marshal, and I thought it only right that he should continue in that position. So shortly after my return home, I announced that I was resigning from the post. My legal expenses had been steep and I needed to make money in a hurry. In addition to that, my mother was very ill and I wanted to make sure she could afford the very best care. And finally, my brother, Billy, had gotten into trouble with the law as well; he was in jail down in Refugio County, charged with attempted murder; he had gotten into a quarrel with another man and seriously wounded him. Since, as usual, Billy didn't have a dollar to his name, I had to pay for his lawyers, and I bought the services of the best I could find. That's why I went back to gambling. It was the only thing I knew.

But gambling wasn't what it had once been, and I did not profit from it as I once had. Beset by financial problems, I found myself relying more and more on strong spirits to dull my disappointment. Then, too, I found it increasingly difficult to sleep at night. No physician could find a cure for that affliction. Often I would prowl the streets of Austin after a losing stint at the tables and sometimes found trouble to get into. One time I barged into the offices of the *Daily Statesman*, rousted all the employees out into the street, and did considerable damage to their equipment—all because they had printed an editorial that cast aspersions on a friend of mine. As a consequence I faced six charges, and paid a heavy fine, and the newspaper concluded that I was a "great curse to Texas."

I think it was that scathing commentary that prompted me to begin writing my own account of my life. It seemed obvious to me that if I left that task to others, I would not get a fair shake. I wanted to explain for posterity why I had done the things I did. Joe Glover and other acquaintances encouraged me to do so. Being the same man who had labored greatly for several days over the letter announcing my candidacy for the post of city marshal some years earlier, I faced the task with some anxiety. But putting all the events of my life—or most of them, anyway—down on paper did not turn out to be quite the ordeal that I had expected. It was easy, really, because all I did was tell the truth. After spending several months on the job, working for a couple of hours every morning, I had recounted everything of any consequence that had happened to me since my arrival in Texas. I didn't think many would be interested in the childhood I had spent on the banks of the River Aire, so mentioned that period only in passing. All that was left for me then was to add to the narrative as one would a journal, to keep it as up-to-date as possible.

Meanwhile, the shootout with Jack Harris continued to haunt me. As part owner of the most popular sporting establishment in San Antonio, Harris had a lot of acquaintances, and his partner Joe Foster was reported in the San Antonio *Express* as saying that if I stepped foot in the Vaudeville again, it would be my last day on earth. Such threats didn't bother me—I could live with them as long as Foster or someone else did not come looking for me with a gun.

I got a lot of information about the sentiment that existed in San Antonio about me from a man named King Fisher. Fisher was a deputy sheriff of Uvalde County. I had met him a few years earlier, and knew that he had come to Texas from Kentucky at the age of thirteen. His father died shortly thereafter, leaving Fisher an orphan. By the time he was twenty, Fisher was already widely regarded as one of the best gunmen in the state. Cattlemen hired him to clean out a gang of rustlers down along the Nueces. But instead of cleaning them out, Fisher joined up with the rustlers, and pretty soon he was the big augur of a gang that, by some accounts, numbered as many as one hundred hard cases. That tells you something about the kind of man Fisher was, I guess, that he could keep that many outlaws under his thumb. For some years Fisher reigned supreme in the Rio Grande Valley. No lawman—not even the Texas Rangers—were willing to even try bringing him to justice. Among the poorer folk he had a reputation as something of a Robin Hood—a reputation, I might add, that he assiduously cultivated by making sure the folks profited from knowing him and protecting him, while at the same time protecting them from his own men.

Eventually Fisher tired of the outlaw life. He found himself a good woman to marry and settled down, announcing to one and all that he fully intended to live out his days as a law-abiding citizen. He took up ranch-

ing, but was an indifferent livestock owner, and finally
settled into being a lawman. He had visited Austin on
several occasions in the past, and since he was partial
to games of chance we had met and become acquainted. I can't say that we were friends, but there
had never been any problems between us.

When I saw him this time, he was little changed
from our previous meeting. He still sported a Mexican
sombrero, a black *chaqueta* embroidered with silver, a
crimson sash and a belt adorned with silver conchos,
and big silver Chihuahua spurs. He carried a brace of
silver-plated Colts with ivory handles in cross-draw
holsters. He cut quite a figure, but then, that was his
intent.

He found me at the Iron Front, and we had a few
drinks and talked about the business I'd had with Harris.

"I didn't know Jack very well," said Fisher, "but Joe
Foster is a man I consider a friend. I spent a little time
in the Bexar County jail some years ago—had a little
too much to drink, I'm afraid, and started shooting out
the streetlights just for fun. While I was there, Foster
had meals sent to me from the best restaurant in town.
If you've ever had the food at the Bexar County jail,
you know what a blessing that was."

I laughed. "Yes, I'm familiar with that jail, King—
and just about every other one in the state, or so it
seems."

"Joe was good friends with Harris, and Jack's death
hit him hard. That's why he's issued that warning about
you coming into the Vaudeville."

"Don't worry, I didn't take offense to it. I want nothing more to do with that place. I wouldn't have bearded
Harris in his den except that the man was on the prowl

looking for me, and I wasn't going to let him catch him anywhere near my family."

"I understand completely," said Fisher.

"Then I have no problems with you on that score."

"Absolutely not." And to prove it, Fisher paid for another round of drinks.

We proceeded to drink and chew the breeze all night long, the conversation turning to our various adventures, of which we both had more than enough to carry us through until dawn. Finally Fisher had to take his leave, stating that he was intending to catch the afternoon train to San Antonio. Then, as an afterthought, he invited me to accompany him.

"There are a couple of new roosts down there that you should look into, Ben," he said. "My feeling is you could come away with a tidy profit if you spent a day or two at those tables."

"I don't know, King, I think I should steer clear of San Antonio from now on. If I go back down there after what has happened, people will say I'm looking for trouble."

"There'll be no trouble as long as you stay away from the Vaudeville, and you've said you have every intention of doing that, and I believe you. You're my friend, Ben, and so is Joe Foster. Believe me, I don't want to see either one of you get into anything."

I told him I would think it over, and we parted company, he returning to his hotel while I went home. Catherine had fresh coffee and breakfast waiting on me. As was her custom, she sat across the table from me while I ate. It struck me how little she had changed in all the years since we had met. I found that pretty remarkable, considering what grief I had brought her, and told her so.

She reached across the table and put her hand on

top of mine. "Being with you, Ben, have been the happiest years of my life."

I shook my head. "I just don't know how you can say that, Cath. I have always felt as though I could have done better by you. Gotten a respectable job and spent a lot more time in your company. Instead, I sometimes feel as though I've spent most of my life in saloons. Even when I'm not in one, I still carry the stench on my clothes. I can still smell the cigar smoke and the raw whiskey. Certainly you deserved better than a gambler for a husband."

"You are who you are, Ben. You can't be someone you're not. I fell in love with you the moment I saw you and I'm still just as in love with you today as I was twenty years ago."

An emotion so strong that it rattled me filled my heart at that moment. "I've been lucky, I guess. Lucky at cards. Lucky when people were shooting at me. But I never have been as lucky as I was the day you agreed to marry me."

She smiled—a smile that flooded my body with warmth—and then rose to fetch the coffeepot and fill my cup. Before returning to the stove, she bent down and kissed me lightly on the cheek.

I told her that King Fisher was in town, and that I had squandered a whole night talking to him, and now was thinking about taking him up on an invitation to visit some new roosts down in San Antonio for a day or two. I could tell that the idea of my being in San Antonio was a source of some anxiety for her, but true to her nature she did not try to talk me out of going. All she asked was that I be careful, and I promised her that I would come back to her safe and sound—and, I hoped, richer in the bargain.

I changed clothes, putting on my best Prince Albert

coat, a new derby hat, spit-and-polished Middleton boots, and sauntered on over to the train depot to find King Fisher there. We boarded one of the passenger trains. Shortly before we were scheduled to leave the station, Fisher remembered that he needed to send a telegram, and disembarked. The telegraph station was located at one end of the depot building—such was usually the case, since telegraph lines generally followed the rail lines cross-country. The train was just beginning to pull away from the platform when Fisher completed his business and leaped aboard.

The train pulled into San Antonio at about eight o'clock that evening. I spent most of the trip writing in my journal, since my conversation with Fisher had triggered a few memories that I wanted to make sure were included in the chronicle of my life. Leaving the depot, we went to the Turner Opera House to see a play in which the famous actress Ada Gray had a starring role. There was much ado in Austin because the play was scheduled to open there in a fortnight; this was my chance to see it in advance of my friends and neighbors.

Considering where I was, I had it in mind to keep a very low profile, but the manager of the opera house insisted that Fisher and I take seats in the front row, so naturally, we drew a lot of attention. Fisher, as always, basked in it. When the play was over, we went outside and discussed what to do next. I wanted to pay a call on the new roosts Fisher had mentioned.

"Ben, I've been thinking," he said. "I can tell you're wound up tighter than a clock. And I know why that is."

"You would be, too, King, if you had as many enemies around here as I do."

He nodded. "That's true. But this is so unnecessary.

I believe that all concerned are reasonable men. I know you are, and so is Joe Foster. I say we both go down to the Vaudeville and straighten everything out."

"I don't know," I said. "I've heard that the Vaudeville will be my graveyard enough times that I'm starting to believe it."

Fisher shook his head in disagreement. "The thing is, I'll be there, and like I told you, Joe Foster and I are friends. I believe we can make a peace here. And besides, who in their right mind would take on the two of us?"

I agreed, but told Fisher that I wanted to find a hotel room and get some rest first. He didn't object, and accompanied me to the Menger. Once I had checked in, he said he would return in a couple of hours and then we would proceed to the Vaudeville. He commented that as far as the show at that establishment was concerned, the later the better, as the performers were known to get more rowdy and risqué as the night progressed.

Arriving in my room, I brought my journal up-to-date before succumbing to a weariness and stretching out on the bed, hoping that I could get a little sleep. The more I thought about the proposed peace mission to the Vaudeville, the better I liked the idea. The last time I'd gone there was to kill a man. This time it would be to bury the hatchet. If I could pull it off, that would go a long way toward quieting critics who accused me of being a person who went out of his way to look for trouble. I had never done that. I had never killed a man who hadn't been dead set on killing me first. To go to the Vaudeville tonight would be seen as a bold and noble action, and I even considered going unarmed, as proof of my peaceful intentions—which would make it far bolder. Who then could doubt that my desire for a reconciliation of the differences that existed between Joe Foster and myself was anything less than genuine? People said that those who lived by the gun were destined to die by the gun. A neat trick, I thought, if only I could prove to be the exception to that rule.

TO THE READER

THOSE WERE THE last words Ben Thompson wrote, for that was the last night of his life.

It fell upon me, his attorney and friend, Joseph Glover, to write the final chapter—a duty I did not relish but for which I suppose no one was better qualified, as I have gone to great lengths to investigate the mysterious circumstances surrounding Ben's death. There are many conflicting accounts, and I am familiar with them all. I am now firmly convinced that I know the truth of the matter. I will relate all I have been told of the events that transpired during Ben's final hours and let you, the reader, reach your own conclusion as to what is fact and what is fabrication.

Let me begin by stating that I have evidence to indicate that King Fisher sent a telegram from Austin to Billy Simms in San Antonio prior to his departure, in Ben's company, for that town. To the best recollection of the telegrapher, all the message said was BEN AND I ARE COMING. So what does this mean? Was King Fisher part of a conspiracy to lead Ben Thompson into a fatal ambush? I would say yes, unequivocally—except for what happened to King Fisher.

True to his word, Fisher returned to the Menger and from there, with Ben, went to the Vaudeville. Where he went and what he was up to while Ben was resting those few hours in his room, I have been unable to discern. On the way, they encountered Jim Brent, who happens to be an acquaintance of mine, and Brent told me that he was sure Ben had no intention of looking for a fight that night. He said that both Ben and Fisher seemed to be in high spirits.

Arriving at the Vaudeville, Ben and Fisher learned that neither Billy Simms or Joe Foster were present at the time. They waited at the bar for a while, drinking whiskey, until Simms returned. Ben and Simms spoke for a moment, and according to the account given by Simms, Ben appeared genuinely interested in making peace. They were joined by Jacob Coy, a city constable who occasionally worked at the Vaudeville. The four of them went to the theater and found seats near the dress circle. In between performances, percentage girls moved among the patrons encouraging them to buy drinks, and Ben offered to buy all around—an offer accepted by the other three men. They talked for a while and then Joe Foster walked into the theater. Ben spotted him immediately, and told Simms that he wanted to talk to him. Simms said that was a good idea and fetched Foster. Ben extended a hand in friendship, but Foster refused to reciprocate. He also refused a drink when Ben offered to buy him one. Most witnesses agree that Foster said something to the effect that it would be a cold day in hell before he drank with the likes of Ben Thompson.

As you have read the previous narrative, you can readily assume that this was not a slight Ben would take lightly, so it should come as no surprise to you that an argument ensued.

There are two different accounts of what then transpired.

One of them is that at some point in the argument Ben Thompson pushed Jacob Coy aside when the latter tried to intervene, and then struck Foster across the *face with the barrel of his revolver. This, at least, is what Billy Simms has sworn under oath. Incensed, Foster launched himself at Ben, and at the same instant Coy grabbed Ben's pistol and tried to wrest it from him. The pistol discharged and the bullet lodged in Foster's leg. That single gunshot was enough to send most of the patrons and performers and percentage girls in the place scurrying for cover. Simms claimed that he and Coy and Foster then opened fire on Thompson as well as King Fisher, and both of them fell, mortally wounded.*

However, several reliable witnesses, a cattleman named Thomas McGee among them, insist that neither Ben nor Foster drew a weapon. Nor did Ben strike Foster. In fact, they say, Foster sat down and spoke to Ben for a moment, and then Ben and Fisher got to their feet, and it was at that precise moment that the shots rang out. Their testimony is that the killing shots came from a private box located at the back of the theater, and that these shots were fired by both rifles and pistols. Ben was shot nine times, and Fisher sustained thirteen wounds. The coroner who examined Ben's body said that any one of the wounds suffered by Ben would have been fatal, and that most of them entered the body from the back. The coroner went further, speculating that at least five different shooters were involved in the killing of Ben Thompson. A highly respected member of the community in San Antonio reported that he was told by several men who frequented the Vaudeville that Simms and Foster had stationed three men with rifles in the private box.

So why, if King Fisher was a member of the conspiracy to assassinate Ben Thompson, was he gunned down as well? As he was struck thirteen times, there can be no doubt that he was an intentional target. But if he and Joe Foster really were such good friends, and Foster actually did arrange the ambush, why was Fisher killed? I doubt that there will ever be a satisfactory answer to that question.

Speaking of Foster, I should point out that he died from the wound he received. The leg was amputated, but gangrene set in, and he perished in a matter of days. So who fired the bullet that claimed his life? It seems clear to me that Ben Thompson did not have the time to draw his pistol. His hands were empty when he was killed. I suspect, as do others, that Foster was hit by a stray or ricochet fired by the assassins he had employed to do away with Ben. If so, there is justice in this world, after all.

The death of Ben Thompson caused a lot of outrage, not only in Austin but around the country. It was not, I think, so much the fact that he had died a violent death—he had, after all, led a violent life, and such an end was to be expected—but the manner in which he met his fate. Particularly in this part of the country it was considered a very cowardly act, since out here a man was expected to do his own dirty work. There remain some who steadfastly defend Joe Foster and his actions; they argue that Ben Thompson was such a dangerous man that no sensible person would have attempted to kill him face to face. There is some merit to that argument, but it does not condone a cold-blooded assassination as that which transpired in the Vaudeville on March 11, 1884.

It is fitting that I make a few comments about the funeral of Ben Thompson. So many people attended the services presided over by the Reverend Smoot that several had to stand outside, and could not hear the Presbyterian pastor's moving words. The funeral procession consisted of sixty vehicles, including a car-

riage filled with orphans from the home that had ben-
efited greatly over the years from Ben Thompson's
generosity. The mortal remains were laid to rest in
Oakwood Cemetery.

As the executor of Ben's estate, I can state that he
left property worth ten thousand dollars, not an incon-
siderable sum, but for the fact that he had a great many
debts—so many, in fact, that in 1887 a court ordered
that his home on Linden Street be sold. I made certain
that Ben's widow received a more than fair price for
it, and am happy to report that some influential friends
of Ben's took it upon themselves to guarantee that she
and his son never wanted for anything.

AUTHOR'S NOTE

THIS BIOGRAPHICAL NOVEL follows the true course of Ben Thompson's life in most respects. Except for one thing—as far as we know, he never wrote an autobiography.

Ben was born November 1848 in Knottingley, a small town located on the banks of the River Aire in Yorkshire, England. He had a brother and two sisters, all younger than he. His father was an officer in the Royal Navy. It is not certain why Ben's parents decided to emigrate to the United States. They had relatives who had settled near the frontier community of Austin, Texas—but the Texas frontier seems an unusual place for a British naval officer to end up. At any rate, to Texas they came. Ben's father made a modest living supplying the citizens of Austin with fresh fish from the nearby Colorado River, but he always longed to return to the sea. Eventually he did, and lost his life there. By all accounts, Ben's mother was well-liked in the community, though some criticized her for being too lax in the raising of her children. By her own admission she could seldom bring herself to punish them for misbehavior. And Ben was a very headstrong boy who early on demonstrated a knack for getting into trouble.

Unlike many of his peers, Ben was well-educated, exceedingly so for the early Texas frontier. He had been schooled in England, and continued his education in Texas when a family friend, San Antonio attorney John Green, arranged for him to attend a private school for two years, until he was fifteen. Ben continued to educate himself while working as a typesetter, first in Austin and then in New Orleans. He was well-read, well-spoken, and a superb conversationalist. But like most boys his age, Ben became accustomed to going about armed. It was not at all unusual to see youths carrying knives and pistols. The event that opens this novel—the shooting of Joe Smith—took place more or less as described. There is another documented event of Ben's early years that instructs us as to his nature, but which was not included in this work. One day Ben accompanied some other boys to the river to hunt geese. They split into two groups. Ben and his group were infuriated when the other group clumsily scared all the geese away. Words were exchanged, and Ben and the leader of the other group agreed to fight a duel. Standing forty paces apart, the two boys fired at each other with shotguns. Both were wounded. Ben was fifteen at the time.

In early 1860 Ben traveled to New Orleans and went to work for a bookbinder named Samuel Slater. There are several versions of what transpired between Ben and the character identified in this book as Letour. I am fairly certain that Ben did get into an altercation on an omnibus with a gentleman of French or Creole extraction. But whether this led to a deadly duel in a deserted carriage house on the edge of the French Quarter cannot be confirmed. It is, however, a legend that persists. Whatever the truth, Ben did not stay long in the Crescent City. He considered going to California, but wound up back in Austin instead, right before the Civil War broke out. Ben enlisted in Rip Ford's battalion and went to the Rio Grande country in time to fight the Mexican bandit leader Juan Cortinas. Later, while part of the garrison at Fort Clark, Ben had an altercation with a Sergeant Vance over rations, and ended up shooting both the sergeant and a lieutenant that intervened. Vance recovered from his wounds. The lieutenant did not. Ben was thrown in the brig. When released to care for a friend who had chicken pox, he deserted. Or so the legend goes. Previous researchers have failed to find any record of such a fight, and what records do exist make no mention of Ben being absent without leave for any period of time. But a San Antonio newspaper gives an account of the shooting in 1863. Whatever the truth, Ben was never tried for killing an officer, and after his initial enlistment term was up, he reenlisted.

When the Second Texas was transferred to the Houston area while a campaign against the federals who occupied Galveston Island was being planned, Ben took part in a whiskey-smuggling operation. He was caught, and once again thrown in the brig. What followed is not clear. Rumors are that he crossed enemy lines to acquire intelligence that proved essential to the success of the attempt to recapture Galveston for the Confederacy. But these are only rumors, and there is no official record to substantiate them. So the scenes in this book involving Aloysius Drumm and Lorelei James are entirely fictional. Something like it might have happened. If so, that would explain how Ben escaped punishment for his whiskey-smuggling escapades. And he did receive an injury to his leg when a horse fell on it. During the attack on the federal forces at Galveston, Ben was ordered to the rear because of that injury, which plagued him for years to come. It's said that Ben took part in the fighting for Galveston contrary to orders, and acquitted himself so bravely that

his superiors could not bring themselves to punish him
for his insubordination.

On furlough in Austin, Ben met and married Catherine Moore. He then spent the remainder of the war
along the Mexican border. While there, he took up
three-card monte and clashed with a group of Mexican
soldiers who lost all their money to him in a cantina
located in the border town of Nuevo Laredo. His
brother, Billy, had enlisted in Ben's unit, and they were
together at the time. When the ranking Mexican demanded that Ben give his men their money back, Ben
balked. He wrote of the experience as follows:

> "Among those Mexicans was Lieutenant Martino
> Gonzales, one of the tallest men I ever saw, a
> black Mexican with the eye of a murderer, that
> danced in a dangerous way, while the corners of
> his mouth twitched spasmodically. I noted him,
> his action, expression, movements, with the ra-
> pidity of thought, and yet as thoroughly as if I
> had studied him for months. I knew that I should
> have to kill him, he kill me, or I have to give up
> the money I had won, and that which I had of
> my own, which surrender I did not mean to
> make."

Ben ended up killing both Gonzales and another
Mexican, and fleeing the scene. He narrowly escaped
capture, as did Billy. His commanding officer, Rip
Ford, sent him back to Austin with instructions to recruit a new company. Ben was in the process of doing
that when Lee surrendered and the war ended. Shortly
after federal occupation forces arrived, Ben was arrested for taking part in an ambush of a detachment
that took place in the hills around Austin. Here again,

some experts claim that no such ambush ever took place. But the Austin newspaper of the time does have a record of the event, and mentions that Ben and several others killed a few soldiers south of town and were arrested for it. Approached while in jail by agents for the Emperor Maximilian, who was fighting an insurrection that threatened his rule in Mexico, Ben bribed a couple of guards and effected an escape. Fleeing across the border, he enlisted in Maximilian's army at Matamoros, served under General Tomas Mejia, took part in several actions against the rebels, and found himself in Queretaro. According to the Austin *Daily Statesman*, Ben

> "became one of the most daring officers in that unfortunate prince's army. For his brave and gallant conduct Maximilian promoted him to rank of major, and it is authentically reported that the unfortunate Maximilian once remarked that not an officer in all his forces possessed the daring of Major Thompson. His dashing conduct in the Mexican campaign is said to be one continual course of startling deeds of bravery, and he became the terror of opposing forces. He inspired the men under his command with something of the spirit he himself exhibited, and the regiment to which he was attached, and which he virtually commanded, is said to have been invincible."

All hyperbole aside, there seems to be no question that Ben saw a lot of action in Mexico, and acquitted himself well. However, Maximilian's cause was doomed (not to mention, in my opinion, unjust) and Ben narrowly escaped capture at Queretaro. He and a friend escaped to Vera Cruz, where Ben eventually found passage on a ship back to Texas. Still facing a charge for the killing of federal soldiers, he attempted to pass himself off as a Mexican, and succeeded for a time, surreptitiously visiting his wife and others in that guise. He was eventually exposed, and had a couple of narrow escapes as the federals tried to capture him. Realizing that they would do so sooner or later, Ben turned himself in, was tried, and acquitted for lack of evidence. (He was not represented by Joe Glover, of course, as Glover is an entirely fictional character.)

At this point Ben embarked on his career as a gambler, and had a concession in The Palace, a saloon run by Phil Coe and Tom Bowles. In 1868 he won Bryan's Blue Wing saloon from a man named Big King in a card game. Then his brother, Billy, shot and killed a soldier named Barnes, and Ben found himself neck-deep in hot water again because he arranged for Billy's flight to the Indian Territory. When these activities were discovered, Ben was arrested yet again. To make matters worse, he threatened the life of a justice of a peace—the details are described fairly accurately in this novel—and was sentenced to a term of incarceration at the prison in Huntsville. Released after two years, he returned to Austin and his gambling pursuits. In partnership with Phil Coe, he traveled to the rip-roaring cattle town of Abilene, Kansas, and participated in the opening of the famous Bull's Head Saloon. By the summer of 1871, Ben had established himself sufficiently in Abilene to summon his wife and small son to join him. On the day they arrived, the buggy in which they were riding overturned. All three were injured, and Catherine's arm had to be amputated as a result. Ben blamed himself, and I do not believe he ever got completely over this tragedy. While he was escorting Catherine back to Texas, Coe was gunned down by the Abilene marshal, Wild Bill Hickok. This prompted Ben to move his operation to Ellsworth in 1873.

While in Ellsworth, Ben was reunited with his fugitive brother, Billy, who was on hand for the gunfight between Ben and Nick Lentz and John Sterling, during which Billy killed the county sheriff. Billy left town while Ben remained behind to face the consequences. The mayor of Ellsworth called for Ben's arrest. None of the local authorities, however, wanted to try doing that. According to a biographer of Wyatt Earp, it was Earp who happened to be on the scene at the time, who stepped forward and volunteered. Ben surrendered without a fight. However, several researchers have failed to find any concrete evidence that Wyatt Earp was involved. For that reason, I declined to introduce Earp into my narrative. At any rate, Ben ended up in custody, but was released on a bond put up by some Texas cattlemen. As for Billy, Ben wrote:

"[Billy] told me that after leaving town, on the day of the shooting, he went out in the prairie and laid down and went to sleep; that he was drunk and that he slept until about 9 o'clock that night. He did not know where he was; that he got up and wandered around an hour or so until he saw the lights of the houses in Ellsworth, when he came on back to Ellsworth about 11 o'clock in the night. . . . He sent over to the Theatre after me, he being near the Grand Central Hotel. I went over there and . . . told him . . . that I would advise him to go out and stay with some of the cattle camps for a few days. And thereupon he left in company with a young fellow by the name of Jack who worked for Frank McGee. I heard

from him every day for four or five days after-
ward but never saw him again until I met him in
Texas."

Upset by the apparent disregard for the law that
some Texans demonstrated, the citizens of Ellsworth
formed a vigilance committee that issued "white affidavits" to individuals like Ben and his friend Cad
Pierce, which warned of dire consequences if the Texans did not depart Kansas forthwith. Ben took the
warning seriously, and decamped. Cad Pierce did not,
and was gunned down by a deputy sheriff named Ed
Crawford, as described in this book.

Now a fugitive from justice in both Texas and Kansas, Billy hid out on the ranch of Neil Cain, near Austin, and in the fall of 1876 was implicated in a cattle
rustling scheme. This embroiled Ben in yet another legal battle. (It may come as a surprise to some readers
that there exists in this book so much about courts and
judges and legal actions; the West has been portrayed
as a lawless place, but that doesn't mean there wasn't
a legal system in place. It may only mean that it didn't
work very well for a number of years.) After much
wrangling, Billy was extradited to Kansas, where he
stood trial for the killing of the county sheriff. Ben
followed, and did everything he could to make sure his
brother got a fair trial. Meanwhile, Kansas kept a wary
eye on the notorious Ben Thompson, believing he was
scheming to break Billy out of jail. In September 1877,
Billy was acquitted. The Ellsworth *Reporter* described
the scene in this way:

"When they came back with their verdict the
court room was full and everyone but the prisoner
seemed intensely interested to learn the result.

Thompson came in . . . smiling as if he was sure that his bonds were about to be loosed. The clerk commenced reading and just as we expected to hear the world 'guilty' pronounced he read 'not guilty,' when all decorum was forgotten by friends of the prisoner who congratulated him on his escape. . . . This was a great surprise to most of our citizens. . . . They expected nothing less than twenty years in the penitentiary for him. . . . This is the way most of our old town residents felt—that he got off altogether too easy—that the taking of human life in Ellsworth was not considered a crime."

I doubt that anyone was more surprised by the verdict than Ben Thompson, who must have thought Billy would languish for many years in Leavenworth.

Back in Austin, still plying the trade of gambler, Ben killed another man, this one a fellow by the name of Mark Wilson, who ran the Capital Theatre. One evening Wilson had a friend of Ben's ejected from the establishment. Ben took offense to that and decided to test Wilson's resolve. He and his friend returned to the Capital some nights later and, sure enough, Wilson ordered some of his men to escort Ben's friend out of the house. Ben intervened and Wilson went to the bar to fetch a shotgun, which he fired at Thompson. The buckshot passing over his head, Ben drew his pistol and fired three times; Wilson died instantly. A bartender then took a shot at Ben and his bullet put a hole in Thompson's coat. Ben shot and wounded this assailant. A newspaper recounted the scene thus:

"A scene of perfect uproar, confusion and screams ensued; the room was filled with smoke

and the floor was covered with blood and lamp
black, and while one man lay dead and another
perhaps mortally wounded, the audience was
making a hasty exit out the front and rear of the
room. Some burst through a front window and
others rushed upon the stage at the other end of
the building and went bounding through the scen-
ery."

There was talk of another vigilance committee, but
it doesn't seem that one was formed, and the law was
allowed to take its course. A change of venue was ordered, and Ben was tried in Galveston, where he was
acquitted. His battery of lawyers convinced the court
that Ben's presence in the Capital Theater that night
had been purely coincidental. I doubt that it was.

In 1876 silver was discovered at the headwaters of
the Arkansas River, and the following year the boomtown of Leadville appeared, virtually overnight. Two
years later Ben Thompson, accompanied by friend
Frank Cotton, visited Leadville to see what all the fuss
was about, as for years the Texas newspapers had been
filled with glowing accounts of the strike-it-rich op-
portunities available there. He met with a string of bad
luck at the Leadville gaming tables, accused the dealers
of cheating, and shot out the lights—a form of protest
on his part, I presume. Not for the first time in his
career (nor the last) he then presented himself to the
authorities and paid a fine for disturbing the peace.

Ben took part in the famous "Grand Canyon" or
"Colorado Railroad" war waged between the Denver
and Rio Grande on one hand and the Atchison, Topeka,
and Santa Fe on the other. He was recruited by Bat
Masterson, who a year or so earlier had gotten his wayward brother, Billy, out of a tight spot in Ogallala,

Nebraska. Ben was sent, as described in this book, to Pueblo to protect the Santa Fe property there. However, his clash with Sheriff Price was not nearly as sensational in fact as I have made it out to be in these pages. Ben and his men did barricade themselves into a roundhouse and company office, and Price did add one hundred "deputies" to his force to take the place. When Price and his crowd marched on the roundhouse—with hundreds of spectators lining the bluffs that surrounded the scene—there was some gunplay at the depot ticket office and a Santa Fe employee named Jenkins was mortally wounded. Price then advanced on the roundhouse. Ben Thompson was caught outside and arrested. Seeing this, the men in the roundhouse surrendered without a shot being fired. Eventually Ben and his men were released from jail, and left Colorado. The Santa Fe paid him $5,000 for his efforts—money that he used to open a string of gambling roosts in various Texas towns.

It was this investment that finally paid off for Ben and made him a relatively wealthy man, so that he could move his family into a nice home on Austin's Linden Street. While there were some who did not approve of his vocation, no one could legitimately question his honesty; he made sure that the games he owned were straight. And, as mentioned in this book, he took part in one of the last expeditions against the Comanches about this time, riding with Burleson's Rangers and very nearly getting killed while out scouting for the hostiles.

The events surrounding Ben's run for the position of Austin city marshal did not happen exactly as portrayed here. He was approached by certain influential citizens and persuaded to run. That he did so because the incumbent was out of favor with the cattle kings is

an example of literary license on my part. Running on
the Democratic ticket, Ben actually lost his first try at
Creary's job. The next time around, Creary ran for
sheriff, making it easier for Ben to nab the city marshal's job. Had there been political approval ratings at
the time, Ben would have gotten high marks from the
people of Austin for keeping the peace. It's not hard
to see why; I suspect very few potential lawbreakers
were eager to challenge him. Finally Ben Thompson
was getting the respect that I believe he had always
longed for—and never gotten previously.

In 1882, Ben received a letter from a detective
agency regarding a murderer suspected of being in San
Antonio, and while investigating this, he ran afoul of
Jack Harris, part owner of The Vaudeville Theater.
Their long-standing quarrel and its resolution was as I
have portrayed it in this novel. One thing I find fasci-
nating about Western lore—as opposed to the actual
events—is how most of the famous gunfights (and this
was one of them) really came about. There was usually
a lot of talk, a lot of strutting and bravado and jock-
eying for advantage, and the violent denouement was
usually almost anticlimactic in that seldom did the adversaries face off in the middle of the street at high
noon. After his acquittal at yet another trial, Ben did
go home to Austin to a hero's welcome. Austinites
called him one of their own, and it seemed a matter of
civic pride to them that he was not "railroaded" into a
conviction by a San Antonio court.

No longer city marshal, Ben returned to his old profession of gambling. He began to drink more heavily
than ever before, and according to accounts of people
who knew him, the once cheerful Thompson became
irritable—which, of course, made him all the more
dangerous. Unable to sleep, he prowled the streets at

night and often engaged in shooting sprees that, fortunately, were harmless. His feud with the friends of Jack Harris continued. One of these was J. King Fisher, a deputy sheriff of Uvalde County. It was Fisher who lured Ben back to San Antonio—and into the trap that claimed the gunmaster's life. The irony of it all—that most of Ben's mortal wounds entered his body from the back, could not have escaped anyone who was aware that Thompson's first serious encounter with the law was the result of his back-shooting Joe Smith when he was a not-so-callow youth of sixteen.

Physically, Ben Thompson stood five foot nine, a slender, dark-haired man who was called by some one of the most handsome fellows in Texas. He took great care in his dress, and was sometimes mistaken for a dandy because of the attire he preferred. Defenders and detractors alike admitted that one of his virtues was a fierce loyalty to family and friends. It was this very loyalty that often got him into trouble. He was also an extremely generous man—his charity guaranteed the welfare of a number or orphan children in Austin. One friend noted that Ben had many enemies, but every last one of them respected him as a man. A testimonial following his death went as follows:

> "By us is his character considered in many essentials to have been great, and his mental and physical endowments extraordinary; that though associations not attributable to his fault may have fatally allured him often into danger and excitement . . . there was a benevolence, honesty and courage in his nature to atone for his shortcomings."

An editorial in the Austin *Daily Sentinel* put it this way:

"Take him all in all, Ben Thompson was one of the most singular of men, and although his hand has sent many mortals to untimely graves, and brought upon his memory the world's frown, I still think that when the great day of reckoning comes and the recording angel reveals our common sins and shortcomings, the record of Ben Thompson, the Austin desperado, will be far from being as black as those who knew him not have tried to paint it."

In my mind, Ben Thompson remains something of a paradox. Without doubt he had grave shortcomings, but he was also possessed of a great many virtues. Other Texas gunslingers—men like Wes Hardin and Bill Longley—were in my estimation cold-blooded killers. I do not believe Thompson was that. But at times he had awfully poor judgment, and allowed his quick temper to get the best of him. He relied on his mastery of the gun to earn him the respect he craved, and that was his biggest miscalculation of all. Because in the end he was more feared than respected. It was probably inevitable that he died as he did, and the manner of his death merely enhanced the legend of a man who was so deadly with his aim and so steadfast under fire that no one in his right mind dared take him on face to face. A dubious distinction, but at least it's something.

JASON MANNING

THE OUTLAW TRAIL

Young Sam Bass lit out for Texas with visions of a cowboy's life dancing in his head. Honest hard work got the Midwestern farm boy on a real life cattle drive to Dodge City. But soon Sam made a fatal choice, and found himself in Deadwood, South Dakota, a place that could turn even the best men bad. Once Sam Bass picked up a gun and robbed a stagecoach, there was no turning back. The law wanted him dead, fate wanted him in Texas, and the outlaw trail waited in between.

OT 5/01

FUGITIVE'S TRAIL

ROBERT J. CONLEY

WINNER OF THE WESTERN WRITERS OF AMERICA
SILVER SPUR AWARD

Scrawny, young Kid Parmlee lit out of Texas wearing a pair of old overalls and riding a swayback horse. His crime: killing a man with an axe handle for shooting his dog. Out ahead lay a land of prairie, mountains, boomtowns, whores, gold, and outlaws. And behind him was a long, twisted trail that was getting more crowded with enemies every day.

"Robert Conley is one of the most inventive
writers America has ever had."
—Max Evans

"Conley spins a fast-action tall tale salted
with Western humor."
—Elmer Kelton

AVAILABLE WHEREVER BOOKS ARE SOLD
FROM ST. MARTIN'S PAPERBACKS